Christopher Wakling

wm

WILLIAM MORROW

An Imprint of HarperCollins*Publishers*

This book is a work of fiction. The characters, incidents, and dialogue are drawn from the author's imagination and are not to be construed as real. Any resemblance to actual events or persons, living or dead, is entirely coincidental.

WHAT I DID. Copyright © 2011 by Christopher Wakling. All rights reserved. Printed in the United States of America. No part of this book may be used or reproduced in any manner whatsoever without written permission except in the case of brief quotations embodied in critical articles and reviews. For information address HarperCollins Publishers, 10 East 53rd Street, New York, NY 10022.

HarperCollins books may be purchased for educational, business, or sales promotional use. For information please write: Special Markets Department, HarperCollins Publishers, 10 East 53rd Street, New York, NY 10022.

This book was first published in Great Britain in 2011 by John Murray, an imprint of Hodder and Stoughton.

FIRST U.S. EDITION

Library of Congress Cataloging-in-Publication Data has been applied for.

ISBN 978-0-06-212169-1

12 13 14 15 16 OV/RRD 10 9 8 7 6 5 4 3 2 1

Also by Christopher Wakling

The Devil's Mask

The Undertow

Beneath the Diamond Sky

On Cape Three Points

Towards the Sun

NORTHGATE LIBRARY
AUG - - 2012

PRAISE FOR *WHAT I DID*

"This is family life today at its most believable: warm and messy, bored and raging, and above all, self-conscious. *What I Did* is every parent's nightmare, but will make you burst out laughing too."

—Emma Donoghue, author of *Room*

NO LONGER PROPERTY OF
SEATTLE PUBLIC LIBRARY

"Gripping, hilarious, tender and a whole lot more, this is, without doubt, one of the books of the year." —*Daily Mail* (London)

"A powerful, poignant and funny novel perched on the precarious line between protecting children and destroying families."

—*Melbourne Age*

"Amusing and unsettling . . . *What I Did* lets us into the mind of a child who is comically literal and utterly at sea in the world of adults."

—*The Guardian* (London)

"Horribly plausible . . . [*What I Did*] brilliantly captures parent-child relations in the raw." —*The Independent* (London)

"Wakling creates believable conflict from the everyday facts of a child going just too far and a parent losing it. . . . The novel is a strong depiction of a family in crisis." —*Sunday Age* (Melbourne)

"A powerful parable of twenty-first-century society . . . a fine, challenging novel." —*Mail on Sunday* (London)

"I loved it! Staggeringly good. Terrifyingly good."

—Lisa Jewell, bestselling author of *Ralph's Party*

"Hugely impressive, gripping, funny, and thought provoking."

—Emily Barr, bestselling author of *Backpack*

"Excellent. . . . Dark but uplifting."

—Alex Preston, author of *This Bleeding City*

For Lucas and Zoë, with love

This is the first bit and shall I tell you why? Okay I will. It is to make you read the rest.

Don't worry, it isn't a trailer. Trailers are the first bits before films which are actually really adverts and Dad says adverts are where they try to get you to buy something you probably don't want. Then again Mum says maybe you do. I often want it.

You want this story. It has already started.

Normally things pull trailers not the other way around, which means they should really come second, so the whole thing is a mistake. And unlike this bit, a trailer isn't really part of it. When you're watching a trailer it won't even be before the right film! That's great, I love that it looks fantastic, let's watch that. No, we can't. It's not here. That is called frustrating.

Dad says they put all the best bits of a film in the trailer to reduce you into watching it, and that quite often the rest of the film isn't up to much, but he is wrong. They don't put the best bits in there, not always. There's no bit where Luke actually blows up the Death Star in the trailer for *Star Wars* but they do have light savers which are magnificent.

Sadly there are no light savers in this story. It is all real. It is about a terrible thing which happens to me. But watch out because the thing you think is the terrible thing isn't really it. Other things come later and they're worse. I'm not going to tell you what they are yet because now isn't the time. That is called suspension.

I also have to warn you that nobody is bad or good here, or rather everyone is a bit bad and a bit good and the bad and good moluscules get mixed up against each other and produce terrible chemical reactions.

Did you know cheetahs cannot retract their claws?

Here is the real beginning.

— Get a move on!

The stair carpet is full of good friction. I am sitting halfway up it with my shoes in my hands because we are going out because it is too early in the morning. You can sit right on the edge of a stair if you want and go a bit closer and a bit closer still until there's not enough friction to hold you back and you slip down bump to the next step. If you start slipping fast enough the stair carpet will be powerless and you will slide down three or four or more steps in one go. Bump, bump, bump.

— Stop that banging.

My shoes have Velcro straps. Rip rip: more friction. If you put your hands inside the shoes it's impossible to do the straps up because your hands are on the inside which makes them not nimble but useless like caterpillars inside cocoons. Unless you press the Velcro shut with your knee or a bit of wall. Like that. Yes, it works.

— I said get a move on.

That is Dad. He is waiting by the front door. We are going to the park. He does not want to go to the park and I do not want to go to the park but we are going out to the park because that's what he thinks we both should want to do because it is so early. Mum is still not back from her night shifting. I woke up very early because it just happened and I didn't realize it so I woke up Dad. When there are dandelions in the lawn you should dig them out with the handle of a spoon to get the root as well as the leaves, he says, and that is what his eyes looked like when he rolled over and opened them: dirt holes. He also smelled of the rusty gate.

— Christ. What time do you call this? he said.

I open up the shoes now and turn my feet into hermit crabs wriggling back into their shells but it is difficult and boring. This banister has a big chip out of it. David Attenborough would know how to interrupt such an interesting sign. It might be a claw mark from the Pliocene area.

— For Christ's sake. What's keeping you? Come on!

Dad is just round the corner by the front door but when I shut my eyes I can see him. He has on a red plaster cast. Shall I tell you why? Because it's red and his hand is broken. It doesn't hurt anymore though. It's fine now. Sometimes Dad says How are you, Billy? and that's what I say: — I'm fine.

The cooker broke Dad's hand. Dad was lifting the cooker and he was doing it on his own which was wrong.

— That was my mistake, Son. The cooker slipped and fell on my hand.

The cooker crushed his hand so he went to hospital.

— And the man there offered me a choice of plaster casts. Can you believe it? He had a set of swatch cards, like I was choosing carpet or curtains. For a second I wondered if it was a wind-up. One grown man offering another a choice of colors for his plaster cast. How can the color be important? God help the NHS, wasting time on that. I chose red. Reminds me of a boxing glove. What do you think?

Mum laughed a laugh that didn't feel like anything was funny and said, — How ironic.

I think it was good to get a red cast instead of a blue one or a yellow one or an orange one or a green one or a purple one or even one that was black. White would have been the most boring. But a white thing is easiest to understand. Nothing tricky going on here just white you can all run along home, there's nothing here to see. Except perhaps an arctic fox.

Chameleons are always changing their color to fit in with the background, which is called camouflage. It's a clever trick, which is not the same thing as lying.

— What are you doing? Come *on*.

People sometimes make their faces play camouflage tricks so they fit in with the background of what everyone else's face is looking like just then. Hey hi how are you, they say. Me? Everyone does a trick smile back. I'm fine.

But tricky is in a way different from a trick and shoes can be very tricky customers to put on, particularly if nobody really wants to go outside in them.

— *Come here NOW*.

Dad comes round the corner and I'm still sitting on the stairs and my shoes are still in my hands and he's cross, I can tell, but he's trying not to be. That is called pressing it. He slaps his good hand flat on the front-room door and a quick hard sound bounces round the hall and I feel myself twitch which is instinctive behavior.

— I'm coming, I say.

— You get me up at the crack of dawn, he says. — And I'm trying to rescue the situation. I'm trying to take us out for a walk, get us some air. But you're on a go-slow it seems. You haven't even put your shoes on!

— I know. I'm sorry. It's friction.

— Eh? Come here.

He squats down and bends forward and takes the shoes out of my hands and grunts as he helps me put them on. Straps too, done. Then he grunts again and rocks back up onto his heels and shuts his eyes and holds his breath a moment. It looks like he's trying to remember some spellings. He steadies himself on the banister and shakes his head as he stands up and holds out the good hand to me. It is trembling and damp. Topical rain forests are very humid.

— Let's get a move on, he says.

We have a beanbag. It does not have beans inside it because it has squashy white bits instead. But don't undo the zip and pull out handfuls of the bits and throw them around whatever you do, Dad says, because that is what an idiot would do because they are a bugger to pick up.

Most of the time, though, we sit on normal chairs.

At the table I sometimes kneel up instead of sitting properly and that's okay so long as I don't wriggle around, and sometimes it doesn't matter if I wriggle around but most of the time it does. For Christ's sake sit still. The table is quite high.

Upstairs where we sleep we have beds. My bed is narrow and Mum and Dad's bed is wide because there are two of them but sometimes Dad sleeps downstairs on the sofa. Everybody has a duvet unless they don't have one in Africa. In the winter it is cold and we had to stick sellotape over the gaps around my slash window and in the summer it would be nice to open the window but Dad says no in case the glass falls out. The frame is rotten so sometimes Dad inspects the window. What are you looking at it for, I say, and he says nothing which means he's concentrating on it. Once he got out a measuring tape and a piece of paper and he wrote down some numbers but I don't think he knows much about slash windows because later he called somebody up who came round to say how much it would cost to mend it and Dad laughed and said you're having me on and the man said you obviously don't know anything about slash windows. I am an expert about animals. Come here, let me look at you, Dad sometimes says in the evening, and he looks into my eyes and says I know you, I know you, I know you. I can see your soul.

We walk up the hill toward the park. It is very boring.

My shoes flash. Everybody was excited by this when I first got them but nobody notices it now and most of the time that includes me. Sometimes when I am bored though I look at them winking away down there and I think well done, keep going, keep at it shoes.

I am best at downhill walking.

The fastest thing there is is a blackbird jet, but the fastest thing there is that isn't a thing is a peregrine falcon, and the fastest thing there is that isn't a thing or a bird is a cheetah.

When a cheetah runs on four legs it counterbalances everything with its enormous tail. Just you watch it go! The tail flies out from one side to the other as the cheetah is chasing an antelope with its head going one way and then changing direction and its tail flying out to the other side to balance everything first one way and then the next. The head stays absolutely still but not the tail, oh no! Cheetahs cannot run as far as wolves but like wolves and unlike other cats their claws are . . . I've already told you.

If I was a peregrine falcon I'd be very careful with my wings. They'd be incredibly delicate. When I did a swoop I would fold them out of the way at the last minute and hit my prey with my talons which are strong because if I damaged my wing feathers that would be a disaster of tremendous portions. I would starve.

Sometimes when we walk around Dad says, — See that lamppost, go go go! and I have to run toward a lamppost. It's okay. I can be a cheetah and run incredibly fast, but I don't have a tail to swish balances with and it is hard to run with your head still, so normally I tuck my arms behind me a bit and go like a magnificent peregrine falcon. When Dad catches up he says — What a specimen, and rubs my head. I quite like running as long as the lampposts aren't too far apart, but it would be better if instead of a lamppost I could run toward something that I could kill.

Today I don't run until we get to the bit of pavement with the shops beside it. The pavement there is flat and my energy levels become fantastic. Does that ever happen to you? It happens to me quite often and when it does it fills me with electricity.

The electricity is a fizzy thing in my arms and legs and the bits called joints where they bend that makes it hard to sit still and Don't move and for Christ's sake just stay put. I sometimes don't feel it but not often because most of the time I do. It's very electric!

Sometimes I do a thing that's very clever which is to look at people and say which animal are you then in my head. There's normally an answer. Like if Dad was an animal he'd be a leopard because he's actually naturally more active at night and he can sleep anywhere in the day, even up a tree, and he's got a very impressive roar and a whole ray of sort-of-grunts, and young leopards like play-fighting and you shouldn't ever get between a leopard and its cubs. Mum would be a fantastic prairie dog. She's never tiring! She can keep on going the whole time, there and back and there and back again. Slow down, Mum! She won't hear you. Last year she ran all the way to Marathon. Prairie dogs are very copulative animals. They copulate together very well in hunts and that is why their hunts are among the most successful in the animal kingdom.

Lizzie is not in our family, but she's nearly in it. She is my cousin and she lives in a street near us with my aunt called Cicely. Lizzie is actually an owl. Owls have big eyes and they don't say much except now and then they sort of hoot, and their head can turn right the way around. Lizzie's head can't do that. I know because I tried to make it once. But she does have huge eyes and she doesn't say anything much except oooh. We saw an owl in the Zoo once sitting on a man's hand. Not far away at all. Right there. It had eyes the color of marmalade with spokes in when you hold the jar in front of a window, which is exactly the same color as Lizzie's when she's looking up at the sky. And when the owl turned and stared at me and blinked and then kept on staring at me it felt exactly the same as when Lizzie sometimes looks at me and blinks, like although she's just little and doesn't speak she exactly knows what I'm thinking.

Did you know there is also electricity in your heart?

Not like a battery although old people do actually have pace-takers but just in your normal heart doing its pulsing, that's electricity. I think I may have too much. I told Grandma Lynne.

— My electricity has escaped from my heart and got sent to other bits of me, I said.

— That will be your nerves, said Grandma Lynne. — Don't worry, it's entirely normal, we've all got electricity there too.

She gave my back a rub when she told me that and I know why. It was to make sure I was very reassuring. And in a way I was but not in the way she meant because I didn't believe her and think okay that's all right then, everyone feels this way, because they don't. What I thought was that's nice of Grandma Lynne to make that up for me to make me feel very reassuring.

Have you ever put your finger in a plug?

I don't think so, because if you had you wouldn't have a finger! It would be black and stuck to the plug. Dad once saw a man who hit a man with a shovel to get the man off a plug he was stuck to with electricity. And so when we were in the supermarket and I fizzed into the jars of green pasta sauce with bits in and couldn't help it and accidentally knocked some off and told Dad, when he asked why oh why had I done that, that it was the electricity, he said perhaps he should hit me with a shovel too.

The thing about the electricity is that it wants you to use it. So now I run away and flap my arms. I hold them out and beat them up and down fast like the wings of a bat which are serrated. Then I run back.

— Hey Dad, I say. Hold your arms like this as if they are wings and flap them like this.

He's looking at his phone.

— Or you can just hold them out without flapping and do soaring if you want, I say.

— Eh?

He looks up and it could be good or bad but hooray it's good.

— Straight out like an albatross, he says, or swept back like a peregrine falcon?

— Wandering albatrosses have a wingspan of up to 3.4 meters, I tell him.

— True.

— They are capable of staining uninterrupted flight for weeks.

— Marvelous. Sustaining.

Dad ruffles my head which is fine, but then he looks at his phone again and his mouth changes. I know from experiments that the best antic now is to do things on my own and probably shut up too. But it's difficult because of the electricity and actually impossible so I put my arms out for wings again and beat them hard like a seagull climbing into a gale or even a hurricane, flap flap vicious hard flap, and he's there too so it's impossible not to say it.

— Hey Dad, you do it too. Go on, flap your arms.

He doesn't join in or even pat the top of my head and say not now, Son, or even do the ignoring, but grabs me by one wing and grips it.

— Don't. I'm not in the mood, he says.

It's hard to think then but albatrosses along with other seabirds are sometimes lost flying into storms. And when they're lost what do they do? They just keep on flapping, of course, until they die. The storm doesn't mind. I would prefer not to flap but I can't and it's annoying, I know that, and Dad sees my free arm flapping.

— Don't ignore me, he growls. — Stop waving that arm about before I . . .

He lets go and shakes his head and I run off up the road with my wings held tight to my sides, controlling my tragedy with tiny movements of my finger feathers only!

— Don't go too far ahead! Dad shouts after me.

Don't, don't, don't. Very boring. And it's going to get worse because look, look, here's a cat flap.

— Don't!

It's not a real cat flap, but a cat-flap sign hanging on a square stand that they stick outside shops to make you buy ice cream and newspapers. Very entertaining!

— Don't!

I won't, but I will, because I'm far enough ahead. He might be saying don't about something else and even if he isn't I have to do it anyway. I have to duck down and push my way through the cat-flap sign to pop out the other side. Victory! But oh no a bit of paper slips out of the sign as it flaps back down again. This is the problem. I jump up and down near it until he catches up with me.

— What part of DON'T don't you understand? he growls.

I pick up the bit of paper and try and push it into the slot between the two plastic halves of the cat-flap sign thing but sadly they have suction. Imagine if you had to put sandwiches together like that, by posting the ham in edgeways between the two bits of bread that were already stuck together with butter. It is too tricky and the paper tears and falls onto the ground again. It has some words written on it. Horse, I think, and Pies.

— Give me that.

Dad bends over to pick up the paper. Some grapes are green but his face goes like the other ones, red grapes. Ribena doesn't come from them but I like it. Even with only one good hand he manages to stick the sign back together again. Prime-apes have posable thumbs too.

— I'm not in the mood today, Son. Not. In. The. Mood.

— Okay I know okay.

He's still at my level. When I grow up I too will have sharp hairs in my chin.

— Are you cross? I ask.

He puffs out his cheeks and slowly shakes his head. — Let's just carry on, he says. First-time rule, understand?

I nod.

The first-time rule is that you have to do what you're told the first time you're told to do it, not the second or third. It is quite boring but worse than that it is sadly impossible to do right the whole time because it only works if you think about the exact things you are being told and not about other things as well, and the thing about other things is that it is extremely hard not to notice them because they are massive and everywhere. At school in Reception Miss Petit said God is like that but she made a sad mistake. God does not exist. He is a segment of the imagination.

— Come on. Hold my hand, he says.

We walk along the pavement a bit more and I think hard about nothing. It's hard. Cracks in the pavement. Cracks.

Then Dad's hand stops so I stop too. We're outside the café and this is why we walked this way round to the park, the slightly longer up-hilly way.

— Look at that. Barely seven o'clock. Corporate tenacity. Shall we?

— Yes, I say. — Yes.

We go in. Dad orders a coffee and I do my best to stand still which is boring. I don't ask. Dad takes a newspaper from the rack and unfolds it on the countertop. There's a picture of a huge gray ship with airplanes actually on it and some people waving. Dad sucks in some air over his teeth and shakes his head. The big words under the picture say STAND OFF something. And below the counter I can see them there in the tray but I do a squint instead of looking and I think about my two feet. If you ask you don't get. Flamingos manage to do standing on just one leg for ages and birds have tiny brains. My brain is hugely developed. It is clever enough to know that the picture in the newspaper upsets Dad because of the new clear bombs. We have them but they're not allowed them so Dad took me on a walk with nearly a million other people to tell the Government to do talking about the problem instead of a war. Some of the people on the walk had incredibly loud drums and a man did a wee in the street before we got to the bit with the talking. Megaphones are not huge phones. Later Dad bought me a Coke with two bits of lemon in it in the pub and was happy. — They can't ignore us now, Son, he said with a four-beer grin. — Not after Blair's mistake in 2003. Even this lot will have to back off now.

The smell in the café is just about as lovely as it is when I put my nose in between Mum's hair in the morning. Her head smells of lemons and chocolate. A basset hound has a more hugely developed sense of smell than I do and so it would like it in here more than I do but only blind dogs are allowed in. I am not blind. Out of my eyes even though they are squinting I can easily see Dad's hand go to the tray and yes, go on, yes, yes, yes!

He's got one, hooray!

He tosses it onto the glass shelf and tells the woman, — That, too, please.

Oh yes, yes, yes.

A massive chocolate coin!

Maybe the whole day will be okay!

I still don't say anything though because I don't want him to change his mind which is easily something he could do. He puts the paper under his arm and picks up the coffee and the lid and the massive chocolate coin which is winking because the lights in here are truly excellent small star-lights aimed at everything. Did you know that stars can tell you where to go? These star-lights are telling Dad to go to the other counter. He walks up to it right near me and he starts ripping sugar into his coffee cup and the chocolate coin is there on the glass sitting next to the lid and I think it's just about as big as the lid and I lean a bit to one side to see if the coin is bigger or smaller than the lid but I have forgotten I am standing on one leg and I fall over. Not right over. I sort of do a half fall into Dad's side. It's okay. Much more massive falls would not hurt me. But sadly I fall into Dad and his arm jerks sideways and knocks over his coffee cup. It goes all over his plaster-cast hand and the paper and up his sleeve.

— Jesus Christ!

I take a few steps away. Dad stands up the cup and grabs for some napkins and starts dabbing and a noise comes out of him which isn't a word or a shout exactly. It's more like a growl inside a box. It makes me shut my own mouth so tight my teeth squeak.

— Here. Let me help. The woman who makes the coffee has come out from behind her bit with some cloths. She allows Dad to run his fingers under the big sink. They are red like the cast which he is trying not to splash. Interestingly the sink doesn't have a tap but a long silver trunk dangling down instead. Dad holds his fingers under the dribble of water for quite a long time, and while he's doing it the woman makes a new cup of coffee and I stand very still indeed. She puts sugar in the cup for him this time and while she's doing that she gives the big coin to me. I say, — Thank you, but I feel sick. He still hasn't looked at me.

I do not eat the chocolate coin. I want to eat it and it wants me to eat it but I don't because he is cross so I put it in my pocket instead. We walk along the pavement. The white bits could be chewing gum which you should not drop or guano which is an excellent word for bird poo. Birds make whole islands out of it and they don't know any better so don't blame them. He is holding his arm with the plaster cast away from his body a bit as if it is still hot but it can't be. Perhaps he is drying it. I don't know and I can't speak yet but I do know this: his arm is making me feel bad.

When somebody makes you feel bad what should you do? Sadly there is no answer to this question, or rather wherever you are the answer is different. If you are in a game of chess the answer is that you should attack back because attacking back is the best form of defense. But school is a different cuttlefish. At school Miss Hart says the first thing you should never do when somebody is mean to you is retaliate back because Jesus wouldn't. If you hit Jesus he just kisses your cheek. Or rather that is what he used to do. He is dead now but some people don't think so because when he was alive he was excellent. The animal kingdom is different from the kingdom of heaven. When a warthog is cornered by a pride of lions it uses its razor-sharp tusks to infect slashing wounds. I found a dead cuttlefish washed up on the beach last summer and it was quite razor sharp, too, but I am less excellent than Jesus because here's what I would do if I had that cuttlefish now: I would jab Dad's bad hand with it.

I walk behind a bit. Then I walk farther behind so that when we reach the zebra crossing — lie down there, zebra, we're all going to drive over you unless somebody wants to walk on you instead — he has to wait for me to catch him up. The flashing-ball lights are pelicans which isn't very realistic because you don't get zebras and pelicans with the same habits in the wild.

— Hurry up.

I slow down a bit more.

— Come on, stop dawdling.

Dawdling is a gentle word when he says it like that and, look, he's holding out his hand to me as I arrive. But do you know what, I am not ready yet, I'm just not, so I don't take it, and he whips the hand back down to his side and says something I don't hear because he says it in a quick quiet un-gentle way, so that although I know that it is mean I don't know what it is exactly, and that's exactly the effect he's striding for.

I walk straight past him onto the stripes.

— Hey! He grips my shoulder hard and spins me around, jerking me back a step in a way that is not nice at all even before he makes it worse by shouting, — You don't just walk out into the road, Billy! Hear me? No matter what!

— But it's a zebra—

— Don't talk back to me! How many times do I have to . . . You wait for me. We look both ways. We cross when I say.

And on *say* he jerks me forward again so that my feet are scrabbling to keep up and you know what, this is very complicated. Shall I tell you why? I will, because you will never guess. There are two things. The first thing is that he hates roads. Or rather he hates the cars that go on the roads because the cars, he says quite often, to get it into my head, and normally he rubs my head when he says it, are modern-day top predators. Saltwater crocodiles, Siberian tigers, Great

Whites. They're out to get you so you have to be on your guard because there's no way I'm going to lose you to one of them, okay? That's the first thing. And the second thing is the even more complicated thing and it is this: he is actually quite *pleased* that I stepped into the road because now he has a proper reason to be cross with me. Spilling the coffee and running ahead and ducking through the sign thing and going too slowly and not putting on my shoes and waking him up early were all bad reasons to be cross, but walking into the road without looking is a good reason, one of the best! Polar bears, sea eagles, Galápagos iguanas. It's such a good reason it means he can be very angry and quite happy at exactly the same time! Excellent!

But sadly it is not excellent for me. For me it is horrid.

I kick out at the road and I miss and hit his shin.

— Ow! Billy! What the—?

He pushes me with a stiff arm across the road and through the railings into the park which is empty except for a man and a dog. In the war they cut down lots of railings to kill people with, but they put these ones back up. The dog has three legs, two at the front and one at the back. If it is a male it won't have to cock a leg to wee but half of the time it will have to turn around to aim at the tree. Girls have to sit down. I don't know what to say about kicking Dad's shin apart from sorry and I can't say that because sorry sticks in your throat when you try to say it. Try for yourself. Sorry is exactly like a fish-bone.

Luckily just then Dad's phone goes off in his pocket again.

He pulls it out and glares at me and says, — Don't go far, to me and, — Yes, to it.

I do as he says this time. It's relatively easy because he's not on me anymore. He's concentrating at something else. Whatever the else is I can't tell you exactly but I can tell you this: whoever Dad is speaking to has something to do with his work and is saying annoying things.

— And there's really no chance of changing their minds? he says.

I go a few steps farther away to the roundabout thing and get on it and go round half a turn and get off the other side. Thank you, roundabout.

— That's what they said, word for word? It's final?

Dad's job is called communications projects. He does it on his own except when he does it with other people. He used to have a different job in a big building where there was a man in charge of him but now he can do his own communications projects for clients at home in his study-office which is in fact a sediment of his and Mum's bedroom. Shortest possible commute, Son. Laptop, phone, know-how, and low cunning. When Dad speaks to people on his phone to do with work his voice sounds different, sort of hopeful and disappointed all at once. If you know him well like me because we are connected, Son, you can tell that he is saying one thing but really he'd like to say something else much crosser. The man in charge at his old office was just called the man.

Now Dad is using a voice which sounds like the one you might use if you got a present you didn't really want at Christmas, so that although what you really want is to say no, no, no that's not the right thing, you've got it all wrong, you can't, because if you're ungrateful for one present you might not get another one ever again, so you say thank you anyway, but it comes out like a mouse peeping from a hole, gray and small and ducking back in again quickly.

— Well thanks very much for all your efforts. Next time, perhaps.

This sounds like the end but it isn't because now he's got his eyes tight shut like he needs to answer a really hard question or perhaps even pluck up the courage to ask to go to the toilet in the middle of Miss Hart's storytime, and the knuckles of his good hand have gone pointy yellow like teeth, and he's carrying on.

This is bad so I walk farther away toward the goals.

The Year Threes from school play football here. They wear boots. Strangely their boots are not boots, though, but instead they are shoes with little teeth knuckles of their own called studs. And here's the evidence: hundreds of tiny holes. I kneel down on the mud and put my fingers into the dents which are slug-size. Sixty million years ago the earth was teething with fossils like this. Yes I am excellent at spotting them in the modern world and, look, here are some more next to these worm-casts. Tracks. Worm-casts aren't like plaster casts at all because for one you can crush them very easily between your fingers and for two they are all the same color. Perhaps these tracks were not made by Year Threes playing football but sand people from *Star Wars*. There's only one way to find out and it's a good thing I thought of it because it means that instead of going away from Dad, which is really what I want to do, I can think no I'm actually following some tracks in search of my very own prey. Don't bother with praying, Son, he can't hear you because he doesn't exist. That said, there's nothing wrong with sitting quietly for a think from time to time.

It's windy on the football-pitches bit of the park and my coat has somehow come undone which gives me two choices. Actually it's just one choice with two bits to it: common mistake, Son. First I could try to zip it up, or second I could run to keep warm. Zips are a right pain. Even when your fingers have come straight out of a nice warm bath zips will defeat them. So two seems the obviously best option, doesn't it? If I run like this, following the tracks by keeping my eye on them, then quite quickly my heart will start pumping blood from the hot bits of me like my knees and ankles to the incredibly cold bits like my ears. And I'll also be faster at hunting down my prey, and this is excellent, because it is called a wing-wing situation.

The football pitches are quite big and empty like Canada.

Canadian wolves are tireless like prairie dogs.

I wish Mum was here but she is working tirelessly.

Prairie dogs, wolves, and Mum. They all use the tireless method of hunting their prey. It is called loping. And since I am a wolf with my nose to the ground loping tirelessly onward it is no problem to cross one pitch and then the next and then cut through the line of popular trees that stand like soldiers at the top end of the big flat bit, with their leaves all shedded off by the wind, so that they're naked soldiers in a way, which is quite funny, or at least it will be when I tell it to somebody, somebody being Ben. Ben laughs the whole time, except when he doesn't, but mostly he does, particularly if you mention naked things, or things that have done a poo, or even a wee. Ben may find it funny, Son, but surely you don't? You're not a baby anymore, are you?

No! I'm not! So why does he have to say that in front of my friend, because he might as well tell Ben *he's* being a baby, only he can't do that because he only ever says things like that to me. Why? I don't know. But I do know I am not going back there even though back there is a long way away now. You can't even see it because of the popular trees.

I switch off my loping tirelessly which is called calling a halt, and I've run quite a long way. There aren't any stud marks here, or if there are they are covered by all these shedded gray leaves. Don't go too far, Son. Stay within sight. He likes saying that but he's not here to say it now and it's a silly thing to say in any case because you could stay really close and hide behind something or go miles and miles away and still be in sight if you were on a salt pan. And I'm six. And there are cars over that side of the park. You can hear them. Their tires on the damp road make a sound as if they are tearing cardboard lids off Cheerio boxes, and I'm hungry.

I reach into my pocket for the chocolate coin. It's there and I pull it out and look at it and notice that it has gone a bit sticky along one edge; you can actually see the melted chocolate grinning out of the gold seam. Go on, it says, lick me but I won't. I won't!

And it's all his fault for making us come out before breakfast.

And I can hear him in the distance, calling my name, and there's something odd about the way he's calling. — Billy. Billy?

He is worried.

I stand up again. And I don't know why. But instead of walking back toward where his voice is coming from through the trees I decide to do the exact opposite and I begin loping tirelessly farther away toward the road with cars on it instead.

One of the best places is the car but watch out, it can also be the worst. Seat belts are difficult to put on. You can pull them across you but if you let go when you're looking for the hole they rush back inside themselves again. Snails also do it, if you touch them. Inside the car we're all together which is good until you need to get away and then that's it, you're stuck, and there's no way you're getting out of there again. But that's not true, not precisely. Because if you're very cunning which is quite like stealthy only in your head, there are one or two things you can say to make the car stop so you can get out. I need the loo can work but not if you say it too often. I feel sick is another one though whether or not that does the job depends on what sort of mood they're in. Birds regurgitate food for their young. What a wonderful trick that would be if you could do it. I feel sick stop the car please no yes I do feel sick no you don't really I do stop it whoa regurgitate. A trick is not always the same thing as lying.

Even once you've stopped the car and been sick or gone to the loo the problem is that you have to get back in again. They can't leave you there. You wouldn't want them to. Many animals, birds and fish, including wildebeests, albatrosses, and salmons, migrate, covering epic distances across the planet in vast schools and flocks and herds. Predators pick off the weaklings which means the old and the sick. And the young. Keep up at the back there! Put your coat and shoes on! Lope!

I go round the edge of a hedge which rhymes and look back round it and I can see he's running too. His red arm is waving back and forth. In PE Mr. Reilly says you should run by pumping up your legs with your arms so well done, Dad, top marks, inflatable. Mr. Reilly has a mustache and colored laces in his shoes. He lives with Mr. Sparks who teaches the Year Fives. They love each other and come to school on bicycles with suspension which is excellent. My lungs hurt. I can hear him shouting at me now from quite far away but not as far away as he was. Bats have incredibly sensitive hearing which is so good they can hear electric eels, but don't touch one. I wish I could stop. No, that's not quite right. What I wish is that I had already stopped quite a long time ago because now

I've come this far I can't stop. No, that's not quite right either because sadly I will have to stop eventually because nothing not even wolves can go on forever, not without pausing for things like water and meat and having a sleep which actually means stopping totally and lying down.

— Stop! Stop, Billy! STOP!

His voice sounds red like his arm. In nature red is used primarily for warnings about danger so I lope on and as I lope I realize a funny thing which is this: I am not in fact chasing my prey with studs on its feet anymore because I am in fact being chased, and nothing chases wolves, so I can't be the predator wolf but instead I must be some kind of prey.

And what does a clever prey do? Easy. It runs for cover. At home where we have beds upstairs they have covers on them which you can hide under in a game but this is not a game but a park which is big and open and desperate. The only cover was behind the popular trees and that hedge but he is already past them with his red arm pumping and I am running too but he is catching up which is called againing.

— COME HERE! STOP! BILLY!

His voice is purple now, very serious.

Reading is very serious too and grown-ups do it as well. Dad likes reading and so do I but not as much as him and sometimes it's something I don't want to do. Most nights he says after bathtime, — We're going to do some reading practice, me and you.

— Why do polar bears hibernate when Siberian tigers don't? I might say, or, — Which do you think has a better memory, African elephants or Alaskan salmons?

He's trying to be cheerful with me so I'm talking about something interesting with him which is nice of me.

— Hmm, he'll say. — Scarcity of relevant food in winter and elephants without a doubt. Clean your teeth and go to the loo. I'll get the book.

Reading books can be quite interesting but they are never as good as when Mum or Dad does the reading and you just listen because the stories are more complicated and therefore interesting then. But that's not the point, he says. The point is to learn how to read for yourself so you can read what you want when you want and make the world your oyster. In his bedroom which is also a study or office he has books from the floor right up to the roof. I'd make the world my lobster if I was limited to crustaceans and had to choose.

But dolphins are far cleverer than lobsters. They exhibit more intelligence than anything else on our planet instead of us, except hold on, what about prime-apes? It is a proven fact that both prime-apes and dolphins have powers of communication but do they read? I don't think they do.

— Come on, sit down, let's do this together, he says.

And I'll sit down but the electricity will probably make me hop up and sit down again with one leg out and roll onto the other knee and wriggle forward or sideways again. I don't know why the electricity picks then but it does and instead of sitting still which is easier if I'm watching television I just find it hard to stop moving.

— Calm down, relax, sit still, he might say. And this is a warning because if I don't the next thing might be a grip around my arm. — Five minutes. For just five minutes, for Christ's sake, *sit still.*

And there are tactics to help you, like thinking you're a cat lying in wait or an owl on a branch or, stillest of all, a croco dile basking under a lamp in the Zoo. Keep still, letters, for Christ's sake, keep still! Reading isn't hard. One letter goes after another and they're just squiggles you can learn and when you know them you look at the word and say it and what it means sort of wriggles through or surfaces like a dolphin which is a mammal too.

— BILLY!

The road is my cover.

I make a final really fast run which is called a sprint for it very impressively. There are no railings on this side of the park because they couldn't get them back after killing people with them in the war. Instead there is a low wall thing which I try to jump over but sadly I don't make it and the brick edge of it bites the inside of the top of my leg very hard which makes me yelp. And it's his fault, not mine: he may as well have leopard-bitten me himself. But I am quickly up because I'm a tough one, very durable, and I'm onto the wet pavement and my coat is sort of falling off because the zip is completely undone but never mind. There are cars parked along the road here. James at school can tell you all the makes if you ask him but I prefer animals. Black car, gap, gray car, gap, red car red car, bus stop, bins. My leg bite hurts. I can hear Dad's feet behind me now and cars ripping more Cheerio-box lids in the wet road and he's panting and I wish I hadn't woken up early and I wish I'd put my shoes on more quickly and I didn't mean to spill the coffee and it wasn't my fault his phone brought bad news so I duck round the back of the bin to get away.

But sadly I'm too slow.

He's got hold of me.

He's gripping my arm.

— BILLY, YOU LITTLE . . . he roars in my ear, so his voice goes black.

But wait! My arm is coming off! Not my real arm ripping

off my body but the arm of my coat sliding off my real arm and sometimes even in the most impossible situations the prey can still get away if it person-veers.

I shut my eyes and wriggle like hell and the coat comes off. There's a lady coming toward us and there's Cheerio noise in the road and I am spectacular. He plunges for me again. I duck and run. Modern cars are shaped quite like trainers. I dart off the curb between parked trainers and I'll make it across the road because sooner or later the wildebeests must cross the river to spite the crocodiles.

Dad's voice goes from black to white. — **NO!**

Something big flashes past screaming horns.

I feel the wind of it just there, like spray off a wave.

I stop.

Then with tremendous peregrine speed he's there. He gets hold of my real arm again and yanks me back through the gap and onto the pavement as the car horn fades.

— JESUS FUCKING CHRIST! he yells.

And his bad hand is pulling at my trousers which are suddenly below my knees which is a very effective technique for hobbling a horse or a wildebeest or me.

And he's yelling NEVER in my face.

And it's cold here for my legs, like on a tundra. They have no fur.

And all I can do is look straight at him as he gets ready to do it.

He pauses.

Then does it.

His good hand smacks me once, then again, and another time, very, very, very hard across my bum and thighs, the backs of my legs.

*

Then there's somebody else with us, a woman. She is shouting, — Stop! but I don't understand why because I'm not running away anymore, I am crying instead. I sit down. The ground is hard and my bum is steam-from-the-kettle hot. I burned my wrist on it once.

— You can't do that, the woman says.

— What? Dad is breathing hard. — What did you say? he says again.

— You mustn't.

— Who are you?

— He's a child.

— I said, who the hell are you?

— You mustn't hit a child.

Very quietly Dad says, — Get away from us or I'll . . .

— You'll what? Hit me, too?

Dad goes very still. Then he says, — Christ, I'm not listening to this. Pull your trousers up.

The woman is quite largely bulgy and she is wearing very white trainers and pink jogging-legging things and a ripply black top. Her face is pink, too, with red lipstick in the middle of it. She is standing quite close to us and she has her hands on her hips.

I am not brilliant at my clothes and suddenly my legs don't work because my energy has involved into sap. I am crying quite loudly. Dad lifts me up by the belt and shoulder and winces because of his bad hand. He pulls my trousers up un-gently and as he is doing that he hisses quietly but loudly, — *Interfering bitch.*

— Pardon?

Dad explodes. — HE NEARLY KILLED HIMSELF YOU FAT FUCKING BUSYBODY BITCH. MY SON! GET

THE FUCK AWAY FROM US. JOG THE FUCK OFF!

Then he drags me past her back into the park.

When you turn the sound on the television off it is called muting it. Swans are also mute and so is Dad in the park and so am I because I do not know what to say and anyway I am not going to say it first. Sometimes we have blinking competitions where the competition is to not blink, and sometimes Dad says Tell you what how about this for a game, competitive shutting-up. He is normally the winner. But did you know that ducks have webbed feet underwater? Although the duck is just sitting there bobbling along, its feet could in fact be going quite fast beneath it very unnoticeably. I have to half run to keep up. Paddle, paddle, paddle, silence, silence, silence, nothing to hear here, nothing to see. Good job, ducks. Dad doesn't let go of my hand. Interestingly I can feel that his own hand is shaking to start with, then it's just hot, then I can't feel anything, not even where my hand stops and his starts.

I am you, Son, and you are me.

We walk home the short way, not past the café, which I hate, because in a way it's the café's fault, and I'm going to put the chocolate coin in the bin when I get home, but then I notice something else, something quite interesting. It is a reflection in the stake agent's window, a moving reflection of something pink. I try to turn round to look at it but Dad jerks me forward so it's not until I get to the corner of our road that I can check and yes I was right! Pink jogging things. Not jogging though, just wobbly walking. It is the woman with a busy body who did interfering and she is coming into our street.

I want to tell Dad about this development but I would be the one speaking first if I did so I don't.

*

I go inside upstairs to my bedroom without talking because I know that is the next thing, to go and wait for him there, but he doesn't come, not straightaway. He goes to his bedroom-study-office and shuts the door. Since it is half-term that should be brilliant because I have time to play with toys and make a fantastic tent out of the duvet and the chair and the edge of the bed, but I don't feel like it. I look out of the window instead. My bedroom has a rubbish slash window which you mustn't touch. The view from it is okay though, of the other side of our street. At the top of the view is the sky. It is gray today like the bit you peel off the underneath of a fish you're going to eat. Then there's the roof of the house opposite which has a thing on top of it for catching television pictures sent from the olden days. Not a net. More like a fish skeleton in fact, and it makes a wonderful perch, hello pigeons, well done keep it up. And under the roof is the house with two windows upstairs and one big one downstairs next to the door. The top windows are like eyes. Unfortunately they have curtains, not a blind, but did you know that some lizards have no eyelids? My window has a rolly-blind and I'm allowed to use it if I want but not yank on it like a monkey on a vine. Sometimes I roll the blind down and up again quite carefully a few times so that our house does some winks, but the house opposite could only lizard-wink back, and it hasn't yet, but it might. Otherwise our house and that house are symmetrical. I spend some time counting the bricks which is boring but helps me not listen to the sound of him moving around downstairs and thinking of him thinking about it because it isn't over yet.

Eventually the footsteps come upstairs again.

I decide that the best place to be is actually sitting on my bed.

There's a knock on my door.

There's no point trying to puff myself up like a toad in front of a grass snake, so instead I just hunch over my knees and barnacle back a bit so that I'm up against the wall.

The door opens.

Dad is there but what's this? He's carrying two mugs.

— What have you got to say to me? he asks.

I don't say anything to begin with, but then I think, hold on, he's actually said something first now, so I know it's all right, I can say my thing now and still in a way be a bit victorious.

— Sorry, I say.

He gives me one of the mugs which is extraordinary because, yes, it is hot chocolate upstairs near the carpet!

Then he sits down next to me on the bed. I take a sip. It is pretty lovely. It makes me think about the chocolate coin which I haven't thrown away yet. I decide I might not. Then again, I decide again, I might, because he's taking his here-we-go breath. But it's only because he wants to tell me very strongly not to run away or ever go in the road ever again without looking, ever, and he does tell me this for quite a long boring time. And at the very end he pauses and says That's it, it's okay now, it's behind us. Best forgotten. But interestingly, before he gets to that bit, or even the strict bit about the road and never, he says something different to start with. Shall I tell you what it is? Okay, I will. After I say sorry he looks at me and rubs his eyes with his fingertips and looks away and takes a sip from his mug and then looks back at me and gulps and says, — Me, too.

Yes, that's right, *Me, too* is what he says.

Can you ride a bicycle? I can, and in the shed there's a bicycle I got for my birthday when I was five with a bell shaped like a football. I don't really like football, but I like riding my bike, but I didn't at first. When I first got it it had stabilizers on which Dad immediately took off, saying, — He doesn't need stabilizers, he's got good balance from that scooter. He'll be fine won't you, Son.

— Are you sure? asked Mum.

I could see he wasn't sure by the way he squeezed my hand three times: short-long-short. That's the signal to say I love you. I was quite pleased about this because I *was* sure myself because it was only a bicycle and I'd even seen very old people riding a bicycle as well as kids who didn't look much older than around four and a half.

— No problem, I said. — I'll give this a go.

We found some sloping grass in the park leading from one path down to another path and Dad held the back of the bike and I got on it. I concentrated very hard; I was very focusing, like a bird of prey with the two bits of lenses in its eye, one for normal-range things and the other for tiny mice cowering beneath hedgerows. Cower, mice, cower. And that was part of the trouble because I wanted to think about the two bits of lens and Dad said Come on, sort yourself out, get your feet on the pedals. Pedals are very simple things but I hadn't really used pedals before and they got in my way. Dad started running with his hand on the saddle and I used my feet to stop the pedals hitting my legs and the steering was quite easy if you didn't try to steer too much, even when Dad let go. But the trouble was the pedals. I couldn't think about anything else and even when that's all I thought about it wasn't enough. They turned a bit and then stopped if I stopped pedaling and then the steering didn't work and the bike was quite high up and wallop, over I went. It was only grass so I didn't mind.

— Are you sure he wouldn't be better off with some stabilizers? asked Mum.

Dad was hot from the running probably. — No, no, no, he said, wiping his face. — No.

I tried again. This time I concentrated on being very poised and very balanced because Dad said, — It's genetic, he's got very good balance, quite loudly to Mum who looked away. Genes are like viruses only smaller. And seals balance things on their noses in zoos. But how did they learn that? There are no plastic footballs in the wild to practice with. In fact there are very few perfect spheres in nature except for the planets we marvel at. A watermelon would be too heavy. The pedals were extremely tricky characters. They were in charge of my feet and not the other way around and trying to keep up with them meant I stopped pressing and even though we were going down a hill with Dad running behind holding me steady and then letting me go, the pedals weren't pushing the bike and it slowed down to one side and I came off again harder this time.

— Son, are you all right? he said in a quiet are-you-actually-hurt voice.

— I'm fine.

— 'Course you're fine! he said for everyone to hear. — Good boy. Jump on again and I'll push you back up to the top of the hill.

Mum arrived and she said, — Are you all right? too.

— I'm fine.

— Sure?

— 'Course he's sure, Tessa. You're a toughie, aren't you. Dad held the bike straight and said Here you are and patted me on the back just a bit hard and over his shoulder a magpie landed black and white in the yellow-green grass and started drilling at the ground. One for sorrow so there had to be two and it was the other one I had to look for instead of getting back on the bike. Where was it? Magpies are attracted to flashy things so perhaps the magpie wanted the bell off my bike. He could have it. No, instead I decided to use it to lure his mate out of hiding like a skillful hunter. Ping, ping. I stood in front of the front wheel and pinged the little silver football boot into the silver ball of the bell.

— Let's try him with some stabilizers, Mum said.

— No need. Stop playing with that.

There was no sign of the second magpie. In New Zealand, which is as far away as America, farther perhaps, they have birds called kia birds which will actually rip your windscreen wipers off! There is one in the Zoo with a curvy sharp beak like a dagger that is curved. They put bits of mirror in its cage to keep it simulated.

— Stop ringing that bell, breathed Dad.

— Jim, said Mum in her warning voice.

I wanted to get back on the bicycle but at the same time I didn't want to get back on the bicycle, and the funny thing was that I wanted to get back on the bicycle and not get back on the bicycle for the same reason which was this: he so wanted me to get back on the bicycle.

— Why are they called stabilizers? I asked.

— Right, said Dad and he picked the bike up and carried it back up toward the path, but not the way he'd carried it into the kitchen that morning. Then he'd carried it like it was made of a fossil or something that would snap but now he carried it like it was the Christmas tree after Christmas when its spikes had fallen off. He walked past the magpie. It was doing more stabbing at the ground with its beak which was sharp but not as powerful or hooked as a kia's. No need to worry about your windscreen wipers or bicycle bells in England. There are no venomous spiders here either. Still the magpie must have had a strong beak because the ground he was jabbing it at was extremely similar to the ground I fell on and that was quite hard ground.

We saw another magpie sitting in a tree as we were getting into the car but I'm not sure if that one counted.

Mum comes home which is excellent but she has been loping around nocturnally for too long and sadly she is dog-tired. She strokes my face and leans against the kitchen door frame.

— Tough one? asks Dad.

She nods her head and does a slow blink.

— Straight to bed, he says.

This is quite good news because it means Dad won't have a chance to tell her about what happened in the park, not yet at least, and sometimes not yet can involve into never. But there is a problem and it is this. Normally when I am at school and Mum has been night-shifting she sleeps in my bed during the day so Dad can function, and I don't mind because I'm not there. In fact I actually like it because after she has slept and woken up and I have come home from school and done things and had supper and a bath and some reading and had a piggy-back to bed, thank you, Dad, I can still sometimes smell her head in my pillow. I don't think about that today though. What I think is this: it will be boring if I can't play in my bedroom during my half-term. Worse than boring in fact, unfair!

— Grab some toys and play downstairs, says Dad, using his highly reasonable voice.

— Do I have to?

— Yes.

— Now?

— When do you think? Mum's been up all night.

— But I was going to make an explosive tent marble run.

— A what? Do it downstairs.
— But I need the ingredients.
— Well fetch them then.
— But you don't understand.
— She's tired, Son.
— But you could do communications downstairs.
— Billy.
— But for a tent marble run I need the radiator thing.
— Enough buts!
— But.

His face is going hard again and Mum has already trudged up the first few steps and I can't help it, it's not me, it's my feet, they just rush up past her stamping, stamp, stamp, STAMP. Quite often this makes him or her come after me very quickly and get cross, but today they don't, and strangely this feels quite annoying, like when you jump on a Ribena carton and it goes hiss instead of pop. I don't get the things I want out of my bedroom, I get pointless things instead, a bathrobe, a babyish book, and some socks.

— I only need a few hours, Billy, says Mum as I barge past her again, and that makes it worse because she uses her voice with cracks in so the inside of me feels sort of melted and scooped out. I nearly say sorry but there's been enough sorry already today, and anyway it's Dad's fault and he deserves it. Still, I don't stamp going downstairs because it's not working. You wouldn't jump on a hissy Ribena box twice either would you? No. Not unless you were an amazing idiot.

I go into the front room and lie on the floor with my head on one side looking under the sofa. When the tide goes out it leaves seaweed in a line on the beach and in this way it is quite like the vacuum cleaner.

I'm still lying there when the phone rings. Not the important phone Dad keeps in his pocket, or even the one Mum carries in her bag, but the old incredibly loud one that lives on its little stand in the hall. It normally only goes off on birthdays when Auntie Lesley calls so it's exciting to hear it and Dad does come two-stepping downstairs as if he's pleased. Only he isn't. His — Hello? comes out more annoyed than excited. Perhaps he's worried the loudness might have woken up Mum. I sit on the bottom step to watch this fascinating development.

— Calling from where? Dad says.

The little voice on the other end does some tweeting I can't hear.

— Is this some sort of windup?

— Chirp, chirp.

— How did you get this number?

— Tweet.

— Of course I'm in. You're talking to me, aren't you?

— Chirp.

— No. No. Absolutely not.

— Ch—

— Good-bye.

Dad bangs the phone back into its holder quite hard but his face doesn't look fierce; it looks . . . whitely frightened. He grips his forehead and stands still for a strangely long time. Our cat Richard is amazing at standoffs so leopards are probably good at them too. When I say, — Who was that? Dad looks at me as if I've asked a particularly hard question like the one about the difference between termites and ants, but we don't look up the answer to this one on the computer. Instead Dad says, — Nobody, and goes back upstairs.

⋆

And later he's still up there when the doorbell rings. I'm not waiting on the bottom stair anymore though. I'm sitting on the edge of the armchair nearest the television which is on because I know how to turn it on now. And the sound is turned almost off, too, because I know how to do that as well. I'm secretly watching an episode of new-series *Batman* which is quite interesting. Suddenly: ring-a-ding! Very quickly like a rat up a pipe I press the Off button and rush out of the front room to answer the door. This is helpful both to Mum and Dad and it is also necessary camouflage. By the way, did you know that the Off and the On buttons are exactly the same one on our television? Well they are, and it isn't confusing.

I open the door and look up and see that there is a lady with a butterfly on the edge of her coat smiling down at me. I do a smile back. The butterfly isn't realistic. It is made from wool or something heavy and bobbly. A knitted butterfly! There's no way it could ever fly properly.

I don't know this woman.

When a person you don't know comes to your door you have to act the right way, which means stand up straight and look at them in the eye, and you have to say the right thing, which is Hello can I help. But there are two things about that. The first is that it's incredibly hard to say things to somebody you don't know while standing up straight and looking at them in the eye, because you always actually want to say nothing and go away. And the second thing is that it is even harder to speak to them normally if they have a knitted flightless butterfly stuck on them and lips which are a quite gentle pink like the clematis, because then it's impossible not to get distracted and start thinking of more interesting things instead, like Hey that butterfly must be incredibly disappointed because there's no way at all that it's ever going to flap up high enough to get at the nectar in that clematis lip with its prebosc-thing. Actually there are three things about saying Hello, how can I help, to strange adults, not just two, I was wrong. The third thing that makes it hard or even pointless is that you know what they're going to say back to you anyway. They're going to say Can you fetch your mum or dad please, or something similar, and that is exactly what this woman with the butterfly goes and says.

— Hello. Is Mum or Dad in?

— Yes.

— Great. Could you fetch them for me, please?

— Which one?

— How about Mum?

— No.

The woman does a small quite nice laugh and says. — Why's that then?

— She's asleep.

— I see. And is your dad awake?

I don't have to answer that question though because at that moment Dad walks up behind me and says, — Just about.

The woman smiles from him to me and back again. She is good at smiling.

— How can I help? says Dad, rustling me behind him.

The butterfly does actually lift up a bit now because the woman is taking an I'm-about-to-jump-into-this-pool-and-the-water-looks-pretty-cold-but-I'll-do-it-you-just-watch-me deep breath.

— We spoke earlier, she says. Sheila Hudson, from the Council's ChildSafe team.

Do you like wine and beer?

I do because I am advancing.

But of course I don't drink beer or wine because I am only six and I don't want my family to go to prison. So you might think hey how can he say he likes wine and beer when he doesn't even drink it? I can answer that question two ways.

No, three.

The first way is this: Mum and Dad and especially Dad drink quite a lot of wine and beer and I like it when they do because it relaxes them at the end of the day and there's nothing wrong with that, Son, is there, especially because when you are a bit relaxed you let people stay up later than normal and watch extra television.

The second way is this: although I don't drink wine or beer myself, they do, which I've already said, and I also said when they drink it they let me stay up late sometimes, but I haven't yet said that they do put me to bed eventually, because they have to, because you can't stay up all night, because if you didn't sleep it would flatten your batteries fatally, and well . . . I can't remember the reason. No, yes, I can. The reason is it smells nice. Yes, wine and beer smell lovely when Mum and Dad kiss you with it at the end of the day. Very cheerful. Lights-out, Son.

And the third way is a secret but I will tell you anyway so long as you don't call the police. Dad sometimes lets me have a sip of his beer or wine to test whether I like them and it's true, I like both, because of my advancing test buds.

Dad goes into the kitchen with the butterfly woman. I walk into it behind them. Look, there's my reflection in the bin. I have a stretched head and a stretched body, too, particularly when I stick my arms out. This is what I must look like if I am hugging a tree and you are its trunk, I expect. Wood has eyes called knots. But I'm not close enough so I go a bit closer and it's quite hard to see all of me then. Impossible, in fact, when I'm actually hugging it.

— Billy? says Dad. — Leave the bin alone.

I un-hug it and step back trying fierce faces for intimidating purposes.

Dad laughs. I look at him. He's already stopped. He'd forgotten to be serious but now just as quickly he remembers again and whap, he's got his I'm-working-run-along impression back on.

Butterfly woman's smile stays put.

— Upstairs. Carry on with your game, says Dad.

— But I wasn't up—

— Now.

Sometimes it's best even if you can win a battle with facts or logics not to bother so as Dad says, — What's all this about then? to the woman I beat a treat because yes it's true animals aren't like humans, they don't fight unless they have to. I pull the door nearly shut behind me as I go.

But I don't go all the way upstairs, no, just up some of them, and then I stop on the stair I always stop on, the one with the loose banister. Rattle rattle. Somebody kicked this banister out once and that somebody was Dad and he was sorry so he stuck it back in with glue again. Slash windows are much more difficult to repair. But sadly even banisters are tricky if you use the wrong sort of glue, or not enough of the right kind, and now the banister is loose again. Still, you wouldn't know it was unless you wriggled it a bit and why would you do that?

Shall I tell you?

Baddies!

Imagine if you were in the house upstairs at night and you heard a suspicious noise coming from downstairs. Well then you might creep downstairs very stealthy, standing on the bits of the steps that join onto the wall, because those bits hardly ever creak, and missing out the second step altogether because sadly all of that step creaks all the time. And when you got to this step here instead of thinking oh Christ I should have brought a light saver or at least a sword you could gently wriggle the banister back like this and un-slot it from the bottom bit, and that would be truly excellent because then you would have a big knobbly stick secret weapon! Take that, baddy! Whack, duck, jab, spin, poke, hit, slash, knockout!

But be careful while you are attacking because you must never stick sticks in your eyes.

I re-slot the banister into its hole which is also called a socket, like you have for eyes and plugs and hips. Did you know that gibbons have ball-and-socket joints in their wrists? This makes them the most outstanding of all animals who make their home in the tree canopy. Hush now, Son. I can hear voices through the leaves.

— That is absurd.

— We have to take all such reports very seriously. I'm sure you understand. We have a duty to investigate all claims of this nature.

— What did you say the woman's name was?

— She's asked to remain anonymous.

— What?

— We have to protect her identity, if that's what she wants.

— I'll bet she does.

Dad pauses. It's not a what-shall-I-say-next pause, though, but the I-better-not-say-anything-for-a-moment opposite. I rattle the banister again. Then I pull it out. Mark in Year One dislocated his thumb falling off his scooter once. Gently: knock, knock, knock. The other banisters are a bit like a xylophone for this one, only all the notes are the same. The pause stops.

— Anonymous, Dad says.

— I understand how . . . difficult this must be for you. My advice is that you cooperate fully with the process. Doing so will help your case. All I'm asking in the first instance is for you to explain your version of events, and allow me to talk to the child in question. Once I've done that I'll have everything I need to make my report. Then we'll be able to take the matter forward appropriately.

— Appropriately.

— You could begin by telling me the child's name.

— I could. Another pause, then: — What did this woman report to you exactly? What did she say?

Dad's voice is very loud even though the door is half shut. It sounds as if he's throwing bits of brick into a bucket. When Butterfly woman replies it sounds very different indeed, all smooth and round. You have to plant daffodil bulbs gently in soft soil.

— As I say, if you could begin by telling me your version of what happened this morning in Alexandra Lane, adjacent to the park, that would be the best way forward.

— You keep saying that. Version. It's as if you doubt me before I've even opened my mouth. VERSION?

Just then, as I'm about to start rattling the xylophone banisters again, I realize I need the loo.

I never do number-twos at school. Don't ask me why because I won't tell you, just like I won't tell anyone at school when I need to do number-twos. It's easy: instead of saying anything I just stop myself needing to go until I get home. But sometimes I can only stop myself needing to go until Dad comes to collect me and then I have to tell him I need to do number-twos. It is better to say so when you're still in the school because Dad says — Righto! very cheerfully when there are people nearby and besides they have toilets there. If you can wait till home that's fine, too. But the worst place to say I need to do number-twos is halfway home because then we have to stop at the café or the woody bit by the park and although he might say — Righto! let's do a sneaky one, he might also say, — Can't you wait? and if you say — No, he might do the thing with his teeth and say — For Christ's sake, why oh why didn't you just do one before we set off? Cows do manure and birds do guano. I already told you about their islands.

There are footsteps behind me and hello what's this, it's Mum coming down early.

— What's going on? she asks. — Where's Dad?

— I need the loo.

— Why is he shouting at you?

Her hair is sticking out at one side like the feathers on the broken wing of a scarlet macaw I saw once at the Zoo, and she's wearing her bathrobe with the hole by the collar. I ripped it by hanging on after a cuddle but I didn't mean to so never mind. She rubs her forehead.

— I need the loo, I repeat.

— Really? she says. — Well put the staircase back together before you go.

I turn to do as she says but the banister decides to be a slippery customer just then and it falls through the gap onto the cabinet thing below. Very clattering. It means I don't hear the next thing Dad shout-says at Butterfly lady, only the bit after it, which goes: — *myself to sodding anyone!*

— Who's he talking to?

— Sheila with a butterfly from the cow sill.

— What?

She steps round me pulling her bathrobe together at the throat. Careful, Mum! It rips very easily because it's not at all durable. Our cat Richard has a bare bit on the back of his neck, too, from his collar which he lost, so now there's just the bare bit. It's quite lucky Dad didn't see me drop the banister on the cabinet because it may look like an old thing you put your shoes in and that's exactly what it is, but it isn't just that because it's also one of his air looms. Ancestors pass all sorts of air looms down and this is what we got from ours. Here you go, you keep it, and give it to someone else when you die! Not ancient ancestors like the dinosaurs. They didn't have things to give away. Just meat and instincts. You there: would you like some of my latest dead thing? No thanks I'm all right. In which case, sorry, you'll just have to make do with some of these prime-ape instincts. Thank you very much, that's marvelous.

Mum goes into the kitchen. I follow behind her bathrobe wings. Hello again, bin.

— Now we've woken my wife, says Dad.

— I hadn't yet managed to sleep. What's going on?

— Billy, he says. I told you to . . . He trails off.

— My name is Sheila Hudson, Butterfly woman tells Mum. She takes a clipboard thing out of her bag. It is made out of the same stuff as jeans so don't drag it along the pavement or you'll get holes in its knees. Now she opens the folder and takes out a little card and gives it to Mum. We have a similar plastic card thing at school which we put in the right box. Here I am, our cards say, completely at school and ready for my packed lunches. Mum takes Sheila Hudson's card and looks at it.

— Tessa Wright, says Mum, glancing at Dad. — How can we help?

— Ms. Hudson was just on her way out, Dad says.

— This is a delicate matter, Butterfly woman tells her jeans-pad thing. — I'm here because—

— Some busybody has been spreading malicious rumors, interrupts Dad. His voice has balloons in it, now. Watch they don't pop! He goes on: — I've told Ms. Hudson there's been a mistake, and she's going.

— Rumors, Mum says. — What do you mean?

— I'll explain in a minute.

Mum's face has gone very still. It's the same face she had when someone crashed into our car in the supermarket park. Let's just drive slowly along here following the arrows shall we? But what's this? Only a car jumping backward straight into our way. Crunch!

— Are you all right? Mum asked me.

— Yes thank you. We crashed!

— Yes. Carefully she took a pen from the glove box. Then out she got, but not in a rush, the opposite in fact, more like a Slow Loris eating an orange: I'll peel this thing, and then I'll eat it, all in good time, just you wait and see. — Can I have your insurance details please?

She blinks at the lady from the cow sill now and says, — Would you mind telling me exactly what is going on?

The knitted butterfly tries to flap free again as the woman takes another breath but it's pointless. — Of course, she says. Then she glances from me to Mum and Dad, moving her head too much as she does it, like the rubbish puppet at Jacob's birthday. All the puppet could do was nod and clap and when it walked it looked like it was going in reverse. Watch out behind there. Crash. Herbivores generally have eyes on the side of their head which would make them very accurate in car parks. Nobody says anything for an odd long second but Dad folds his arms and this makes Sheila Butterfly take another flightless breath. There are loads of birds in Madagascar which can't fly at all because of the useless predators.

— I think it would be best if we three had a discussion in private, the woman suggests.

Dad stares at her. Then he walks over to the bin and says, — Snack time, Son. What do you fancy?

— Orange juice without bits in, I say very quickly. — And a chocolate chip biscuit.

— Coming up.

He opens the cupboard and takes out a glass. I stand on one leg because suddenly this is brilliant. But Dad is going underwater-slow. I can swim a width without breathing, nearly. Orca is another name for killer whale. Like peas, they come in pods. Come on, Dad, we're all waiting here with baited hooks. But something isn't right at all. Have you ever seen two strange cats on a wall? Well Mum and Butterfly remind me of that. They're both standing way too still, watching each other, and waiting, waiting, waiting, while Dad makes a slow-motion snack. David Attenborough has a camera that he uses to catch the droplets polar bears shake off their top-predator necks. And Mum is chewing her lip. Don't eat it, Mum, we have biscuits. But waiting for them to arrive is so boring I decide to stand on the other leg.

No, no, no! How can a highly intelligent human being do something so slowly and still get it wrong? That's orange squash, not juice, and a very incorrect digestive biscuit. I open my mouth to say hold on hold on hold on that's a mistake you've made there, Dad, but I don't, because my instincts tell me that anything I say right now will be bad for the whole species.

Mum and Butterfly watch as Dad pours out the wrong drink and sits the wrong biscuit on a plate. Anyone would think he was doing fascinating experiments. It's not even for them! At last he puts the snack down carefully on the kitchen table and pulls back a chair and gives me an odd smile. — There you go, he says with the balloon still in his voice. — There you go.

I take a bite of digestive. Chameleons aren't just camouflage experts: they have killer tongues. And it's not only the biscuit which tastes odd right now. Everything does.

— What's going on, Jim? Mum asks again.

— Perhaps we could talk next door? says Butterfly.

Dad growls: — This is Billy's house. You can say what you have to say in front of him.

I take a little sip of squash. It's all right. I would have preferred proper juice though, even if it did have to have bits in.

But hold on, what's this? Butterfly puts her jeans file down on the side quite firmly and stands a little bit straighter up and says, — No, that would not be appropriate.

And something about the way that she says it sends a cat message to Mum, because she jumps off the wall and sort of swoops down on me with a headlamp smile and picks up the plate and glass and swishes me past Dad — too slow, Dad! —through the door into the front room. — Tell you what, she says, — you can finish your snack in front of the TV.

How about that! Yes, yes, yes, truly excellent news.

I say, — *Life of Mammals*, please.

— Which one?

— *Meat Eaters*.

— Again?

— Yes please.

She sighs but I can tell she's not going to argue and she immediately proves me right by saying, — Okay, coming up, and launching into highly effective mode. She whips the DVD out of its box and slots it into the little tray, thank you tray, red light, in you go, blue light, and zip zap yes, yes, yes, that's the right episode. Swelly music. Zebra's eye. Yes!

Do you like David Attenborough? Of course, because everyone does, and so do I. I like all of him. But if I had to pick the bit I like best it would be relatively easy: I like his voice more than his other bits. God does not exist. But if there was a God, which there isn't, because of the evidence, which there isn't enough of, Son, he would sound exactly like David Attenborough, and Dad agrees with that. He might even have noticed it first. I've watched the DVD of *Meat Eaters* so many times I know nearly all the words.

But even though I do the thing of saying what David Attenborough says exactly when he says it the voices from the kitchen interrupt me just after the first kill. Not all of the words make sense, especially mixed in with *Meat Eaters*, but some do.

— Calm down, Jim. Please.

Truly explosive pace.

— Something, something, child protection, something, duty.

The fastest of all land animals.

— Explain myself to a fucking stranger.

Keep its head still even at such speeds.

— Please calm down.

But the impala is no slouch.

— Assessment team, something, work closely, something, police.

Cubs look on.

— Something, silly something, ahead and call them.

Long tail acts as a counterbalance.

— Jim, please . . . Cup of tea . . . He's not serious.

They go quiet for a while then and I get to watch the excellent sequence including the bit Dad calls the money-shot in peace and quiet, right up to the distended belly. It means fat.

But just after that, no, no, no, at the part with the cub with the bloody head from sticking it into the zebra's insides, no, no, no, the DVD starts jumping. Not this again. The screen goes all flickery like Great-Grandma's bad eye. Old people always go wrong in the end and in that way Dad says they are just like everything else. That's the thing about everything, Son: it all falls apart in the end.

I wait.

The cheetah cub jabbers his face in and out of the stripy stomach a thousand tiny times.

Come on come on come on you can do it.

But no.

After a bit the cub stops trying to get to the next scene altogether.

When I was vertically a baby I posted some crackers into the video slot and ever since then I am sadly not allowed to touch either it or the DVD machine.

So I slide off the sofa arm and go for help which is called summering reinforcements.

The kitchen door is shut.

They are still talking behind it.

Mum says, — Of course I believe you, Jim. That's why I see no harm in letting Miss Hudson talk to him.

— What's the point? hisses Dad. — He ran away . . . straight into a fucking road.

Imagine the stillest thing you can imagine. A swing with nobody on it perhaps, or a hammer that's fallen down the back of a sofa. That's how still I go when I hear him telling. *It's in the past.* That's what he said. He said what I did was *forgotten.*

— And if that's the case, Mum begins.

— What do you mean *if* that's the case? Are *you* doubting me now, too?

Another thing that stays very still is a bear when it is asleep and I'm glad I'm not a bear because they hibernate in caves from the autumn right through the winter and all the way to the spring and sleeping is very boring. You just lie there with your eyes shut waiting until the morning. But hold on, maybe I am not right about bears because in fact they only have to go to bed once for the whole winter and then they are asleep and it isn't the bit when you are asleep that is bad, it is the bit when you have to go to bed and when you are lying there waiting, waiting, waiting, staring at the shadows on the floor and down one side of the picture, which aren't moving. I have to do that every day.

— Of course not, says Mum. — But if this is the situation we find ourselves in we don't have a choice. We've nothing to hide, for God's sake.

Butterfly woman starts planting more daffodil bulbs after that and I don't hear all of it, only the bit at the end where she says, — Consent of just one parent is sufficient. I can't hear what other horrible thing Dad says about me in reply to that because he's using very evil muttering, which is not nice, because that's what Miss Hart says: It's not nice to mutter.

I back away from the door and up the stairs to my step. But I'm so angry that he told on me, instead of keeping it forgotten like he *promised*, that I don't walk normally, no, no, no: again my feet by instinct go stamp, stamp, *stamp*.

Rabbits signal warnings of distress in much the same way.

But before I've even sat down next to the banister he's out through the kitchen door and after me and I immediately feel two things at once. Shall I tell you what they are? Okay then, I will. First, I am cross with my feet for doing stupid babyish stamping again, because I know it drives him to destruction, and I don't want him to be angry with me again, because I suddenly remember the hot chocolate. And the second thing is the opposite, and it's this. He made my feet stamp by lying and I don't care about having hot chocolate near the carpet, or even the snack and juice which he got wrong anyway, idiot.

Sadly it's the second thing I feel the most and to prove it I look straight up at him as he comes across the hall and I lift my feet and do one big vicious thump with both of them at once. Take that, stairs.

Dad stops.

He is three or four steps below me and our heads are on roughly the same level which is called staring your enemy eye to eye.

I am so angry that my anger clips his because among other things my hair feels like a billion tiny spikes sticking into my head.

Dad leans forward.

He is feeling something huge, too. It has made his eyes all narrow and watery as they look at me very hard.

He knows me.

I can tell this because how else would he know precisely what to do to infect maximum damage on me now? He reaches out and slowly brushes his hand backward through my hair and although it may look like he means it nicely in fact his hand just jabbers the billion spikes.

It is also two things at once: lovely and agony.

But before I have a chance to say either sorry or I hate you he's gone up the rest of the stairs past me three at a time.

His bedroom-office door shuts.

Click.

Sometimes when I go to school I say I don't want to go to school I don't want to go to school I don't want to go.

And in a way I wish I didn't say it, but it's exactly the same as when you shut your eyes instead of letting a fly fly into them. You can't stop them blinking and they can't stop it happening either, they just see the fly coming and whap, they shut. The word for this is reflux. Fly, whap! reflux. They're shut.

Reflux is another instinct from the ancestors, like when salmons swim upstream to get back to where they came from. Or at least they try to incredibly. The journey is fought with difficulties. The salmons may know the way but they don't know what might happen on the journey. Somebody else may have moved the river into a canal or put a dam in the way. Damn that dam. Damn isn't a bad word but you can't say it at school. Even if you get upstream to school, there might be a bear there fishing with its claws.

Sometimes when I say, — I don't want to go to school, Dad says, — And I don't want to work today but hey, off we go, and he says it out of the side of his mouth like it's all a very annoying joke.

Or sometimes he sits down next to me and rubs my head like he did just then, and says, — Son, I understand but that's just the way it is, we don't have a choice here, you have to go.

And the voice he uses then is more like we're finishing up at the beach and everyone's disappointed that we have to go home.

But sometimes his voice will go all bright like the sun you mustn't look at directly and he'll say something like, — Well hold on now but they have splendid toys there and there's so much to do and you love it when you're playing with . . . all the toys, and all those friends, yes with all your friends, you just love it, I know. And for a little bit we both know that he can't think of the name of anybody at school until he tries hard and carries on. — There's Toby, he says, — and Simon, or Nick, which one is it, your other special friend there? You like playing with him, don't you, I know you do. And his voice is so brightly colored it's not nice: he's like a chameleon stuck on orange in a green rain forest when he says that. Bad camouflage.

Mum comes out of the kitchen next. She sees me on the stairs and says, — Oh, I thought you were watching—

— It stuck.

— I see. Well, never mind. I'll put it back on after you've had a chat with the lady, Sheila. She's come especially to see you. You can watch the rest later. That's a promise. Okay?

— I want to watch the rest first.

— Well, she says, — You can't. Not just now. Once you've had your chat, okay?

I do a small growl.

— What's the matter?

I don't really know so I don't say anything. Mum takes my hand. Hers is cool like the other side of the pillow. Mum sits me on the sofa. She turns off the television with the mote control and squats in front of me.

— So Sheila will ask you some questions, and it's nothing to be worried about, you just have to answer them truthfully, okay? She's a very nice lady. You'll be a good boy with her, won't you?

— I want to watch *Meat Eaters*.

— After she's spoken to you, I promise.

— Predators please, now.

— Billy.

— Now!

— No. I really need you to be good.

— My head feels electric.

— God, not now, Billy, please.

— But—

— You have to be sensible.

— But—

— You will be, won't you?

Mum sounds extraordinarily pleasing now. Please, please, please.

I growl again a bit harder this time and kick my feet against the sofa to demonstrate superiority. Mum pinches her forehead for a second, squeezing as if she thinks that's going to help her decide what's next to say.

But then the shape of Butterfly woman is in the front-room doorway. Too late, Mum! She stands up with her eyes begging for mercy which is brilliant, victory to me, and she backs away.

Butterfly sits down on the coffee table just in front of me. She puts her jeans folder down beside her and smoothes the front of her skirt out and does another smile.

— Hello again, she says.

It's hard to look at her face because when you feel shy faces are like bad magnets, very repulsive, so I look at the woolly butterfly instead and say, — Hello, to it.

— What's your name? she asks in a slow just-in-case-you-are-stupid voice. But I'm not the stupid one here! She is. They told her my name and she's already forgotten it.

— Billy.

— Billy. That's nice. I'm called Sheila.

Let's all tell each other obvious things all day shall we? No, let's not. It's very boring. Never suffer fools, Son. But then again don't be rude. It would be rude to say yes you keep telling us you're called Sheila, don't worry we've got it, I know. So I don't say that. Instead I concentrate hard on saying something nice about her name, too, and this is what I come up with: — The she-lions do most of the work in a pride.

She laughs. — I know! That's true. But how are you, today, Billy?

If she wants to talk like this I suppose we have to talk like this: — I'm fine, thank you, I say. — And how are you?

— I'm fine, too.

— Good, I say. — Tigers are bigger than lions.

The butterfly wiggles then and that's because when you laugh your chest shakes. Good luck, butterfly. Your only chance of flying is if this lady here takes you to a space where they have zero gravity.

— And how is your day going? she asks.

— Normally, I say.

— Normally? What do you mean by that?

— It's a normal day.

— I see. And what makes a normal day for you?

This is a strange question but don't worry, I know the answer. —Twenty-four hours, I say.

The butterfly struggles pointlessly again. It's easier to look at the woman's face now. She's doing more normal smiling.

— I thought you meant that there has been nothing unusual about today for you, she says.

— There hasn't, I say, — except it's not actually normal. She looks confused, so I explain: — It's half-term. Normally I go to school. I'm in Year One this year which is normal because I'm six. But today I'm not at school and that's normal, too, because it's a normal half-term day. Schools normally have half-terms in the middle and now is the middle. Everything is normal.

— Everything is normal, she repeats, but her smile has faded. It sounds like she doesn't believe me. This is annoying but maybe she is right. Is she right? Yes, I think she is! If you're in the wrong, Son, it's best to admit it.

— Except that my hairs hurt, I admit.

— Your hairs?

— The hairs on my head.

She's sitting next to me on the sofa now, with one leg bent up under her bum so she can sit sideways and see me. Yoga has nothing to do with yoghurt. Sometimes Mum does pilots which is quite similar.

— Your hair hurts? Why is that?

— Because of Dad.

She reaches across to the coffee table and picks up her folder.

— Why do you have a cloth one? I ask. She looks confused again. — Jeans, I say. On your folder. Normally they go on legs.

She opens the folder and says, — It was a present. Pretty silly, hey?

— Why do you use it then?

She smiles and shrugs. — Billy. Do you understand why I've come to visit you today?

— Yes.

— Why?

— You're delaying my predators.

— Excuse me?

She's staring at me superhard now which is suddenly very tiring. And it's Dad's fault. She wouldn't be asking me all these questions if he hadn't told on me.

— What do you mean, predators? she says.

— There are two kinds of thing, I explain. — Prey or predator. If you're prey you must run away or use other defenses like camouflage or armor. But predators don't stop trying just because of that. They still want to tear you apart because of nature.

— I see, she says, but from the stiffness around her mouth, very concentrating, I think she probably doesn't see at all.

— And I'm here to stop these predators, you think?

— Well they're pausing because of you, but don't worry they'll start up again after you've gone.

When I was very little, vertically two or three probably, I used to like writing nonsense in small notebooks. I didn't call it nonsense, though, I called it writing and I learned it by copying Mum and Dad, because they write with pens, too, but normally I had to write with pencils. Dad used to give me these small notebooks from work so they must once have belonged to the man, and when Dad didn't have any of the man's notebooks to give me I made my own by folding bits of paper and sort of sticking them together with sellotape or sometimes staples. Careful there, Son, that thing bites. Mostly those books came apart. But anyway, whenever I had a note-book I would sit down and do hundreds of squiggles in it because I didn't know real letters yet because I was a very young idiot. Now when I write I do it using proper letters in words, but back then ages ago I just did little up-down-and-across marks with gaps. Everyone said well done keep going that's great, until my friend George's brother, Felix, who is in Year Four now but wasn't then, said no, that's not real writing at all, it's just total rubbish.

Butterfly writes some stuff very quickly in her jeans folder and smiles encouragements at me and what I think is this: So what? You're a grown-up and grown-ups are supposed to be able to write quickly, and anyway what you're writing is probably still total rubbish. It makes me cross to watch her, but hold on, that's not fair, because it's not her fault, it's Dad's. If he hadn't told on me to her we wouldn't have to wait here while she writes in her stupid book and I could be watching David Attenborough instead.

— Your hair, she says. How did your father hurt it?

— Viciously.

— What do you mean, though? Describe what he did.

I push my fingers through the front tangly bit of my hair but feel a bit silly so I tug on it to make the feeling feel worse.

— I see. And has he done this to you before?

— Oh yes, quite often, I say.

The woman prods her cheek with her tongue and writes something else. Then she says, — Can you tell me about your morning, Billy? In the park. What happened?

I have a think then and shall I tell you what the thought is? Okay, I will. It is this: I think Jesus was wrong. Not completely wrong, because he was excellently kind, and particularly impressive on humans, but he was wasn't impressive the whole time. He was rubbish at animals. Apart from fish. He made thousands of them out of bread. And that's fine. But I am not a fish. And I'm not an animal, either. I am a human and so are you, probably. Well done, Jesus. But what about our ancestors? Yes, yes, yes, they were animals, too. And that is why sometimes we still have to do what animals do when they are cornered. What's that, then? I will tell you, but first I will tell you what animals don't do, or do hardly ever, and it is this: you hardly ever see an animal showing you its other cheek. Silverback gorillas least of all because sometimes they're too busy beating their chests. Which is a signal for what exactly? That's right: it's a signal to say, you there watch out, you're annoying me and if you do it again I am going to rip your arms out of their plug sockets. That's right, bugger off, or I'll retaliate.

Dad told on me, and he got to go upstairs to do his own thing, so I decide to tell on him, because maybe then this Butterfly woman will flap off and let me watch TV.

— What happened in the park? Butterfly asks again.

— Dad chased me.

— Why?

— Because I ran away.

— And why did you run away?

— Because he was chasing me.

Butterfly woman does another smile, very reassuring, and says, — Okay.

— He was the predator and I was the prey.

— Predator?

— Then he attacked me, I say.

— He attacked you?

— He caught me first. But once he'd caught me he swiftly attacked me, yes.

— How do you mean?

— He hit me.

— Where did he hit you?

She really is stupid, so I use a slow voice to help her: — Next to the park, I say.

— No. Whereabouts on you did he hit you?

— Everywhere!

— And did that hurt?

Is she a complete idiot? — Yes, I say slowly. It was agony.

She writes some stuff in her boring pad again now, and then finally says, — I see.

Well done, Butterfly, it wasn't that hard was it? We got there in the end! She pauses and sticks her tongue into her cheek again and writes down something else, and I wonder will she ever, ever, ever go away?

Not yet it seems because she's got more questions.

— Can I ask you to do something for me, Billy?

— What is it?

— Can you show me exactly where you were hurt?

— Why?

— So that I can help it not to happen again.

I laugh at her then and she says, — Why are you laughing?

— You think you can stop Dad? He is more powerful than you! Most males are.

She smiles again. — There are ways of helping.

— Okay.

— But to be helpful I need to know where he hurt you.

This is probably a test. I bet Dad has told her to ask me to undress because he knows I'm slow at clothes and probably thinks I won't show her properly and will get into trouble instead. So I start getting undressed. I concentrate very hard and I do it like Mum says, super-efficiently, step-by-step.

— You don't need to take . . .

But I do! She can't fool me! I am already there, undressed.

And now that I am naked I can show her my spectacular wounds!

Butterfly looks at me. She sucks some air in over her teeth when I point at the wall bite on the inside of my leg, and she's also impressed by my other bruises, like the stairs one on my back, and some of the red bits, too, I think, because she looks hard at all of them, like you might if you saw an amazing painting of an otter perhaps. I don't say anything. I just point. The wall scrape wins I think: it's gone bright dark purple-red all around but there's still some blood in it.

— Is that from this morning? she asks.

— I don't want to tell you.

— Why?

— Because it wasn't my fault.

— Don't worry, Billy. I know that.

— No. It was Dad's fault instead.

— How exactly?

— He got me by a wall.

— He did what?

— I was running away from him and he was chasing me, and then he was about to catch me by a wall, and because he was about to catch me and I was trying to escape, the wall bit me.

— The wall bit you?

— Yes, because of him.

— Because of him?

— They used the railings from the wall to kill people with in the war. He told me that ages ago. Did you know that there's a banister on the stairs you can hit people with if you like?

— Right. A banister. No. Has somebody hit you with a banister?

— No, I say. — But if they did I'd run away.

— Have you ever done that? Run away?

— Oh yes but he caught up with me, like today. He always does.

— I see. What are these marks here, on the backs of your legs?

— I don't know. It might be because of always getting hurt on the stairs.

— You get hurt on the stairs. How?

— There's not enough friction in them. I could push you down them easily. Anybody could. And when you get pushed down them it hurts! Did you know a wolf's jaw muscles are strong enough to bite your thighbone in half?

— I . . . no. I didn't. But Billy, how did you get these bruises here?

— They don't hurt. They're just normal bruises.

— And these ones on your back here?

— Normal.

— I see, she says, handing me my T-shirt. — Thank you. Good boy. Thank you.

— I am a good boy, I say, getting dressed. — I hardly ever retaliate.

There are three boys at school who do ganging-up. Mostly it's against me but I don't mind and only two of them are in my class. The other one isn't but he is in my playground at break time. They are called Rufus and Joe and Eddy and they live in a close which is actually quite far away which they don't realize is a joke. Eddy is not in my class. He is the ringmaster and he has curly hair. He sends the others in to hit me first. Sometimes they will say something first like, — Hey you idiot you are a wildlife freak, but mostly they won't say anything at all. They just run up and push me over and that will be the first thing I know about it.

Retaliation is very interesting because mostly it's wrong, except when it's right, and then it can actually be your duty to stand up for yourself and let them have it, Son: don't let anyone push you around. Duty is called compulsory. But at other times it is very important that you don't fight back at all and instead use Jesus's weapon of choice which was his cheek, which he kept turning, which wasn't at all pathetic. Luke Skywalker has a light saver.

School is the place where the rules are very easy. Everyone knows them. You mustn't hit anyone or do aggression. Absolutely not! Not even rough-and-tumbling. If you kids must fight why not join the judo club? The teachers are in charge at school so you do have to do what they say, although this can be extremely tricky because sometimes they aren't looking and at the end of the day you have to stand up for yourself, Son, or bullies will keep doing it for ever.

Did you know that there is an extra sense some animals have for checking whether prey is in fear? I think Eddy is one of those animals. There's Billy sitting playing with his Tiddlos, just let me check whether he's in fear. No. Well he should be. Attack!

When it last happened I jumped up very fast and the nearest one was Joe so I grabbed him very noisily to show that I was up and he was down because he was. I tripped him over very easily using judo. But Eddy and Rufus got me from the back and I realized that they were working as a pack. I made a tremendous roaring racket to show I wasn't afraid and it wasn't camouflage, I really wasn't. It was quite good fun actually. I spun around but one of them had a finger in my ear and that hurt so I sat down on him and there was a crunchy feeling of the gravel through him. Then something hit me on the cheek but I don't know what it was. I didn't see it. All I saw was the playground, very close, very miniature, but no worm-casts, just sandy concrete. Next my neck felt nasty and then I realized what was going on and tried to wriggle out of it but I couldn't. The zip was done up. Of my coat. They were pulling me across the playground by my hood.

Obi-Wan Kenobi has a hood but nobody would drag him anywhere by it because he would defeat them if they did. If you strike me down I will become more powerful than you can possibly imagine. Feel the Force, Billy.

Unfortunately I didn't have time to use my Force because Miss Hart used hers first. She saw me being dragged across the playground by my hood and she retaliated at the predators. — Stop that! she said, and they did. Her weapon of choice is taking away your gold stars.

Butterfly's weapon would definitely be her folder, probably. Get back, get back, or I'll jeans-folder you. She is filling it up with words now. If it was a rifle this would be called loading it with ammo. I want a catapult. — What about a dogapult, Son? Dad said when I told him, which was annoying and not funny because dogapults don't really exist. One day I'll be allowed a catapult but not yet because they are like sticks and the God they had before Jesus. He didn't exist either but he did make some laws and the main one was that you had to poke out other people's eyes if they poked yours out first. Careful there! If you wave that stick in my face I'll take one of your eyes out with my catapult.

— No, I normally don't retaliate, I tell Butterfly again.

She looks up from her jeans and tries another smile but it's a weak one and suddenly I think she might either be confused or upset which is bad because it means she's even less likely to go home.

— It means poking somebody else's eye out, I explain. — But don't worry because I won't do it unless I have to. How long are you staying?

— Does that happen often, Billy? Do you try to fight back?

— Sometimes retaliation is the only option, I say.

— Really. Did you retaliate today?

— No. I promise I didn't. It's half-term. Will you go away now, please?

She closes her folder like Mr. Kneele closes the Bible when he finishes reading bits of it to us at school. Slowly. It's a great book, the Bible, full of tremendous stories. Bedpost of Western civilization, Son. Just don't take it as gospel. That's a joke. I still don't understand it. Perhaps I shouldn't have asked Butterfly to go away.

— Sorry, I add, looking at the dead TV. — But I'd like to be on my own now please.

She straightens my trousers because I've sort of pulled them up half facing the wrong way, which is nice of her. Then she tells me some stuff about how sensible it would be if she arranged for somebody to check my bruises to make sure they weren't still painful tomorrow or the next day and I do some nodding in time with her butterfly which flaps a bit as she stands up, because yes, it looks like my nodding is helping the butterfly to drag her away. Some eagles can lift up whole lambs but this butterfly isn't really doing the lifting at all. Its an octopus allusion. Still, off you go butterfly. Take your woman. Open the kitchen door. Get Mum. Bye bye.

Mum comes back into the front room straightaway and turns the television on again. Hooray. There's the little cheetah cub, still at it, dipping its bloody head in and out. Mum immediately fast-forwards the DVD to the gray wolves and goes right back to the kitchen again, shutting the door to say more things to Butterfly and leaving me to watch the whole of the pack hunting the caribou from the start of the chase to the exhaustion bit at the end in the deep snow, oh yes, oh yes, oh yes!

Actually the end bit is sad. Red snow.

Another sad thing happened in Tesco with Mum a few days ago. Shall I tell you what it was? Okay. I had my Tiddlos with me. Do you know what they are? They are small plastic things that you can have which are very small, smaller than thumbs, and they are made out of the oil which comes from the middle of planet Earth which is where you get plastic. Each Tiddlo is very different actually. Some look like an animal and others look more like a robot and some of them look like people and some of them look like nothing but you can still tell they are Tiddlos. Father Christmas made me mine but Andrew told me most of them come in packets of three from a shop. Andrew has thirty-nine Tiddlos which I believe in. Louisa says she has a million, which is not true.

I have three Tiddlos.

If you count to a million you will die. Yes, before you reach a million, you will become extinct.

The Triassic area was two hundred million years ago and this explains why the dinosaurs that roamed the earth then are all gone.

One of my Tiddlos is green and has a face like a saber-tooth without its teeth, but not just an ordinary cat. He is Saber.

Another of my Tiddlos is orange and hasn't got a face at all. He looks a bit like a tiny spade. I call him Sandy.

And the other one of my Tiddlos is pink which at first I

didn't like until Dad said he liked its robot armor shell because it probably made that Tiddlo more invincible than the others. He is called Vince because that is what Dad called him.

Dad says Tiddlos are amazing. — No doubt some bloke's got himself a kidney-shaped swimming pool by churning out these gobs of pointlessness, he said. — Amazing.

Anyway, Tesco is very boring always, apart from the day I'm telling you about, because of the freezers which have very bright white lights to buzz above them a bit like the light in *Star Wars.* And I had an idea. I held Vince and Sandy up to one of these lights to check whether Vince was actually totally pink or perhaps a bit orangey like Sandy, and that is what I was doing when Mum saw me.

— Hang on to those little tiddlers, she said.

— They are called Tiddlos.

— Yes, hang on to them.

— I am hanging on.

— Because you'll be sad if you lose one.

— But I won't lose one anyway.

— Put them in your pocket. They'll be safe there.

— This is an experiment. I'm checking to see the—

— Yes and the result will be sadness if the experiment goes wrong. Put them in your pocket.

— I won't drop them, I'm just checking the—

And that is when it happened. Just when I saw that even in the brilliant light-saver light Vince was totally pink, and just as I was having a feeling like getting out of the bath when the bathroom is cold, a sad shivery feeling, just exactly *then*, Vince fiddled out of my fingertips and dropped down into the freezer and I could actually see him bounce off a packet of something and skiddle between two things and disappear.

Mum put her hands on her hips.

She looked at me.

Then she looked in the freezer.

She moved some boxes.

She leaned right over into the freezer, toward the bottom.

Her coat went up and I could see a bit of her back between her pants and her jumper, and as I stood there looking at her skin which is prawny pinkish but not as pink as Vince I could tell that . . . that was that.

My Tiddlo Vince was gone.

And I could feel it coming up, a hotness in my throat which went up, up, up behind my eyes. And my mouth was opening because it had to help with the breathing. I couldn't hear myself yet but I knew I would soon, when I got enough breath. I breathed in.

Then the crying shouted out.

In and out, and in and out, loud to soft as the crying part ran away into the distance.

Finally I stopped.

And I was thinking why did it have to happen? And is it her fault for saying it might? And if it did why did it have to happen to Vince, my Tiddlo Vince, which Dad liked, and which was pink, which made me not like it as much as the others, which made me feel better when I thought of it, but then immediately worse.

— Oh love, said Mum. — Oh love.

— Don't . . . tell . . . him, I managed to say. — Vince is . . . gone for . . . ever. He will be . . . very . . . very angry.

— Who will?

— Dad.

— Dad? Don't be daft. It was just a little thing.

— Father Christmas brought it!

— Of course. But I'm sure the shops have copied Santa's

idea by now. They copy all of his ideas. I'm sure we can replace it in time.

— But please . . . please don't tell . . . Dad about it.

— Why? Her scarf smelled nice, like under the hot-air thing in a café.

— Because . . . Vince was . . . his favorite . . . and he'll . . . think I . . . did it on purpose.

It's hard talking when you're cry-breathing and much easier if you put your head into her chest and don't talk or even try not to cry.

And then later when I was watching *Insect Hunters*, Dad got home. I heard the door go. There was a change in the house. It got smaller all of a sudden, like the pupil of an eye when you shine a light into it. Cats have slit pupils. I don't know why exactly. Actually it's because of car headlights.

And I heard him come in and felt the house-pupil going narrow and then I remembered Vince who I had forgotten about, but I didn't remember him immediately, or even Tiddlos, I just had a feeling which is hard to explain but I will try. It went something like an empty noise and a hot pillow when your legs are tangled and it still being dark when you open your eyes. The darkness became a Tiddlo-shaped hole and then there was Vince, or not Vince: there was Vince not being there.

And I realized peregrine fast that I had done an idiot thing. I'm not talking about losing Vince. I'm talking about asking Mum not to tell Dad I lost him. Because Dad would find out anyway. And when he did find out he'd be crosser than if I'd told him.

That's what he says and it's true! He's always saying it.

— The worst thing is a lie, Son. I don't care what you've done, I just care if you don't tell me.

*

Now Dad comes into the front room and quietly sits down next to me to watch the last of the *Meat Eaters*. This sofa is quite old. The springs aren't really excellent anymore. When Dad leans back next to me the seat cushions sort of dip down and gravity means I go that way, too, and his arm is on the high bit of the back, so I end up leaning on him with one ear against his chest. Lub-dub, lub-dub, lub-dub. Sweatshirts don't have buttons which is good because buttons dig into your ears. Mum must have found a way to get rid of Butterfly in the end, so everything must be okay again, and that must be why Dad is happy to sit back and watch David Attenborough with me without saying anything right up until the end: yawning lion, swelly music, flying words. He watches in silence with me until the BBC yo-yo comes to a stop. Then he reaches for the mote control and . . . off.

Lub-dub, lub-dub, lub-dub.

— What did you tell her, Son?

— Who? I ask, sitting up.

— You know who. The woman who came to speak to us.

I shut one eye and line the blurry tip of my nose up with the edge of the curtain, and one leg sticks itself out straight as the other one wriggles back up under my bum. Then the legs swap over so I shut the other eye and move my head so that the curtain-nose-line works the other way around. I'm not sure what the right answer is anyway.

— Stop wriggling about and tell me. Whatever you said, it's okay.

— No, I say quietly. — It's probably not.

— If I say it's okay, it's okay. Do I look like I'm about to be cross?

— No.

— Then tell me.

— I'm sorry I said it, I say.

— Said what?

— Will you really not be cross?

— I'm nothing if not a man of my word. And I say there's nothing you could have told her that wouldn't be fine by me.

— Okay then, but . . . I'm sorry.

— Spit it out, Billy.

— I told her that I wanted her to go away. But I didn't mean it nastily. I hadn't even got to the gray wolves because the cheetah cub was stuck, and she kept asking me questions. Go away just sort of came out.

Dad's red arm drops down round my shoulder and he pulls my head into his chest again. Lub-dub, lub-dub, lub-dub. Eventually he says, — Don't worry about it. I told her much the same thing.

This makes me feel immediately good, like going past the top bit of the hill on my bike. Freewheel! The top bit of our hill is called its summit, and freewheeling means you can control everything with the brakes. Take a rest, tricky pedals, I'm on the brakes now.

— Did you chat about anything else with her, though? Before you asked her to leave.

— Not really.

— She must have asked you some questions.

— She did but they were boring.

— I see. Still, can you remember what they were?

— I had to explain food chains, I think. Some grown-ups don't know very much.

— That's true. Food chains, eh. Anything else?

— Would you like a game of chess?

— Not just yet, Son.

— She didn't even know that it hurts if you fall off a wall. She was quite kind with my trousers, though. I said thank you before I said go away and then I said sorry. That's really everything I can remember. Would you like a game of chess now?

Lub-dub, lub-dub, lub-dub.

— Okay. Fetch the board.

Back when the house was a cat's pupil because Dad had come home I knew I had to be truthful straightaway so I went into the hall while he was still taking off his coat. Some hooks on the rack are too high for me but I use the toolbox. Tooling is very human and prime-apes have been known to use basic tools as well. I ran up trying to tell him about Vince immediately because then it would be over and out and said, but Mum got there first and said to Dad, but really to me, about Dad, — Here he is, hunter of elk, trapper of furs, fisher of . . . fish. Dad! Good day?

And a lot was waiting in the air before he turned around from hanging up his coat with the burn in the sleeve from the bonfire, and the funny thing was that it wasn't just a lot waiting in the air for me. Mum had a face which was a little bit too happy and a little bit too stuck on. And Dad turned round and noticed.

— Ah the weather girl, he said. — Don't you worry, low dispersing, clear skies ahead.

Mum gave him a hug after that and even put her chin on his shoulder for a second. Then she saw me standing behind them, and winked.

But that made it even worse! Because then it was all down to me and my news about Vince the Tiddlo, which would make everything . . . worse! So I half didn't say it but I had to be truthful so it half came out anyway.

— Dad sorry I wish I was more careful, not an idiot, Vince . . .

— What's that, Son?

— I didn't mean to, it was an accident and . . .

— Slowly. He bounced down, squatting on his heels, bounce, bounce, bounce, and his face was second-beer friendly.

— It was an accident. Tesco. The freezer. I lost my Tiddlo. I lost Vince.

Dad looked up to Mum and shrugged his shoulders and shook his head. — What's he on about?

— Those little plastic collectibles. You know the ones, she said.

Dad turned back to me and his eyes went narrow and for a second it could have been a bad face, narrowing sharp to come up with something that might cut you. But then just there around his eyes there were creases. He put a hand up to his mouth and nodded his head with a serious I-see look, but there was definitely a smile behind the hand. Some nontoxic creatures dress themselves up like the ones that are actually venomous who they are pretending to be. More camouflage. I didn't like the smile. Sharp narrow would have been better actually. He thought I was funny.

— Son, he said. — Son.

He pulled me into his neck which smelled of outside, of leaves, raking, the mud that comes up. I wanted to pull away and go upstairs but at the same time I didn't. I could feel his chest tight with something that was holding onto itself. Was he trying not to laugh? Or was I wrong? Maybe he was trying not to cry? Human behavior is extraordinarily complex. Lub-dub, lub-dub, lub-dub.

— Son, he said again, more softly. — I am very sorry for your loss.

*

We play chess quite often and I know how the knight moves. Over there, that's right, and up one. And while you're at it fetch your mate. He can do the same thing in that direction. Along two and up a square. Pincer movement! Dog legs! We play for a bit because Mum has gone back to bed. When I was vertically four Dad instructed me on how to set the board up and what all the pieces are called and which squares they're allowed to move to and I made a very idiot mistake involving seafood.

— Pawns, son, P . . . A . . . W . . . N . . . S: noble foot-soldiers. Never to be confused with the scavengers of the ocean.

He generally likes to hear that mistake again and occasionally when we play I make a joke about it to keep him hugely amused but I don't say it today because I can tell he's not in the mood. Sadly I can also tell that he isn't really concentrating on our game. Shall I tell you how I know? Okay. It's because he wins it too quickly and then he wins the next game fast as well. It's not particularly fair and normally I would say something like hey that's not fair, my brain is not fully developed, but I don't today because he's not in the mood for that either, I can tell. After the third game in which he really easily captivates me before I've even got my pawns in a wedge he checks his watch and then jumps up and says, — Christ I nearly forgot.

— Forgot what? I ask. It rhymes.

— We're supposed to be having tea with Cicely and Lizzie. He pulls out his phone and says, — Find your shoes and coat.

I put them on and stand by the door, very quickly.

And off we go round to visit Cicely and Lizzie. They live in a house you can walk to which is useful. Conkers also have something useful called a spiked shell for defense. Echidnas are rarer than hedgehogs. Cicely and Lizzie's house is quite like our house because it has a front door and a kitchen, and even some cupboards that connect to each other which are brilliant for hiding in because you can go in one door and come out of another one, but we don't have anything like that in our house, and the other thing that is different is that their house isn't a house at all! It's flat, instead. Flat like a slice. Another way you can look at it is to say hey, look, this is only a part of a house, it's not meant to be a whole one, which creates the word apartment to use instead of flat, whichever you prefer. Both words make brilliant sense. So I don't understand why Dad and Mum always say let's go to Cicely and Lizzie's *house*, which doesn't make any sense at all, but that's still what they almost always do say.

Mostly Dad, actually, because it's normally me and him who go visiting.

Which is sad for Mum because Cicely is her sister. But that's the way it goes: Mum simply has to work too tirelessly to go round and visit people like her sister Cicely as much as Dad and me do.

Normally we go there at lunch or dinner because Cicely is a fantastic cook. There's a fox who is fantastic in a story with no tail. He is called Fantastic Mr. Fox.

Can you count to a hundred in tens? I can. It's easy, and here's how: ten, twenty, thirty, forty, fifty, sixty, seventy, eighty, ninety, one hundred.

Six is one more than half of ten.

But Lizzie, who belongs to Cicely, because everyone in a family belongs to the other people in it, well Lizzie isn't even three! Which means she's got to carry on living for five times all the days she's lived already before she'll even get to ten years old, and it will take ten of those ten years to make a hundred. You have ages to go, Lizzie! Neons!

The first thing I do after Cicely opens the door and says, — Hello Billy, is say — Hello, back. But the first interesting thing that I do is run in to the main room to look at the fish. — Hi fish, I say. The fish open and shut their mouths. This is because they are sucking in water to pump through their gills and get the bubbles out of it to breathe with, and not because they are trying to speak. Only an idiot would think that a fish could speak. They can't. Neither can Lizzie. She is too young to say anything yet, and she can't suck the bubbles out of water either. Still, Son, you were rabbiting on for England when you were her age.

Rabbits can't speak either except in *Watership Down* which is actually quite a frightening film. There is a snare which Bigwig puts his head into, and Hazel nearly dies of bullets in a log. The sky turns red and runs down into a field. I watched it with Dad near Christmas when I was still five and kept seeing the bloody field when I woke up. Actually it was when I was asleep, and it woke me up, so Mum came to settle me back down again. — Jesus, Jim, what were you thinking?

Lizzie doesn't have a dad.

She must have had one once because babies don't just arrive on doorsteps. The stories about stalks aren't true. You need a father and a mother, which equals a male and a female, who must do some mating with sperms and an egg. It is truly miraculous. — When you popped out, Son, that's the closest I've ever come to believing in God. Four weeks in and I was reviewing my thoughts on hell, too. That's a joke.

In fact it wasn't God who made me, but Dad and Mum, and I think Mum did most of the work in her room. Cicely did most of the work making Lizzie, too, and now she's doing it all because Lizzie's dad doesn't exist.

Still, Lizzie has a tank of topical fish. I open my mouth and shut my mouth in time with the big one and see Lizzie's reflection in the glass of the fish tank coming up behind me. She is carrying her drill in one hand and a circular saw in the other, and she is wearing her little yellow work helmet. She gives me the circular saw. I follow her into the little hall place where she has a small workbench thing next to the shoe rack, and I press the trigger a few times to whiz the little thing inside which makes the buzzing noise. We do some pretend making for a bit and as we do it I give Lizzie a running comment tree.

Shall I tell you why?

Okay, I will, but it is a secret, and the secret is this: it may sound stupid talking to somebody who never says anything back because what's the point of that, but I still say words to Lizzie even though she cannot speak yet because I'm doing it on purpose! It's a project. I am going to be the first person Lizzie says a word to. I know I am, because I am the one mostly filling her up with the speaking ingredients.

— What do you think, Lizzie? I say. — Shall we make it long or short, like this or this, with this hook thing here called a hook, or a screw which is twisty and a screw? It's up to you. Do you like sawing? I like sawing, with a saw. This saw is circular because this is a round bit called a circle, with teeth, which makes it a saw.

Lizzie smiles at me and says nothing back. Then she immediately decides she wants the circular saw. But instead of saying Hey, can I have a go on the circular saw now, Billy, please, she just bursts into tears and drops her drill and slumps down in a heap and her head goes back and her face crumples up like a crisp packet if you hold it over some flames. Never play with fire, Son: it's addictive as well as dangerous. After her face crumples up Lizzie's mouth carries on being a crisp packet: the hottest bit in the crumply middle melts into a hole you can look into or scream out of.

Lizzie screams.

She has very small teeth.

Two of my own teeth are new. There's a wobbly one in my top gum, too.

I guess that Lizzie wants the saw, and I give it to her just as Dad and Cicely come out of the kitchen to see what's going on. Cicely sort of gathers Lizzie up and strokes her hair and Dad looks at me with his hands on his hips.

— She wanted me to give her circular saw back, I explain.

— Why did you take it from her in the first place?

— She gave it to me. It has little teeth and so does Lizzie, I say.

— What's that?

Lizzie stops crying almost straightaway because she thinks the circular saw is incredibly interesting. She makes the whizzing sound happen and struggles away from her mum and shows me the round fake blade spinning and grins at it.

— Don't wind her up, Billy, Dad tells me, dropping his hands to his sides. — We've had enough aggro for one day.

Cicely's knees crackle as she stands up and turns back toward the kitchen. — Not going well, then? she asks Dad.

The kettle clicks off in the kitchen. With the light coming in through the window like that you can see the steam clouds pillowing in, but I don't feel hot. No. I feel shivery all of a sudden. Is Dad planning to tell on me here, as well? I walk around Lizzie's noise banging at her workbench and half follow the grown-ups in time to hear Dad say, — No, not particularly.

— Want to talk about it?

I immediately think of something fascinating to say about how in Yellowstone National Park, which is in America, which is across the Atlantic Ocean past Cornwall, though you could get there by going the other way, but it would take you longer . . . and then I forget what the fascinating thing was. Before I can say anything anyway, Dad is opening his mouth to tell her. No, no, no! Steam! From blowholes in the ground! Whales, dragons! I stumble forward, but too late.

— Not really, says Dad. Just that sort of morning. You know. Nothing to tell.

— What's the matter, Billy? Cicely asks me.

Nothing to tell!

— Would you like some juice?

— Yes please. Orange without bits.

Cicely pours me some juice. Her hands work exactly like Mum's, very smoothly, but her fingers are longer. While she's pouring and I'm watching there's a thump in the hall and Dad goes out and then he comes back in holding a parcel for Cicely. She looks at it one way up and then the other and takes the bag off.

— What lovely wrapping, Cicely says.

It's red.

Danger, danger!

She puts the present down.

— Aren't you going to open it? Dad asks.

Cicely does a little quick smile and glances at me and her fingers speed up folding the bag thing into the bin. She is shy! This is very odd because a present is nothing at all like walking past Mrs. McCabe, the head teacher at school, in a corridor which is empty because it's only you that needs the loo.

— Not just yet— Cicely begins.

But she is interrupted by Lizzie who has crept into the kitchen and now starts to cry again. Not melted-crisp-packet crying this time, more like a dog tied up outside a shop. — What is it? Cicely asks her.

And what I think is this: it's obvious, which means easy in your head. I open my mouth to tell everyone but Dad says, — Shh, and anyway there's a more interesting thing to think about which I heard on the radio in the car to do with experiments they did on dogs, experiments which proved that dogs can do more than ten different kinds of barks which people completely understand. Even people who don't have dogs! I'm angry. I'm sad. I'm excited. I'm . . . I can't think of the others. But Lizzie isn't a dog, she's even cleverer, she's a human, even though her brain is not yet hugely developed. It will get there, just you wait and see. There are whole countries in Africa, too, and the people there are less fortunate, so we pay a pound to wear our own clothes to school every now and then. It helps them develop. I wore my fuzzy spider's-legs T-shirt last time it happened and Freddy called me babyish. I ignored him until I realized I had a plain white T-shirt in my PE kit bag and put it on instead. Spider's-legs is too small now anyway. It would probably nearly fit Lizzie. Next time we come round I'll bring it because I know exactly where it is. She is still crying, but louder now and I don't actually like the sound of crying so I take a risk and ignore Dad's shhh and say, — She just wants to open it herself.

Obvious is the opposite of oblivious, I think. Oblong has nothing to do with it.

I turn a chair round so the seat bit is facing Lizzie and yes, what did I tell you. She climbs straight onto it up to where the present in its wrapping, very nice, very red, is sitting on the table. She reaches for it. Her hands remind me of starfish but squids have excellent suckers. Have you seen *Finding Nemo*? I have. Nemo only has one fin so he'd be terrible at opening presents but his dad never gives up the search.

— It's for Mummy, darling, Cicely explains. — Mummy's present.

Lizzie grabs it anyway. Also obvious: it's all so obvious.

— She wants to unwrap it for you, I say.

— But it's not for her, says Cicely.

— Yes, I know, I say, and I go on, nicely slow: — But Lizzie doesn't care. It's the unwrapping bit she wants to do. I know this because when I was small I liked tearing everything off everything, too.

Cicely glances at Dad again and it really does look as if she would prefer to open the present herself, which isn't like Mum, who always lets me open everything, even Cheerio boxes. Careful you don't spill them! But if Cicely wants to do something to stop Lizzie from opening that present then she should have done it sooner because Lizzie is already into the wrapper, very quickly nimble, rip, rip, rip. I'm impressed: by the time she is as old as me I bet she'll be better than me at zips.

Inside the wrapper is a white cardboard sleeve thing with a blue velvety box inside that and with yet more impressive speed Lizzie slides the blue box through the white one and pops the lid. Cicely sees what's inside and takes a deep breath. And I guessed right: she didn't have to worry about Lizzie stealing her present, because Lizzie loses interest in what's inside the box immediately. All she really wants to do is have another go on the sparkly red paper and silver ribbon, which has slip-slithered under the table. Down she slides to fetch it.

Cicely is still peering at the blue box's insides. Some tribes read entrails to see if they're superstitious, or tea leaves. And I lean forward to see what all the fuss is about and I see it. A necklace curled on a little cushion thing. Boring!

— Why don't you teach Lizzie how to do cat's muddle with that ribbon, suggests Dad.

— Not muddle, cradle!

— Not with little Lizzie it won't be, says Dad. — Take her to her room and see what sort of new knots she can produce.

Cicely still hasn't said anything. This is not at all like her because she's normally very chatty as well as polite. Perhaps she doesn't like the necklace, or its cushion. I take one of Lizzie's hands, very hot, very small, and lead her through the hall. The door swings shut behind us. I pick up the circular saw from the mat where she dropped it, but she doesn't care about it now, which is good for me, because the way it whirs when you press the trigger is in fact quite interesting. There's the fish tank. The one at school had a bubbly filter, too, but someone turned it off by mistake. Fatal, Son. Lizzie has already lost the tail of silvery ribbon so no cat's cradle for us but it doesn't matter because I will spend the time doing something better anyway, teaching her to get ready to speak by explaining animals to her using the alphabet. A is for adder. B for bison. C, crayfish. D, E, F, and G. She pretends she's not listening but I know better. Off she goes, inside her tent thing. Goldfish have a very short attention spam, too.

At school it is often quite boring. They teach me things I know already and to prove it I will give you some examples for instance.

For instance one day Miss Hart got out a box of vegetables

and held them up and asked us what they were. The first thing she held up was a carrot. Ta-da! A carrot. Then she held up . . . a cabbage. And then she held up a tomato which is not a vegetable because it is a fruit. I put my hand up and down very quickly because I could see her mouth getting all ready to tell some unsuspecting prey that fact and I didn't want to say the thing that might spoil her thunder. I sat on the mat with my hands under me but on the mat and listened to Alice say, — Tomato, and Miss Hart say, — Yes, and did you also know it's actually a fruit? I shut my eyes and opened them again as a test. Yes, absolutely everything that I could see at that moment of time was quite boring.

Dad says that it's my job to keep things interesting. I mustn't blame the boring feeling on anybody other than myself is what he says. I shut my eyes on the mat again and here is what I thought.

Radish.

Celeriac.

Palm heart.

Later I am at home in my own bedroom which is better than Lizzie's. Hello house opposite, any lizard winking? No. Lizzie: lizard. Neither says anything; they're both on mute. Did you know that Galápagos iguanas have black skin to absorb heat stored in rocks, but I only have a radiator? If I fetch my colored pencils from the drawer next to my bed and put a piece of paper on the Hungry Caterpillar book because it is biggest and the most firmly flat, and if I sit with my back against the radiator like this, brilliant, I can do a warm drawing on my lap. I have lots of paper. Galápagos iguanas are hard to draw but I person veer. If you press a normal gray pencil hard enough you can almost make it go black.

Dad's voice is gray-black at Mum downstairs. — Follow-up medical? She said what? Beyond a joke.

I press my pencil down harder and keep shading in the rocks until little gritty puffs of lead start coming off the end. It looks like the tip is burrowing into iguana world.

Mum's voice is colorless: whatever she says doesn't make it all the way up the stairs.

— Of course I'll take him, won't I, Dad shouts. — It's not like we have a fucking choice!

Something inside me decides to stop shading in the rocks and put my drawing down instead. Butterfly had a jeans-pad but I've only got plain paper and a caterpillar book to rest it on and I'm trying to create something spectacular, not write horrible notes. And that's what they're talking about down there, her, her and me, her and me and Dad and what I did. I feel the hollowness rush inside me as I realize this because it is evidence of lies, more lies and yet more lies. He said it was over but he is still cross and he hasn't stopped talking about it at all because he was *lying*.

I close my bedroom door. Shutting hard is not the same as slamming.

Mum gives me my bath before she sets off for her night shift. There's bubbles in it. I also throw lots of plastic toys into the water, including the two Tiddlos. Shall I tell you why? It's for defense. When I was smaller Dad used to get into my bath because it saves energy and anyway it's fun, and sometimes he still gets in with me. But he never likes baths having plastic toys in them as well as me because rolling around on those buggers hurts like hell, Son; ouch, they're murder! Well they don't hurt me so there!

Normally these days when I jump out of the bath I dry

myself because I'm six, but Mum is there with one of the large towels for grown-ups today. She folds it around my shoulders and pats me dry very softly, as if I was made out of tissue paper wrapped round old people's bones instead of young bendy ones and highly effective skin. Arms up. Legs apart. Something about the gentle way she's touching me makes me go still and breathe more slowly. I feel smaller again, vertically minute. She smoothes everything dry and then turns me round to face her and I see she is biting the inside of her lip.

— These bruises, she says.

— They're fine. Can I have some milk?

— But they're worse than . . . The state of your back. God, Billy. The inside of your leg.

— Don't worry, Mum, I tell her. — I am durable.

— What? What did you say to that lady about how you got these?

— I don't want to talk about her.

— But —

— I really don't really.

— Listen to me, Billy. That lady is very important. Understand? And she's worried about you because somebody saw . . . somebody said they saw . . .

I'm holding my sides very tightly and shivering a bit even though I'm actually quite warm, because it's a sort of tactic for making myself not hear what she's saying, because *I just want her to stop talking about it*.

— What's the matter? asks Mum.

— It's forgotten!

— What is?

— It! Dad said! So I don't want to talk about it!

She gathers me up in the towel again then and leans into me and strokes the back of my head while I cry a bit. The towel doesn't taste as nice as it smells. Dad used to eat Shedded Wheat when he was a boy, with hot milk, and cats occasionally suffer from fur balls. I calm down. And Mum, using a very soothing voice, and without taking my head off her shoulder, says that it's all okay, it's all fine, and all I need to do is tell the truth about what happened in the park, how I got the bruises, to the doctor the nice lady has arranged for me to see in the morning. Dad will take me. And yes, I can have some hot milk. I just have to tell the truth tomorrow and it will all be tickety-boo.

Do you have dreams? I do. But I can never remember them.

When I wake up the following morning the light is already coming through my blind which means I may be nearly late for school which makes me quickly roll over and stick my head back under my pillow like a lizard going for cover under a rock, only this rock would be useless defense because it is soft. Talons would punctuate it: it doesn't even smother out all the morning light! I shut my eyes and remember all of a sudden that it's not school today, it's excellent half-term instead, which means I don't have to hide under a rock to keep the day away or do the thing that always happens next anyway, which is getting out of bed to make a start, Son, because we all have to.

Eyes open, whap!

This news that I don't have to leap out of bed immediately is so exciting that I immediately do leap out of my bed.

And I didn't wake Dad up early today either because it's late and I've only just woken up so I can't have. The news just keeps on getting better!

But have you ever had cold hands? I have, and once Mum

suggested that a good way to warm them up would be to put them in a basin of warm water, but sadly I let the hot tap run for too long before I pressed the plug lever down and the water in the basin wasn't warm anymore because it was hot. Only I didn't know that. Basin sounds a bit like bison and yet I don't think you get water bison only water buffalo which doesn't matter. What mattered was that I plopped my hands deeply into the basin of hot water without knowing what I was doing, and unfortunately my hands were too cold to tell me about the mistake quickly enough. They sort of knew something was wrong, and so did I, but it was like we were shouting at each other across a windy park. What's that, hands? I can't quite hear you. Shout louder! Then, and it felt like ages later, but Mum said it was probably just a few seconds, my hands started screaming at me, and I knew exactly what a stupid idiot I had been, and I burst into tears.

And that's exactly how I feel this morning after I realize I haven't woken Dad up early, which is good, but suddenly strangely bad. Because, because, because . . . because I woke him up early the day before, which was awful, because of something I can't quite remember which happened after that, until I nearly can, and then do . . . which makes the whole thing come screaming back at me very loudly and with agony, too.

For breakfast Dad makes porridge with golden stirrups. I always want a second spoonful of stirrups because the first one is inefficient and normally Dad says no way, one's enough, Son, and then gives me a second spoonful anyway, but today he gives me spoon two before I've even asked, which is so excellent that I nearly ask for a third, but I strain myself very wisely and don't. He is concentrating on the radio, which is full of people interrupting each other because it is the morning.

Today they are arguing about the new clear threat which the first man says isn't going to go away on its own. The allies have to show we mean business. But we don't even know for sure they have the capability says the other man. There's not enough evidence.

— Precisely, mutters Dad.

— Like for God, I say.

— What's that?

— No evidence.

Dad laughs unfunnily and says, — Exactly. But it doesn't stop people believing.

After breakfast we take the bus into town. I sit next to Dad on the window side and he looks out, too, leaning on the top of my head with his chin. It is not scratchy this morning because he has shaved it.

Shop windows are like televisions, very full of adverts. The bus stops by one which shows a massive picture of a lady on a beach bending over with a measuring tape around her waist. Dad uses his for slash windows. We wait for people to climb on and off which is called boarding and is very boring, and I stare at the picture and try hard to work out what it is trying to make me want. Not the measuring tape because of the beach, and not the beach because of the measuring tape, which only leaves the bendy thin lady. She is staring past the bus with a two-headlamp smile on her face, very pleased.

— We don't want one of those, do we?

— What's that?

— A bendy lady.

Dad laughs and says, — Oh I don't know.

— We've already got Mum.

He stops laughing and says, — Of course, you're right.

Then his phone rings and he checks it and winces and sucks in his cheeks and lets the ringing happen again before he presses a button anyway and holds the phone to his ear with his eyes shut and says very cheerfully, — Morgan, hi! So, where do we stand?

The bus rolls forward. Good-bye bendy woman. Dad's good hand is on my knee. It stretches into a waiting starfish, much bigger than Lizzie's, then gradually balls up into a fist.

We arrive at the hospital and go slowly up the front steps with Dad still talking very pretend cheerfully on his phone, and we come to a halt in the hall. Actually it's not a hall but a bigger bit called a lob-in where they lob in all the sick people. In you go, go on, into the bright lights and excellent colorful pictures. Here's one of a whale grinning. But sadly the artist got the eye wrong. It's way too near the blowhole and it's all long and slitty. His brush must have slipped. As a result the whale's smile looks a bit fake. Dad's phone snaps shut behind me so I turn round and tell him about a superb species of fast-swimming and edible fish.

— What's that?

— Red snappers. David Attenborough says —

— Not now, Billy. He shoves his phone hard into his pocket and takes me over to some plastic chairs which are cleverly bolted onto the floor. It is all squares. You could play chess in here if you had any pieces. Chess is like kitchen roll, very absorbing. It will take your mind off anything.

— Do they have any pieces? I ask Dad.

— Enough about species, Son.

— No, no, no. If we have a game we can mop up the bad news from your phone.

He plonks me onto a plastic chair and squats down in front

of me. In baseball, which they play in America, which is near Cornwall, they have a man who squats like this the whole time. Dad shakes his head and pinches the top of his nose.

— Okay, Billy. Listen. This is important.

— I know, I say.

— We're going to see a doctor.

— I know. And I'm going to tell the truth.

— Right. Good. The doctor wants to look at you and ask you about your bruises. How you got them. And it's very important that you tell him—

— The truth.

— Yes, the truth. The *simple* truth. No stories with it, okay. Just answer the questions. Honestly. And *briefly*.

— What's briefly?

— In as few words as possible. No wittering on about nature or whatever. Clear? The plain truth.

— All clear, I say. But the truth doesn't always help. You told me that —

— Did I? I did. Well . . . not always doesn't mean never. Understand?

— Yes.

— Good, right. He looks me straight in the face. Our eyes are the same gray color because mine came out of his, but right now I think his are more shiny, like cutlery. A cutlass is a type of sword but it doesn't cut less. — I can't believe this is happening, he whispers. He looks away for a moment. When he turns back he's smiling at me to be reassuring but it doesn't work because the smile is as fake as the whale's.

Soon we are in the waiting area with the babyish Thomas the Tank Engine toys and boring magazines and, look, here's Butterfly, she's come, too. Dad spots her pushing through the swing door and goes stiff-tall in his little seat because like a dog or a deer or a rabbit or any creature really his body movements have many purposes, including for saying things like Oh no, danger danger, don't come any closer, stay clear!

Butterfly doesn't get it, though. She marches straight over, smiles, and sits down opposite us, bag on her lap, a corner of jeans-folder poking out of it, very alert, like an Alsatian's ear.

— Great, she says. — I'm so glad we're all here.

Dad nods.

Butterfly leans forward toward me and says, — Dr. Adebayo is a very nice man.

— How long will this take? Dad asks.

— Not long, she says, still looking at me. — He's a very gentle doctor. Do you know, he even keeps his stethoscope on the radiator, to make sure the silvery end is warm!

— What's a—

— He'll just want to ask you some questions and look you over like I did yesterday, okay?

— It's a medical instrument for listening to chests, Billy, explains Dad.

— Oh. I thought . . .

— It was some sort of dinosaur. 'Fraid not. No.

— Carnivores use slashing motions—

— Not now, Billy.

Butterfly is still smiling but with confused eyes. She goes off to the lady at the desk with her bag bouncing under her arm. In Scotland they play bagpipes by squeezing their elbows together tightly. Top marks, Butterfly, inflatable.

The doctor appears. He offers Dad a hand to shake, then switches to the other one with a silly-me laugh when he sees Dad's red plaster cast. Very friendly. He takes us into another room, which is in fact two rooms connected by a door with a window in it. The door is open. Here's another little low table. This one has Legos on it. Sadly the bricks are too big for highly detailed work, but never mind, I'll manage.

— Build me a bridge, says Dad.

— Okay.

— And while Billy's doing that, says the doctor, — perhaps you and I could have a chat through here.

Dad pats me on the head and follows the doctor through the door, which swings shut. The glass has little wire squares through it, which would be great if you wanted a massive game of noughts and crosses, but I prefer chess, and for that you'd have to color half the squares in black, like the floor. Dad is standing very straight. He looks as if his belt is done up too tightly; I'd like to go and tell him to undo it a notch, but I know I'm not supposed to interrupt so I don't.

He's explaining something very stiff and quiet to start with. I can't hear it. So I construct some pillars for my bridge.

But then he says things loudly enough for me to hear.

— Of course not!

— Then don't in sinew ate it!

— That's ridiculous!

I need longer bits than they have here to connect the pillars up but these short bits will work if I join them with reinforcements so I keep trying anyway. At least I have something to show Dad when he eventually comes out, still done up too tightly, but pleased with me all the same; I know because he kneels next to me and squeezes my hand long-short-long. It's a sign.

The doctor appears in the doorway.

— Okay if I have a chat with Billy next? he asks Dad.

— Yes. Leave that, Billy. Come with us.

— If you've no objections, and Billy doesn't mind, it might be helpful to talk to him one to one. Just through here.

Dad lets out a sort of low sharp sigh and says through gritty teeth, — Of course. As I said. We have absolutely nothing to hide.

— Very good.

— I'll be just here, Son, Dad says. — No need for you to worry about a thing. Okay? Five minutes. With the doctor, here. Just be . . . I'll be right . . . outside.

— Okay, I say, and I give him an I-know-what-to-do wink.

The doctor has a lovely watch, very silvery, with a red hand that goes round smoothly without stopping. Actually, looking carefully, I see that it moves in tiny jerks. Tickety-tick. Seconds are short things. Very *brief*.

— So what have we here, then? Let's just lift that up and I'll help you take it off. Now those. There we go. How old are you then, Billy? Let me guess.

It's an easy question to start with, so I answer: — Six.

— Is that right?

I've told him the truth but he must think I am lying and he does, yes, because look, he's checking something on a screen.

— Well then. Six! Let's have a look at you. Turn this way. And lift up your arm. And let me just look at . . . Yes, yes. That's right, I see. You've been in the wars, haven't you?

— No.

— Does this hurt when I press here?

— No.

— And this?

— No.

— Well you're a brave boy saying it doesn't. This scrape here looks nasty. And . . . recent. Can you tell me about it?

— Yes.

— Good. Good boy.

I look at the doctor's face. He has very dark eyes, like tarmacs.

— Well then. How did it happen?

— Actually I've forgotten.

— Well, I bet you can remember if you try. Have a think about it for a moment, and then tell me how you got hurt here, and here, and here. Can you do that for me?

— Yes.

— Excellent.

Once there was a very rich man who pressed eyes into the tarmacs of roads. Cats' eyes. It must have been a hot day when he did it because they stuck in and they're still there, winking. Everyone gave him ten pence afterward to say thank you, well done, now we can see, marvelous, you deserve to be rich.

— Tell me, then. Was it all at the same time?

— Yes.

— And when was that, then?

— Yesterday.

— Yesterday. Good boy. And . . . what happened yesterday?

Last summer some of the tarmacs on our road melted. I know because I trod black stuff into Cicely and Lizzie's house. It wasn't my fault but I felt bad. Their house is actually a part of a house. A part of one.

— Where were you, then?

— Out.

— Out. Whereabouts?

— Outside.

— Okay. Outside. At the park, perhaps. Did this happen in the park?

— No.

— Okay. It's okay. You can take your time. It didn't happen in a play park. On a road?

— No.

(And it's really quite interesting this, using the littlest words possible for my answers, while being truthful, too. It is interesting because otherwise it would be very boring, because Butterfly and Mum have already asked about these bruises and now that Dad's given me permission I'm allowed to do what I want to do which is say as little about them as possible. It actually happened on the pavement but he hasn't asked me that.)

— Was there anybody with you when you got hurt? asks the doctor. As well as tarmacs for eyes he has lovely brown skin on his arms, and undone shirtsleeves rolled up above his elbows, and his big silvery watch slides up and down his quite thin wrist when he moves his hand about. I put my head on one side to look at it and the next thing I know he's undoing the strap bit. — Here, he says. You can have a closer look at it if you want.

— Thank you.

— Watches have very delicate insides, he explains. — But the watchmakers are very clever; they protect the workings with strong casings and toughened glass. Now. Was anyone with you when you got these nasty bruises?

— Yes.

Can you tell me who?

— Yes.

— Who, then?

— Dad.

— Okay, Dad. And what was he doing when it happened?

— Shouting.

— What about?

— Me.

— And why was that? Why was he shouting about you, then?

— He was cross.

— I see. Why was that?

— Because.

— Because of what?

— Just because.

— Okay. Is he often cross with you?

I put the watch down on the side and say nothing. How often is often?

— Don't worry. Nobody's cross now. Tell you what. Do you know what this is? It's a ruler, for measuring how big things are. I'm just going to measure these bruises. And see this, this picture of a person-shape, well this person-shape is like a little version of you, and I'm going to draw the bruises on it. Here. Here. And here. This is your back, and this is your front.

— Where's my face?

— Good point. I'll draw you one.

The doctor's thin quick fingers draw a picture of a face on one of the person-shapes, but it's a stupid smiley face, not very realistic, which is a shame because that's what I have to tell him when he asks.

— How's that, then? Better?

— No.

He laughs and says, — A critic, eh. But he carries on measuring bits of me with his ruler thing and jotting down things on the people-shapes, and although he's a friendly man with a watch something about the way he's doing everything makes me cross. He thinks I'm ever so slightly an idiot. I'm not. And I even know some jokes. Would you like to hear them? Okay:

What goes ha, ha, bonk? Easy: a man laughing his head off. And what do you call a blind deer? Easy again: no idea. Do you get it? I do. And I know some more, too, including this one: What do you call a man with a seagull on his head? Very easy: cliff. Do you understand? It's because seagulls live on cliffs. And what do you call a man with a spade in his head? That's simple, too: Doug.

Dad told me another one after he told me that.

— Try this one, he said. — What do you call a man *without* a spade in his head?

— I don't know, I said. — What do you call a man *without* a spade in his head?

— Easy, said Dad. — Douglas.

I still don't get that one.

And another thing I don't like about the doctor is that he keeps asking me what I did to make Dad cross.

— What was it, then? What happened?

— Nothing.

— Come on now. You've already said he was angry. Clever boy like you: I'm sure you can remember why.

— *Nothing.*

And this is the truth because it's what Dad said afterward, and even if Dad keeps telling people about it I won't because he said that it was all in the past, Son, that we could forget it. *So I have.*

— But something must have happened. This must have hurt.

— I've forgotten.

— Really. You've forgotten? How's that then?

— Because.

— Because of what?

— Dad.

— You've forgotten why he was cross because of something he said since?

— Yes.

— What did he say?

— Forget it.

— Well, it must have hurt. I'm sure he wanted you to feel better quickly. That must be what he meant. I'm sure you're allowed to remember how it happened, and tell me. What hurt you here? It's all right. You can tell me.

— A brick.

The doctor pushes his papers to one side and turns his turning chair, which looks excellent because it's got almost no friction, and swivels right round to face me properly. — *A brick?*

— Yes. A wall brick.

— What happened with this brick?

— It hurt me.

— How?

— It wasn't my fault.

— No, no. I'm sure it wasn't. But whose—

— Dad's—

— fault was it, Billy?

— Dad's.

— What did he do with the brick?

— Nothing.

— Did he hit you with it?

— No.

— Or throw it?

— No

— Okay. So it *wasn't* your Dad's fault, then.

— Yes it was!

— How, though?

— It just was!

The doctor's thin fingers do a long heavy wipe of his face, and when they've finished he takes a big breath and lets it out through his quite wide nostrils which have hairs inside, very ticklish. Being brief is reasonably hard and the doctor isn't giving up. He's like the ivy on our garden wall: we're always pulling it off but it keeps growing back again.

— Okay. Let's go slowly. You say your dad was to blame.

— Yes.

— Well, tell me simply. What did he do?

— Got cross.

— I understand that. And you don't want to tell me why. He was just cross about something. But what did he do?

— Hurt me.

— How?

— He just did.

— But he didn't hit you.

— Yes he did!

— He did hit you? What with?

— Nothing. He didn't.

— Nothing. He did, or he didn't. This is . . . The doctor digs his fingers into his tarmacs now, and he's trying not to show it, but failing: he's even perhaps almost nearly being frustrating. — So, you weren't running away, and he didn't catch up with you, and he didn't smack you for running into the road?

I think: *He knows. He knows. He knows.*

It comes out as: — No, no, no!

— He didn't smack you? He didn't—

— No!

— So the brick you mentioned . . .

— It was a whole wall. Not just a brick.

— But he didn't hurt you?

— Yes he did!

— But not with the brick?

— Yes.

— He hurt you with the brick?

— He did! It was his fault! The brick bit me first. Because of him! Then his hand hit me, too. That hurt as well. Afterward!

As I say this I realize the doctor isn't just winning because he's won, and something inside of me changes color, from glowing yellow to flat purple, and a wavy feeling rolls up through my chest into my face. It feels hot and heavy and miserable. I look down at my legs. They are still bare. And the next thing that happens is very shameful, sorry Dad, babyish: I start to cry.

— It's all right, says the doctor, very softly. — Here. He slides a big box of tissues across at me, but it's tricky to pull one out because loads of others come with it, and I get in a muddle, which the doctor eventually helps with; he holds an open tissue out to me, then wipes my face for me with it, saying, — There we go. Don't worry.

— Dad said use small words, I say.

— What's that?

— He said be brief.

— Really.

— Yes.

— Why do you think he said that?

— I'm not supposed to tell you.

— I see.

— We're supposed to forget everything and put it behind us.

— I see.

— I'm not allowed . . .

The doctor shakes his head and blinks at me kindly. How hot does it have to be to melt tarmac do you think? You could manage it if you had a heat wave like last summer. Mum has a hot thing she uses for her hair, but I don't think she would like the black stuff sticking to it. Do your fingers have eyes? Neither do mine and in the winter it gets cold which is all right apart from the gloves because gloves are a pain unless they're mittens. Shall I tell you why? I already have. It's because I don't have eyes on the ends of my fingers and sadly without eyes they are rubbish at looking for finger holes. The doctor reaches his hand out to mine. I'm not sure what to do at first but then I pick up his watch from the table and give it back to him.

— Not supposed—

— It's okay, it's okay.

— To say much.

The doctor clicks his watch back up onto his wrist and slides his chair away.

— You've said enough, he says.

I am good at swimming because it's important. Otherwise if you fall into a canal you'll drown. Once I did fall into a canal in fact because of some swans who I was feeding for the Queen, because she's the only person allowed to eat them. Swans have incredibly thick necks and powerful beating wings, so I gave them some stale bread. There were some other people doing it, too, but I wanted the swans to like me best so I stood nearest to them, right at the edge where even the grass leaned out a bit, and I fell in. I would have started swimming very quickly if I'd had the chance but before I got going it was already too late: Dad was in the water with me trying to get us both out. It didn't work to begin with. Both of us went right under instead because canals have steep sides. Then it did work and I was on the edge with the other kids again, only they were dry and I was wet. Dad climbed out after me and he was wet, too: when he stood up water spouted out of his laces-holes. We borrowed some bin bags from a pub to sit on in the car and we went home with the heater on. Mum was quite cross with Dad for letting it happen. Dad normally gets angry about accidents like that, too, to teach me a valuable lesson, Son, but do you know what? No, because you weren't there. But I was and I can tell you that when he pulled himself out onto the bank after me he didn't shout at all because he was too busy just lying there laughing.

Back in the waiting bit there's Dad sitting opposite Butterfly but they're not chatting, no, because it looks like he's trying to work out what his fingerprints mean instead. Superman can blow things up with his eyes. Watch out, fingers! Butterfly is pretending to read something boring, just blinking at it, and moles can barely see but don't worry, they feel their way very effectively. She leaps up and steps toward me saying, — Great, well done, Billy, I'm sure you were a good boy for Dr. Adebayo. But Dad is already up with a hand on my shoulder.

— Okay? he says.

— I'm fine.

Dad glances at Butterfly and growls as he walks us past her, — You've finished with us. We can go now, yes?

— I'll be in touch, she says.

We catch a bus back through town. It's raining. I watch the drops on the window for a while. Hardly any of them are going anywhere. I put my thumb on one, hold my breath, count to ten, let it out, and look: the drop hasn't moved.

— Dad, I say.

— Yes.

— Can I ask you something?

— Of course.

— Because I need to ask you something.

He turns me round to face him and nods: — Fire away.

— Is it mongooses or mongeese? I say.

And then it's absolutely brilliant because shall I tell you what happens next? Okay, I will. It's this. We don't go home. No. That's what he said we were doing but he changed his mind instead and . . . instead we go . . . we go . . . we go . . . to the cinema . . . instead! The cinema! Dad just sees it rolling backward out of the bus window and hits the bell button on the yellow plastic rail thing. The bus slows. We get off at the next stop. The puddles are jumping like someone's throwing handfuls of gravel into them. Take that, puddle, all full of spitting holes, take that!

And it's not a birthday or even a weekend!

But in we go all the same, into the lovely glowing front part and there's the ticket machine and a man behind his glass thing and that woman who weighs the sweets which, pound for pound, must be more expensive than truffles, Son. But look, he's buying us some anyway. Great scoopfuls! In they go and I don't even know what film we're going to see, and neither does he really, I think, because when I ask he checks the ticket before telling me.

— It's supposed to be good, he says. — Tall alien people. Econonsense. And a fellow in a wheelchair. Look at this; we even get these uncomfortable glasses. It's 3-D.

3-D means not 2-D. 2-D is 1-D less. 1-D doesn't actually exist because it's only a dot. Imagine if a picture in a book got up and walked off the page into the room saying hello there, have a look at the other side of me, all round me in fact, I've got no thin edges, because I'm a right round thing: that's 3-D.

Dad and I sit down the front in the middle, hunched in the dark in our seats, which Dad sort of turns into a sofa by lifting up the rest thing between us so that his arm goes round my shoulder and my head goes just there under his chin.

It's brilliantly under-the-duvet-dark, and in among the sweets there's even some cola bottles, and it just keeps getting better and better because look, look, look: he's pulled it out of his pocket, his phone, and he's switching it . . .

Off.

And it's adverts.

And then for a second it's quiet.

Before . . .

The screen is quickly there, enormous and incredibly loud and that's it, we're going, it's started, and we're right inside it, with things flying past us and a soldier guy in a wheelchair in a box on a planet with gigantic trees that twist for miles above the ground that lights up when you tread on it or run off a waterfall because he's lost his gun to find the girl one to help you escape the dog things with six legs that leap into the sharpened stick which jabs straight out of the screen as they're bark-biting and making me duck because they're really quite frightening me this bit with the moving ears and amazing snarling scaring him and Dad's chest is warm in the quiet bit that comes afterward lub-dub-lub-dub until they run up a tree and slash what's that bullets horrible man armored suit thing noise and big doing hitting again too with the man in the box coming back out for his wheelchair as the tall blue one flops asleep before it wakes up again and runs off into the mountains with the others in search of the dragons which will kill you unless you plug your tail in quickly and fly them down to attack the vicious helicopter planes and the massive wedge ship thing which throws bombs at the huge brilliant tree because apart from her and him they're horrible humans who want it to fall over while they drink coffee watching with a scar on his head until the man in the wheelchair goes back in his glass box to do something about it but really it's the brilliant blue things that fire the best arrows which sometimes can go through the cockpit glass but mostly can't depending upon whether your dragon is red massive or blue medium size before the mating bit which leads up to the biggest fight which makes the funny pipe music turn off for the crashing wallops to make the seats vibrate but it's okay because Dad's arm is still there even when the totally evil scarred guy jumps out of the thing using his armor suit to whack and wallop and have oxygen so he can try to grab the wheelchair guy who is still asleep wake up for God's sake until the blue one plugs his tail into the roots and makes the okay music swell up swell up swell up so they can live there for as long as they want after the film ends.

Writing comes then and the lights round the edges glow orange.

I sit up. Dad stretches.

— Verdict? he asks.

— Brilliant.

We walk the rest of the way home because it has stopped raining and exercise is good for you. Some people have dogs. If you're one of them you have to take your dog for a walk every day because if you forget it will chew the furniture and make you fat. But we only have a cat, Richard, who does his own thing, Son. Miss Hart at school gives us gold stars for being like Richard. Doing independent work it's called: in deep end dent. My reading age is impressive but Finn is a month younger than me and his is truly spectacular.

Dad doesn't say much while we walk and neither do I. I hold his hand and when we go past shops with cat-flap signs outside I don't even have to try not to duck through them, I just don't. When things are fine it's called harmonious and that's funny because it is vertically the opposite of harmful.

I like the beach. Do you? Probably, because normal people do, and the best beaches are near America in Cornwall with waves on them, because a beach without waves is like one of those daft hairless cats, Son. Try stroking one! Pointless. But watch out, you have to be careful at a beach with waves on it because waves do what they want to do, and sometimes all they really want to do is slide on in up the sand and steal a child or two. So don't go too far without me, Son, do you hear? It's the treacheries' fault. There are in fact hundreds of treacheries near the beach, like cliffs you can fall off into sharks' mouths with teeth that all point backward. Don't even bother trying to pull them out because they'll just grow back again sharply. Other things to beware of include currents, killer whales, and jellyfish, particularly the box jellyfish from Australia, or ones with huge ten tickles from Portugal. Yes, look out for anything tickly at the beach, and anything in a small Australian box. Some killer whales play tennis with seals and our cat Richard does the same only he uses mice. Very bloodthirsty: you might not like it, but it is in fact a fact of nature. And keep out of the wind, too, because as well as blowing you off cliffs and creating huge waves that steal children the wind will spoil your lunch which is normally a picnic. Sandwiches with sand wedged in them are horrible. Thanks for that, wind. Did you know that Cornish people used to live underground? Well they did, and it's cold down there, so they kept their lunch warm by wearing it under their hats in pasties which don't have seams like sandwiches and are therefore much more sensible for the beach. Here come the Cornish people out of their tunnels with their excellently designed lunch under their hats for a brilliant picnic. And if they want they can shout, too, because that's the thing about a wavy beach, Son: it has a restful sound track. Shout all you like, the sea hush will soak it up. Stamp, too, if you want. The sand won't mind. That's it. Run around, jump up and down, shout and scream to your heart's contents, and when you're finished we'll go for a swim.

And here's Mum sitting at the table very still with the kitchen door open, which means she can see us taking our coats off in the hall, and me putting my shoes away, but instead of jumping up to come and say hello and perhaps rubbing my head like she does after school on a normal day she just keeps on sitting there watching us and waiting until we are finished. The house is very quiet. We go into the kitchen where the quiet makes sense because there's no radio on and yet it still feels bad. Dad doesn't say anything either. But this silence is an incredible tactic which Mum is the best at because it doesn't matter how long you just wait wait wait she'll still be waiting longer for you to speak first and eventually Dad does.

— Hello, he says.

— Hello.

— You okay?

Mum drums her finger on the table. — Where have you been?

— Film! I say.

Mum bites her lip and looks at Dad. He nods and shrugs.

— There were cola bottles and blue things and a tree blew over with huge bullets, I say.

Mum gives me a little nodding smile but quickly looks back to Dad, and I'm hungry anyway so I sort of sneak sideways to the cupboard to look for a snack.

— You went to the cinema? she says.

— What's the problem?

— You had a nice time?

— What is it?

— You didn't think to call me after the medical?

— Well, I . . . thought you'd be sleeping.

— What did you see?

— *Avatar*. They were reshowing it.

I find the biscuits and check: they're not even looking, so it's incredibly easy to take one. Two, in fact.

— I hope it was good, she says, and Darth Vader has a funny voice, too, so that even when he says fairly nice things like *Obi-Wan has taught you well* he still sounds pretty unfriendly, and that's the same as Mum, because it's obvious that she's not really interested in the blue aliens or the guy in the wheelchair or the big fallen-over tree. In fact she means almost the opposite. *I don't care if it was good or not* would have been more truthful.

But Dad doesn't seem to get it.

— It was fine. Distracting.

— Wasn't it violent?

— I suppose so, in parts. Vicious use of panpipes, that's for sure.

— And now is the time to take Billy to a violent film. Today. In the middle of this . . .

— Tell you the truth, I wasn't really thinking. I wanted not to think.

— No, you didn't want to think, or return my calls.

Dad reaches for his phone now and the two of them are totally absorbing, like chess, so I actually decide to eat a third gingernut because nobody is going to notice and there are no nuts in gingernuts anyway and even if there were I am not like Connie in the other class who is allergic. Dad pulls his phone from his pocket, holds it out to Mum, and his thumb presses some buttons.

— Sorry, he says. — I switched it off.

— Yes, she says. You would, wouldn't you. Today. It makes sense.

— Look, the medical was fine, wasn't it, Billy. Billy? Come out of there! This'll blow over, Tessa. He was only with the doctor fifteen minutes.

— So that's all right then, says Darth Mum.

Dad's voice goes warning-loud then but it's okay, I'm nowhere near the biscuits now. — Look, he says. It's not as if we've done anything wrong.

— No. I'm sure not.

— What's that supposed to mean?

— It'll all be fine, I'm sure you're right.

— It *will* be.

— Yes.

Dad's phone starts beeping.

— And those messages won't alter anything.

Dad's thumb starts doing more buttons.

— Not even the one from me . . . telling you they've already rung us. That woman, the one who was here yesterday.

She says the doctor has some concerns. And because of that, because of that . . . they've decided they have a duty to investigate us, this family, further.

Dad's thumb stops what it's doing and he drops his phone onto the tabletop. Clonk. He sits down, plants his elbows on the table, drops his head into his hands. His fingers prod wrinkles into his forehead as his face dips lower, lower, and lower, until his fingers are digging into his hair. He has nice hair, Dad. It's the color of straw. But oh no, it looks as if he's going to pull some out.

— Stop! I say.

It works. His hands drop down as he glances up at me. — Come here, he whispers.

I've eaten too many biscuits so I do as I'm told. He lifts me up onto his knee and sticks his nose in my ear first, then my hair, then my ear again. He grips the back of my neck and holds me reasonably hard.

— Whatever happens, he says quietly. — Whatever happens, you must remember none of this is your fault. You hear me? You've done absolutely nothing wrong, Billy. Promise me you'll remember that. *It's not your fault.*

— What's not? I say. It rhymes.

— That's it, says, Dad in a small voice. — Precisely.

After that I go upstairs to fetch my stretchy lizards. I've got three. Two are the same blue-gray color but one is gray-green different although they are all quite similar. Stretchy. Pull them like that and they will stretch to more than twice as long and shrink in the middle to half as thin, but watch out you don't yank them about too hard, Son, or *snap*, you'll have a leg off.

How hard is hard? Not that . . . because that's fine . . . and so is that, even though the bit by its shoulder has almost gone see-through . . . but it's still fine . . . even probably when I pull it harder still, like . . .

Snap.

No, no, no. I can't believe it! But it has happened. It's terrible and I did it and now I've got two bits of one lizard, a leg and the rest, in two totally different hands. And my stomach feels very small and hard, like a Brazil nut. Perhaps if I put the pieces under my bed and push them like that toward the wall . . . But no, no, no, I can't, I mustn't. Instead I have to drag them out again and make myself take them downstairs to show everybody because if I don't I'll have done something worse called a lie. And although my stomach nut is horrible and both my hands know and tingle that they shouldn't have done what they did, and I really, really don't want to tell Dad or Mum, a strange tiny part of me is actually okay. Shall I tell you why? Because at least it happened to the gray-green one which was different anyway, and not the blue-gray other ones which are an amazing pair.

Down I go.

But I stop on the broken banister stair.

Because they're still talking and it is rude to interrupt anyway, which isn't the real reason.

— You told your mother?

— I had to speak to somebody. You weren't answering.

— Your *mother*?

— This isn't just going to go away. She knows people.

— I can't believe it.

I squash my lizard's leg-stumps together hard. You can barely see the join. I could just keep squashing it together like this forever and nobody would notice but it would be difficult at night when I go to sleep. Some batteries are rechargeable.

Dad's still talking. — What did you say to her exactly?

— All I know. That somebody saw you belting Billy in the park. That he's covered in bruises. That they're saying somebody — meaning you or me, presumably — may have hit him with an implement of some sort.

— Implement?

— That's what she said.

— What fucking implement?

— I don't know.

— This is insane.

— I know.

— Insane!

— So you haven't hit him with anything?

— Jesus, Tessa.

— Well?

— You're actually asking me this. I don't believe . . .

— *You* don't believe *me*?

Superglue! It's amazing, and Mum has some, because she mended my cup with it, the one Grandma Lynne gave me when I was born. Peter Rabbit. Mum actually cried when I told her I'd broken the handle off. Anyway it's mended now but I'm not allowed to drink out of it anymore so in a way it isn't mended which is confusing. But nobody drinks out of lizards so the glue will mend it, probably, and then my stomach Brazil nut can forget all about it. I jump down the last two steps, thump, and rush into the kitchen.

— But it's okay! I say.

Mum and Dad are standing at opposite ends of the kitchen table. If they had a little net and some bats and the right kind of really light ball they could play table tennis standing there like that, but sadly they don't look like they want a game.

— It's fine, I tell them, holding out my snapped lizard. — We can use your glue to put him back together.

— Billy. We're talking, here, says Dad, but kindly.

— Yes. I broke my lizard, though. Sorry! Superglue . . .

— Give it here, says Mum.

— Let's have a look, says Dad. — I'm not sure glue will work, Son. He may have to be a wounded lizard from now on.

— I'll mend it, says Mum. — Now run along.

— It's not fixable, Tessa. Dad's voice has scratches in it. Have you ever licked sandpaper? I did once but I'm not going to do it again.

— Run along, Mum says again, very calmly. — I'll mend it.

Dad leans forward, both fists on the table, plonk-plonk. He shakes his head. — Jesus, he says.

— Are you cross?

He keeps his eyes on Mum and says, — With you, Son? No. Not at all. Do as she says now. Run along.

I put the lizard bits on the table between them. It's confusing, but at least I'm not a liar and they're not cross with me. And out I go, as far as my step. I don't want to go all the way upstairs because I'll see the other lizards there and even though it was the gray-green one now there are only two. So I sit down and wobble the banister out and hold it across my lap for defense instead.

Once, I was wearing my shark trunks in the swimming pool, because they are excellent, even though they're unrealistic, because all the sharks are swimming in exactly the same direction, and in the wild that would not happen.

Anyway, whatever you do, don't jump into the pool until everybody is ready.

Fairly often, especially when he is in a good mood, Dad will finish doing up his own trunks and look at me standing on one leg ready in the changing room and say, — Shark shorts, eh. Shall we play the game? And this is excellent. And it is also what happened on the day I'm talking about. He was helping me put my goggles on. They are tricky customers because of the rubber which is very gripping but unfortunately a bugger for tangling in your hair.

Dad had his own goggles up on his forehead, very blue, and he sorted out mine eventually and said, — What about it?

— Okay, I said.

What he meant was shall we play the shark game now? And what I meant was okay, let's play.

Here's what happens. First of all I swim off in one direction. Then he swims off in another. Then I sort of swim around a bit and he swims back very stealthy, normally along the bottom, a top predator shark. Then . . . when I am unsuspected . . . he attacks! I have to try and defend him off by whacking him on the nose to confuse his radars. It's excellent.

On this day he swam off a long way and I swam off, too, and he didn't come back for so long that I started looking at the black lines. With my head under the water they were very still, but when I stuck my head out and looked down they were all wobbly, which was interesting, even if I tried looking at them with one eye shut. Then somebody else was in the way so I swam round them and decided to see what the ceiling looked like if I lay on my back. Some lights and some metal-pole things and a slit of window showing brown clouds. I leaned my head back a bit so I could look up through the water to check if the ceiling would also be wobbly then, and it was, and the cloud was greener, but sadly some water went up my nose because that's what happens when you do that.

And I really had forgotten.

And that's when Dad struck.

Whap!

I didn't see anything. I just felt the grip around my leg and arm and down I went, yank, and I was thrashing, and half pretend-punching through the water, very weak but trying anyway to see if I could erupt his shark radars, but I couldn't, and I was up again, and the water was double up my nose now, so I was half yell-help-scream laughing, and I didn't take a breath, but down I went again for the death roll. Over and over I went fighting until I got a nose-whack in, and then Dad swam down and off again with bubbles silvering up behind him, and I was swimming up again, too, because what I really needed was a huge big breath . . .

And that's when he struck.

Whap!

No, not Dad this time, but the lifeguard man in his clothes from the tall chair on the edge. He wanted to save me. But I didn't really understand because I didn't really need saving. Instead I thought it was another pretend shark attack so I did some huge excellent pretend struggling, including some nose whacks which didn't work because they didn't make him go away at all. He dragged me to the side of the pool instead and lifted me very strongly up onto the tiled edge, saying, — Stop! Stop! Stop! It's all right! You're okay!

— I know I am, I said.

— You're okay?

— Yes. I thought you were another Great White attacking.

— Lifeguard. I'm the lifeguard.

— I know, I said. — It's brilliant. But your shirt is very wet. At home we have a drier, but mostly we hang things on the line. It's my dad, normally, who is the shark.

— Your dad?

— Yes, him.

Dad was arriving then up out of the water and onto the side, too. He looked small next to the lifeguard, and worried: he pulled his goggles up but one side snapped back down wonky into his eye.

— What is it? he asked when he got it straight. — You're okay, yes?

— I'm fine.

— He's fine, Dad said to the tiles.

— He wasn't a minute ago, said the lifeguard.

— Yes I was! Tell him, Dad! You're the shark!

— Come on, Billy. Thanks so much.

— Did you pull him under on purpose?

— No, no! We were playing a game.

— Yes you did! I said. — You even did the death roll.

— I had an eye on him, said Dad. — He was just playacting.

The lifeguard peeled off his shirt and began wringing it out. Lots of water wriggled out of it, probably because it was so absorbing. He looked quite a lot younger than Dad with his top off, very pink muscled, and he sounded more important.

— Kids must be supervised at all times, he said.

— Of course.

— Not ducked.

— I didn't . . . of course. Come on, Billy.

We started walking away with Dad holding my wrist not gently and the lifeguard calling after us, — Anymore ducking and I'll have to ask you to leave.

I sit on the steps with my banister gun sword, very well defended, until eventually from in the kitchen I hear Mum say, — I've got to make up the spare bed.

Dad says nothing back to start with. Then he says, — Come on, Tessa. There's no need for this.

— There is. She's staying over.

— Who is?

— My mother.

— What do you mean?

— She just wants to help.

There's a long silent bit next, very long and quite deadly, like a poisonous snake. Taipans are the most venomous. Here one comes, slithering out through the half-shut kitchen door and up the stairs to envenom-hate me. No way, snake! Don't bother trying. I am too well defended.

But it isn't in fact a snake that comes out of the kitchen next; it's Dad instead. His eyes have shrunk. They blink at me. — Put your shoes on Billy, he says softly. — I need some air. We'll take the football.

On Saturday mornings I play football but I don't have any football kit or shin pads. Tom from my class has both. But football isn't about the uniform, Son, or to do with my class, or even school, at all. It's just normal, like the rest of Saturday, so I wear normal shorts because I am a beginner. Tom is in Level Two where they play proper matches using goals and a pitch and cheering. Football is a very running sport. That's the bit I like because it's the bit I'm good at because I've got a proper motor. Yes, you've got a great little engine on you, Son. In fact it's a heart, because I'm organic, and if Dad wanted to give me a better compliment about running he wouldn't choose the car to compare me to but a gray wolf instead. Look at him go! Back and forth, forth and back, tireless, keep at it! Lope!

Sadly the ball part of football is tricky.

Do you like soft-boiled eggs? I do.

With the ball part the thing that you have to do first is called trapping it. Clod the coach is always telling us that. He is French. — Ready? 'Ere you go! Trap eat. Trap eat! What Clod means, and I know because he has showed us, is that we should put our foot on the top of the ball and hold it there, trapped. You're going nowhere, ball, so don't even think about it even though you're very rolly. Come back here!

I have actually thought of a much better trap using a box and some long string.

Although we don't play games like Tom with shin pads does, we do other stuff as well as trapping the ball, like kicking it round some markers on the floor and back again. You have to imagine the ball is attached to your boot with very sticky spit because that's what it's called: dribbling. And remember, actually spitting is rude, so whatever you do don't spit the ball right out, feet. Okay! Keep going, that's right. Dribbling.

Then at the end we do actually play a small game without the proper goals Tom has or much cheering, and it really matters which team you're on because some of the very little kids wander off. Jake's brother, Tim, for example. Come back, Tim; we need everyone on the team to help, not just some of us. I switch on my tireless loping anyway but the ball is a bugger and doesn't go in the right goal for me very often. Never mind, Son; the engine on you! I was watching. You ran that little heart out.

Today in the park I do some running around after the football as well, trying my best to make Dad pleased, but sadly it doesn't work. He stops kicking the ball to me quite soon and we walk about instead for a while. Quite a long while in fact. By the time we arrive home again the sky is plug-hole dark and my stomach is vertically empty.

But then, brilliant, we open the door and Grandma Lynne is there!

She sort of swoops down and pulls me into her buttons before I've even undone my Velcro shoe straps. It's nice but uncomfortable and I feel suddenly shy. She holds me away without letting me go and looks me up and down with a big crinkly smile. — Billy! she says. Then she stands up and straightens her jacket and turns to Dad to say — And Jim, of course. I'm so glad you've brought him home.

Dad hangs his coat on the hook and mine, too. — Lovely to see you, Lynne, he says.

— Well I had to come. Straight from work, as soon as I heard. It's outrageous!

— It'll blow over, says Dad quietly, walking past us into the kitchen.

Grandma Lynne watches after him as he goes, shaking her head, her eyes very wide. It's only the kitchen, Grandma Lynne, nothing to worry about. She's wearing one of her smart suits; that's why the hug wasn't comfortable. And now she's bending down on her stiff knees in front of me to ask, — Are you okay, darling? Are you sure you're okay?

— Yes.

— You're sure, though.

— I'm fine.

— Good, good. That's good. My beautiful boy.

I feel shy again when she says that because boys are supposed to be handsome not beautiful, but I don't tell her that because it would probably be ungrateful. Instead I say, — Do you always take your suitcase to work?

Her eyebrows runkle up. — Briefcase, do you mean?

— No, that. I point at her suitcase in the hall.

— That's my overnight case.

— But you said you came straight from work?

She smiles at me again and says, — Funny little thing! But when I turn around I see Dad leaning in the kitchen door and he winks at me which is a sign.

Do you know some things about Grandma Lynne? I do because she's my grandmother and here is a selection from them. First of all, she has a car with a map that moves on a screen in it, and she keeps sweets in the glove box, but she never eats them herself because she concentrates on yogurts for breakfast. She doesn't like the Grandma bit of her name much and once she asked me to call her just Lynne, but Mum laughed behind me when I tried it and Dad said I didn't have to bother after that. Grandma Lynne listens to music without any words in it and is very important because her job, which is being a curator, says so. Curators look after things. Her hair is brilliant shiny-black like crows' wings, and she was once married to a man called my grandfather, but he went away from her ages ago and then, before I was even born, he died, and now Grandma Lynne doesn't have to have a Christmas tree because she can enjoy ours and Cicely-and-Lizzie's instead. There are more things about her, too, but I haven't selected them.

Mum makes me supper. I eat it. It's normal.

Then, excellent: *The Private Life of Plants*. It's an old one, but David Attenborough is fully involved in it. Grandma Lynne even bought me some Smarties to eat while I'm watching the surprisingly violent plants. Crawling, climbing, flying, thieving, fighting, killing: they do all of it! And Mum and Dad must both have forgotten the film Dad took me to earlier because having this as well might give me square eyes.

But it doesn't matter to me because it's not true. I've never seen anyone with square eyes in my life, or animals, and Dad once told me he agreed. — Old wives' tale, Son: they're compulsive liars! When some plants let out their seeds it's like bombs going off, and apart from the bit with the doctor this is probably the best day of my whole life.

Sadly everything ends, and that includes plant life, and I know how to turn the television off, so I do, which is sensible. I sit on the sofa in the quiet. This arm and cushion is quite stainy. It's my fault, because I was a very leaky baby and then when I was older I started drinking Ribena un-carefully in cups without lids. Mum keeps a throw over this sofa but it has scrunched off because I've been sitting here, and that's what Dad says about the throw, always: — What's the point? The moment you sit on it the thing comes off. And anyway Mum never throws the throw on, she smoothes it, so it should be called a smooth. Except that it's quite tickly. I burrow my legs under it; they're roots feeling for moisture. Any old Ribena down there? No. Still, now I'm planted I can't move, which means I'll have to sit here and wait until somebody comes along and harvests me for bed. It's not my fault is it?

Grandma Lynne is talking in the kitchen. — Things like this. They snowball. You have to react quickly to stop them getting out of hand.

She's right. The only way to deal with a dandelion in your lawn is to dig it straight out with the handle of a spoon. If somebody just cut my top half off two more of me would grow back through this throw-smooth in no time.

— I agree, says Mum. — But what should we do?

— Take some advice, says Grandma Lynne. — Find somebody with the expertise to put our case.

She's still talking about her case which reminds me to feel happy because she's staying the night. In the morning I'll probably have hot chocolate because she'll have tea in her bed. The spare room is right next to mine and the walls in between them are thin. It's called stud partitioning, Son; basically it's rubbish. I can even hear the spare bed squeak when she sits up in it in the morning. It's like the signal; squeak, she's up: go, go, go! Some people eat their whole breakfast in bed on a tray in case they drop bits.

— What do you think, Jim? asks Mum.

— I think I'll fix us another drink. What will you have, Lynne?

— I'm all right, thank you.

— Jim? says Mum.

Dad: — Nonsense. The bottle's open.

— Really, says Grandma Lynne. — I'm fine.

— We can't afford lawyers, says Dad. — I don't think we need one anyway. There's no *case* to argue. It'll fizzle . . .

— I disagree, I'm afraid, says Grandma Lynne. — You need to be pragmatic. She's using her slow important voice, very like the woman on the radio who reads the news. — Listen, if it's a question of money . . .

— No. No. Thank you. We'll handle it.

Mum: — *Jim*.

— There's no *Jim* about it.

My legs have heated up under the throw-smooth, which must mean that plants have warm roots. It makes sense. Even in winter: that's why they call it a blanket of snow. Sled dogs can sleep under one no problem, using their tail to keep their face even warmer. And carrots are actually roots, and so are potatoes, I think. But why aren't there any of them in the

Antarctic? No idea: no eye deer. It's true though; there are no vegetables at the Pole at all, not even parsnips.

Normally vegetables grow in patches.

A large patch of silence has spread itself out over in the kitchen.

Grandma Lynne plants some words in it, still very this-is-the-news carefully, to see if they'll grow: — I don't see why you won't let me help.

— Please, says Dad. — It's my problem.

— But I *know* a good solicitor who'd act for a nominal—

— *No thank you*, says Dad, in a voice which reminds me of the noise our cat Richard once made when Dad's friend Alan brought his excellent floppy-eared real spaniel into the house, very low and keep-away-from-me growly.

— Well, says Grandma Lynne. — I don't know. It's almost . . . she runs out of word-seeds.

— What's that supposed to mean, Lynne?

— I'm just saying.

— Saying what?

— Refusing help in this situation smacks of . . . I don't know . . .

— No, go on. What?

— It's just so *perverse*.

—*Perverse?* What are you getting at? Why don't you just say it straight out?

— It's not what it means to me that matters . . .

Dad's not keen on any of what Grandma Lynne is planting here, I can tell. The silence which comes next belongs to him. It feels like a large deep hole. Yes, he's got his big spade out and he's dug up all her word-seeds and now he's off to take them to the tip. Here he comes, stump-stump-stump into the hall. He sees me lying on the sofa and says, — Jesus, are you still up? Why didn't you say it had finished?

I don't know why but instead of saying sorry I do something silly: I duck all of me under the throw-smooth and pull it tight over my head.

— Get upstairs. Now, Billy.

Dad's voice is like car doors slamming in the quiet but I still can't help what happens next, which is this: I burst out laughing and hold the throw-blanket tighter still over my head. It's shaking because I'm giggling and I wish I could stop but I can't.

— NOW! roars Dad, and suddenly the covers aren't there anymore because he's ripped them right off. And he's very upset. I can tell because he's got me by the wrist and he's dragging me up off the sofa. Mum and Grandma Lynne appear in the doorway behind him. — *Just do as you're bloody well told*, he hisses.

— Ow, I say. — You're hurting my arm.

— Jim! yells Mum.

And Dad lets go very quickly, his hand spread wide, as if my wrist has suddenly turned cold enough to freeze his fingerbones, which it hasn't, because when I rub it the feel of it is only a cross between tingly warm and normal. Still, I burst into tears, because it's all gone horrible.

Next to Mum I see Grandma Lynne saying nothing. She can't really; she's too busy pressing her hand to her mouth. Then Mum steps into the gap between me and Dad and gathers me up and Dad un-freezes and backs away muttering, — Get him upstairs and into bed now. I'm going out.

— Where? asks Mum.

— *Just out.*

⋆

Do you like toothpaste? I do. The spicy grown-up type is actually my favorite now, but when I was very little and Mum or Dad put their extra-minty paste on my brush by accident it made my tongue feel too cold and too hot at the same time. I used to cry. But I'm much more coping now, and I've even got a buzzy brush like Dad. It's invigilating.

Also when I was little and Dad was doing my teeth for me he gave them names and called them out as he brushed each one: — *Arthur, Ben, Charlie, Dave, Eddie, Freddie, George; Harry, Ian, Jimmy, Keith, Larry, Marcus, Nigel; Otto, Peter, Quentin, Robert, Simon, Terry, Unwin; Victor, Walter; Xander; Yuri, and Zac.* It took quite a long time, particularly with the ones at the back of my mouth, which he always got to last . . . and . . . had . . . to . . . think . . . about. XYZ. An alpha bite. When my first baby tooth went wobbly and I told Dad he stopped in the middle of Tesco and looked at me for quite a long time.

I asked him what the matter was.

— Nothing, he said. — I'll glue it back in tonight when you're asleep.

Some people are scared of the dark, but I'm not.

I don't like funny noises at night, though; they bother me, so after I say good night to Mum I lie there listening for the normal noises instead. The most normal noise is the television but it's not on tonight: if it was I'd be able to hear some we're-so-happy laughing or screechy tires or dun-dun-dun music or HEY, IT'S GONE LOUDER NOW, BECAUSE IT'S AN ADVERT noise! None of that for now. Instead there are one or two cars slushing along the road outside and a dog barking and the voices downstairs: Mum and Grandma Lynne. I listen hard but can't hear the words, just the sound of them: a few very usual little bits together with some less normal this-is-the-news speeches from Grandma Lynne. It is all quite reassuring I suppose, but I wish I could hear Dad's voice as well. I can't, though: he's still *just out*. Just out isn't so bad. It's the opposite of totally out, which means a long way away. He's probably sitting on the wall outside, or maybe the front step. I do some yawning because it can actually make you feel sleepy as well as the other way around, but it doesn't work, so I listen hard again and hear the boiler creaking. Fine. Not as interesting as a helicopter or siren. Those things show that society is doing its thing, Son, and all is as it should be. You can try counting sheep if you want. Or shepherding counts. German shepherd is another name for Alsatian. Old-fashioned shepherds had crooks and policemen use Alsatians to catch them. Stop, thief! Go on boy, on you lope! Alsatians are one of the wolfest types of dogs. Breeds. Breathe. There goes the radiator, pinging softly. Underwater sounds. I roll over and push an arm into the underpillow coolness . . . and . . . ping . . . the pipe . . . hush . . . steps . . . cat . . . purr . . . tar . . . mac . . .

— Billy?

It's Grandma Lynne. I roll back over and sit up to say hello.

— You're still awake, she whispers, pushing me back down.

— Yes.

She bends over and kisses me on the forehead. Lovely smell, plus wine.

— I just came to see if . . . she trails off, says nothing for a while.

— Do you like Alsatians? I ask eventually.

— Listen, Billy. I'm worried about you.

— I'm fine. They keep German sheep.

— Yes, but Billy. If you need somebody to talk to . . . little

Billy . . . Grandma Lynne is always here. You know that, don't you?

— I'm not that little.

— Of course you're not. I didn't mean that.

— I'm six.

— You can tell me anything you like.

— Okay, I say. — Can you get Dad in off the step please?

— Good night, Billy.

— Good night.

After that I fall asleep. And guess what, I have a dream! I'm not going to tell you about it though, because, Son, other people's dreams are boring.

The next not-boring thing to happen is a loud slam-bang noise that wakes me up in the middle of the night. I jerk up, very what's-going-on? It's darkish on the landing and I am distorted. Then another stumping noise comes up from the dark downstairs and I do some big gulps. I could cry out but that would attract attention like an idiot. And I realize very sadly that it is too late for other tactics because they're already inside, so there's no point; I couldn't reach my defensive banister even if I tried. If prey can't fight then flight is the other option but . . . I go for camouflaged hiding instead. Dark on the landing, dark under my duvet. Go!

But there's a problem with that because how will I know? The robbers could turn my bedroom light on and see me bulging, and I wouldn't be able to see them because it would be dark inside my bulgy bit. Look, there's a kid inside a duvet. Let's steal him, too. All right then, why not. And I can't even breathe properly because I've curled up into a ball and it's made everything prickling hot, the backs of my legs where they're pressing the other bit, and the underneath part of my chin which is rubbing up against my neck. I can't hear either! I'm breathing too loudly and the duvet is a scratchy bugger which you shouldn't say at school so I stop breathing for as long as I can and . . .

— I'm sorry.

It's Dad. He's on the stairs. Creak, creak.

— So sorry.

I peep out from under the covers. The landing light clicks yellow. — Shh, says Mum.

— Tessa, says Dad. — I'm . . .

— Shh, she says again. — Jesus. Look at you.

— So, so, so . . .

— Shh! You'll wake—

— Sorry, Dad goes on in a huge whisper. — It's all my fault.

— Shh.

There's more foot-padding noises on the carpet. Then Dad does a famous racehorse wee and after that the toilet flushes. Mum and Dad's door snips shut again. I lie there panting and wondering why I haven't called out and I think about doing it now but decide not to, no, and I don't know why. I don't know what he was sorry about, either. Sometimes you do have to say sorry, though, even if it was an accident, like when Jindal knocked his water-pot over on my arctic tern painting, only Jindal refused to say it then because he said Beth jogged his arm anyway. Jogging is like loping and Beth's dad is a fireman; he probably never makes mistakes. The house goes deep-black quiet again, nearly. There's just the sound of Grandma Lynne laying back down on her bed next door: squeakety-squeak.

Once Casey told me Fuck in the playground so I gave him some advice and it worked. Do you know what my advice was? I said Fuck wasn't allowed and that Casey should tell a teacher he had said it before a teacher found out.

— They won't find out, Casey said.

I laughed even though it was serious and said, — Yes they will. They are teachers. Teachers find things out.

Casey was trying to do something else but he still looked a bit worried.

— I'll come with you, I said.

It's easier to own up if you have somebody with you. The easiest is when it's Mum but we were at school so actually neither of our mums were there. Casey didn't really want to come but I helped him. He's quite weak. I used battle of wills and person veering.

We walked up to Miss Hart. I went first and Casey camc afterward. — Miss Hart, I said. — Miss Hart, Casey said something bad.

Miss Hart has tiny lips like on a fish. She pressed them together into a funny little smile. A fish smile is an unusual thing because they are very inexpressing creatures unlike prime apes.

— Really. Well I'm sure he won't say it again, will you Casey?

I couldn't see what Casey said to that because he was still behind me, but it didn't seem right yet. He hadn't told her what he'd said.

Miss Hart was turning away.

— Fuck, I said.

Miss Hart turned back round again very fast like a diamond-back rattlesnake, and I looked for Casey so that he could explain, but he had run away like a gopher into the long grass.

It was all right in the end. Miss Hart gave me a biscuit.

*

Dad stays in bed until late the next morning but Mum and Grandma Lynne are both sadly already downstairs when I wake up, so I don't get to have hot chocolate in the spare bed. When I realize this I'm nearly angry; my feet feel hot and ready to stamp. But luckily I stop them because Grandma Lynne jumps up with a watermelon smile when I walk into the kitchen and says how about some pancakes then?

— Pancakes!

Mum says, — What a *great* idea, I'll help.

— We'll all help! says Grandma Lynne.

And Mum starts diving around in the cupboards like a dog retrieving birds from bushes, Alan's spaniel perhaps, though he mostly retrieves socks, and anyway he never gives them back, and she's talking as she does so, saying — Here's a wooden spoon, and a nice plastic bowl, and some flour, and eggs, and milk, let's have some milk, too, and butter, a new pat, and the scales . . .

It is called a running comment tree and is not like her at all.

I nearly shout Hey Mum I know you know where everything is; you put it there, remember! But I don't.

At least she's incredibly cheerful, which must be why Grandma Lynne is as well, or perhaps it's the other way around. Anyway I don't care. I just help, too, like Grandma Lynne suggested. I do some of the mixing and nobody notices two things. First, that I am still in my pajamas, and second, that occasionally some of the mix spills out of the bowl, which is normal, but normally it makes somebody say Hey watch out, you're spilling it. Nobody says that at all today. So I just push my pajama sleeves up my arms and stick the wooden spoon straight in! And for a second it looks like that's too much, because Grandma Lynne reaches into the bowl and lifts my hand out; but it's not to say Hold on, Billy, you're making a mess. No. Instead she just turns my arm over gently above the bowl and looks at a small red mark on the white bit, there.

— Does that hurt? she asks, pressing it.

— No. It's normal.

The scales aren't normal ones, though. They're excellently interesting, much thinner than the ones in the bathroom. Measure, measure, measure, scale, scale, scale: Spider-Man scales things in a different way and fish have them for other purposes, too, including waterproof swimming.

We make pancakes. Lots of them. Here you go, Grandma Lynne, have another with some lemon and a slurp of maple stirrups, fantastic, and I'll have another one, too, and Mum, because there's more mix, so let's keep them coming, Mum, keep at it, even though I'm quite full up, but never mind because we're having a really pancake brilliant time!

Then the kitchen door swings open and even the pan spattering on the cooker goes shhh. Hello Dad. His hair is up in blades and he's got gray skin to go with the iron filings sprinkled up his throat and round his bunchy jaw. He stops in the doorway and sways there a second and blinks at Grandma Lynne like he's forgotten who she is.

— Morning, he mutters. — I need—

— Pancakes! I shout.

— No, Son. His teeth bite down. — Not just now—

— But there's loads of mixture left. I've had three and Grandma Lynne has had four at least.

— Great. But I'll start with a coffee.

His mouth is having a good go at smiling but his eyes are dandelion roots again, or better still, radishes, radishes somebody cross has stamped into the mud.

— We were just making Billy some cheer-up pancakes, says Grandma Lynne.

Dad's smile twitches wider. — So I see.

— Why don't you go back to bed? says Mum.

Dad shakes his head a tiny bit and moves into coffee mode, unscrewing this and washing out that and tapping the black stuff out of this into that after filling the other bit with water and screwing it all back into one piece with the flame going and setting it down on top. Normal. He sloshes some milk in a mug. Pauses. Then he looks like he's remembered a birthday and says, — Anyone else like a cup?

— Yes please, replies Grandma Lynne unusually quickly.

— I'm all right, says Mum at exactly the same time.

And after that there's just Dad fiddling super slowly with mugs and milk on the suddenly noisy kitchen worktop in the long-lasting otherwise silence.

Being quiet is tricky. Even when you want to be silent, somehow noises happen. Either your foot slips out from under you and hits the table leg or you say something like, — What about broken promises you never told anybody about, do they still count? . . . The words just come straight out before you've even thought them. In class Miss Hart often makes us all sit still quietly just to have a think about what we've learned and even when that happens it's hard not to say Hey I've learned this or that or whatever it is. Leo is worse at silence than me because he has a special teacher called Mrs. Cassidy just to help him with it. But I don't have her and if it wasn't for Leo I'd definitely be the worst! Leo hates oranges and is allergic to sand, crayons, and PE, too.

And did you know another thing, about bells?

It's obvious: they're normally noisy.

We have them at school to tell everybody what to do next, only they don't really work. When the bell goes off I know it's time to stop what I'm doing so that something else can happen, but I always have to say Hey, there's the bell, what's happening next?

Dad likes bells.

Actually that's not true.

He likes a song about bells, though, bells you have to ring unless you don't do it because you've forgotten your perfect offering.

I don't know what that means, but it rhymes.

And so does the next bit in the song, the important bit about there being a crack in everything.

Which isn't really true.

Don't worry though, because it's only a song. And songs are like stories, Son. They may not be factually true, but it doesn't matter because something inside them is probably truer.

Shall I tell you what's inside?

Okay I will. Light!

That's what the song says, anyway. The cracks in all the bells and songs and stories are there for a reason, to let the light get in. So we can see how everything broken is excellent.

Dad explained it. He said — Everything falls apart, Son. And that's okay, that's how it's supposed to be. We're all imperfect. You included, and even, believe it or not, me! But don't worry. Our faults make us who we are. The cracks are illuminating.

And I understood that, I actually did. Because it made sense. Once I even had a Lego cat figure with ears that swivelled until I dropped it and one of them chipped off, making it non-symmetrical and therefore rubbish. We couldn't even glue it.

Don't worry, it's just *flawed*, Son: that makes it more realistic. I wasn't allowed to throw it away. Instead I still had to like it because Dad told me I had to, so I tried, and it worked, sort of. And that's what the song about cracked bells means: if you drop things, including bells and Lego cats, they will break, because most of them have cracks anyway, because that's just the way things are. It all makes perfect sense. Sort of.

Anyway, it is quiet in the kitchen for a long time. We don't have anymore pancakes because Mum turns the knob down on the cooker. Gas lives in the gas pipe and oxygen is a gas that lives in pipes, too: windpipes. If broccoli goes down the wrong pipe it can be fatal, even though broccoli looks like lungs. It also looks like trees. Brocco-lung, brocco-tree. Leaves do quivering in the wind and Dad's good hand is quivering when he picks up the spoon to stir his coffee. He could use that spoon to dig out his dandelion-root radish eyes, but of course he doesn't. It would hurt.

— Why not take that back to bed, Jim, Mum says.

The quiet gets louder.

— You might as well just sleep it off.

Dad smiles hard enough to show off the pointy yellowish teeth at the sides of his mouth when Mum says that. He shakes his head and says nothing more loudly still.

— What shall *we* do today, anyway? Grandma Lynne asks me. — How about a trip to the Zoo?

This is excellent news, so excellent I sadly can't help what happens next. But it happens. I sort of throw my arms backward and push out with my legs to signal yes I'm excited and my chair tips swiftly up onto two legs. Too swiftly. It goes past the edge of balance utterly. One minute I'm there sitting at the table, the next I'm on the tiles incredibly noisily.

Everybody panics.

Me because I've hit my shoulder and elbow on the floor impressively loudly, and Mum because she's my mum and emergency go-go-go she needs to get across the kitchen to help-help-help, and Grandma Lynne because she's Grandma Lynne and she wants to be involving, too. Dad snaps upright as well. I see him there at the edge jerking back from the kitchen surface with coffee all over his shirt. And I'm rolling onto my side and Mum is there above me and Grandma Lynne is behind her with her crow's-wings hair flapping, but Dad is already between them bending over me, his eyes as red as the plaster cast, a hand under my back, hauling me up.

Everybody speaks at once.

— Are you—

— Jesus, Billy—

— The poor little—

— What have I told you—

— Thing.

— About swinging back on the—

— Okay?

— Bastard chair!

And Dad's chin is sharp-edged on my face for a while, wet with something, and Mum keeps pulling at his arm, and it really didn't hurt that much, but there's no space to say anything, none at all, because Mum is saying, — Give him here! and Dad is going, — No, no, no! and Grandma Lynne is begging, — Please! and I am too busy trying to breathe.

And that's when the bell goes off.

The doorbell.

Ringer-dinger-ding, a crack in everything.

Grandma Lynne steps backward. Dad's got me tight on his knee, so tight it's actually making it tricky for me to connect my windpipe to the oxygen supply efficiently. And Mum has one hand on her hip and the other in my hair. They're both going — You're okay, you're okay.

— I am, I am. Sorry, sorry, I say.

The bellringer dings again.

— That's the doorbell, I explain.

At least Grandma Lynne's got the idea; she's halfway out of the room and across the hall.

— Leave it, Lynne, says Dad. But she doesn't seem to hear him because she prefers what Mum says instead, and that's the actual — No, answer it, opposite.

Grandma Lynne made Mum in her room. Not her bedroom, but the room next to her stomach. All female mammals have one. And all babies start out from there with stretchy umbrella cords. Sadly there is no cord between Mum and Grandma Lynne anymore, but they're still more connected than Grandma Lynne and Dad, and that's probably why Grandma Lynne finds it easier to understand Mum's instructions. She smoothes her hair wings and goes to open the door.

Mum follows her. I hear some normal hello-do-come-in stuff and there's some slow shuffling-through-there noises and then the kitchen door widens and Mum and Grandma Lynne come back in with the Butterfly lady behind. She has somebody else with her as well. A giraffe.

Dad breathes out hard through his nose and I can smell too-old-oranges and drain. A man came with a whizzy thing to unblock ours once, but sadly the whizzy thing got stuck so he had to get another one.

Dad keeps hold of me. The Giraffe is quite interesting because of her extremely reaching neck and narrow shoulders and stretched long arms. She is holding a black boxy briefcase in one hand. Perhaps there are bricks in it and that's why her shoulder is sloping down so hard. No, because the other one is doing it as well. She looks round the room over everyone's heads while Butterfly gets herself all ready for a speech. It's a kitchen, Giraffe; no acacia leaves here, no matter how high you look. No, not even up above the clock, we're very sorry.

Grandma Lynne is fiddling around behind the wicker chair, looking for something. What is it? Her bag. She takes it to the far side of the kitchen table and sits down very quietly. Don't mind me, she means, I'm completely out of the way: I do the same thing when there are crisps in a bowl and I want some but know they'll say no if I just take them. And Mum has backed up against the units to give the visitors space. Sadly it looks a little bit like she's scared of them. Don't be, Mum. Prairie dogs have nothing to fear from giraffes so long as they keep away from their highly kicking legs. And butterflies aren't a problem either. Unless . . . I don't know, so I ask, — Dad, are any butterflies poisonous?

— Probably, he replies very quietly.

— So, says Mum.

Butterfly clears her throat. — This is my colleague, Rommi Godwin. She's also on the ChildSafe team.

Giraffe does a strange sideways-nod thing. Her hair is cut in an excellent wedge shape into the back of her neck which makes it look even longer. She reminds me a bit of the blue things in the film, minus a plug-tail. And Grandma is fiddling with something inside the mouth of her bag, and squinting at it like a very obvious spy which means it must be her phone.

— What are you here for? Dad says, low and cross.

Butterfly fights back with a smile. — As I explained to your wife yesterday . . . she looks at Mum like they're very good friends . . . — our visit to Dr. Adebayo has progressed us to the next stage in this process. That's what we're here to explain, in person. And we're here to reassure you, as well, that we have Billy's best interests at heart. We really do want to find a constructive solution to this difficulty.

— Progressed us to the next stage? spits Dad. — Solution to this difficulty? Speak English.

— Jim! says Mum.

— No, no, it's all right. Butterfly fiddles with her hair halo. — You're right. I just think, as before . . . she smiles at me . . . — it might be best if we discuss the detail without Billy present. It's really a Mum-and-Dad chat, this.

Dad shifts under me. Did you know the world is made up of plates? Not like the plates you eat off and then have to wash up, no, much bigger ones. They float about on fiery lakes of larvae with buildings on top; Big Ben for example. Every now and then one of the plates knocks into another and probably breaks and that's when the larvae squirts through. Stand back, stand back! It's gonna blow. Dad breathes hard through his nostrils again, straight down my neck, hot ticklish, and says, — He's going nowhere.

Butterfly's lips do her straight-line smile. She looks at Mum, but there's no help from her because she's caught in some headlights. Quick. Don't just stand there. Get out of the way! There's a horrible bit in a film called *Crocodile Done Deeds* which I was allowed to watch once, where idiots shoot kangaroos with flashlights on trucks, until one of them isn't a kangaroo in fact but is Mick Done Deeds with a gun instead, shooting the idiots back which is excellent. But where's Mick now? He's hiding . . . in Grandma Lynne!

— I think perhaps it would be wise to do as the lady asks, Jim, she says.

— And I think perhaps it's my decision, Dad says back, very

friendly, very calm. But it's all camouflage! He's actually vibrating a bit in his seat: I can feel it through my back. And everybody else is a grown-up so they should surely understand better than me that it's time to stand very well back and turn off the searchlights and put your giraffe head in an emu hole. Here's more evidence: low growly Dad words with unusual gaps in them: — Whatever you have to say . . . about me and my son . . . you can say . . . to me and my son.

Now Giraffe does another of her strange sideways head-jerk things and her eyes go blinkety-blink, and she says — We can't force you to exclude Billy from this conversation, but not doing so may well have an impact.

Mum's crept round the units to us and now she puts her fingers on Dad's shoulder. They slide down his arm and stop on his hand, which clenches tighter around my own wrist. — Please, Mum whispers. — Please.

— Impact, says Grandma Lynne. — What do you mean?

— It won't be considered appropriate parenting.

Dad snorts.

— Please, Jim, says Mum again.

— *Nowhere*, Dad hisses.

Grandma Lynne's hands are clutching and de-clutching on the kitchen table; scratch-scratch goes one of her rings against the wooden top. It doesn't matter because the table is old. I'm even allowed to paint on it and last week on *Blue Peter* they showed how to milk a cow. Gently squeeze its udders. Scratch, scratch. — Tell you what, says Grandma Lynne. — Why don't I make a pot of tea and you can explain where this is all going?

— We don't have a teapot here, I say. — Just bags and mugs.

Butterfly laughs very enthusiastically, like I've told a no-eyed-deer joke or something.

— It's true, I say.

— Of course, she nods. — A mug of tea would be lovely.

— I'm afraid now's not the time for tea, says Dad.

Giraffe shifts about on her hooves looking this way and that for lions in the tall grass and Butterfly's straight-line smile zips shut again.

Dad goes on: — Just get to the point.

— Yes, well, says Butterfly. — The point is this. Having examined and talked with Billy, Dr. Adebayo has some further concerns for his welfare. And the doctor's concerns . . . I don't want to be alarmist, but you should realize the seriousness of the situation . . . require us to take further steps to make sure he's all right.

— What further steps? asks Mum.

Giraffe leans forward now. They have incredibly soft mouths, like horses, and similar big yellow teeth. — Under Section 47 of the Children Act, if our initial investigation has concluded that Billy is at risk we have a duty to proceed to a Child Protection Case Conference. This will be attended by Dr. Adebayo, ourselves and other representatives from Child-Safe, Billy's schoolteacher, and any other interested professionals. You are encouraged to attend, too. It is recognized that parents have an important part to play in the decision-making process . . .

— You *recognize* we have a part to play? says Dad. — That's fucking priceless.

— Jim, *please*, says Mum.

He ignores her. — But what if we don't *recognize* you? What if I don't think you've any right to interfere with me, with my family, *at all*?

— Of course we recognize . . . Mum starts.

— No. We. Don't.

Giraffe's lips peel back. She pauses before speaking. Acacia trees protect themselves using their most vicious thorns, but despite having velvety-soft lips giraffes aren't bothered. They eat the leaves up all the same. — If a Section 47 Inquiry is obstructed, Giraffe says slowly, — and Billy is considered at risk, the Act envisages it may be necessary to apply for an Emergency Protection Order under Section 44.

— What does that mean? Mum asks.

— It might mean removing Billy from the perceived threat so as to ensure his safety. Giraffe says these words like she's telling Mum one of her Tiddlo's will go up the Hoover if she doesn't tidy them up. Butterfly still wants to be Mum's friend, though, because she does very reassuring smile-nodding at her as she goes on, — Which is precisely why you're so right to want to cooperate fully with the process.

Mum is nodding hopelessly, still very caught in the headlights, while Grandma Lynne's fingers are still gripping at each other so tight, tight, tight that her rings look like they're about to pop off. Rattle-scrape-rattle goes the wooden tabletop. And just next to my ear I'm sure I can hear Dad's teeth grinching as he clamp-bites them together. We have a salt grinder that makes the same squeaking noise because it's got a rubbish plastic mechanism, Son.

— And if we do as you say, Dad spells out super slow, — if we come along to your kangaroo court, and listen to you chatting about what some anonymous stranger in a park has to say about us, and what the doctor thinks he knows as a result of a ten-minute chat with Billy, and sit there while you come to the same ridiculous conclusion that he's at risk . . . what can we expect you to decide for us then?

— We can't prejudge that, says Giraffe with a kinder face. — And in any case—

— No, no. I bet you can't, Dad interrupts. — But surely you have a *duty* to inform us of the likely eventualities?

Giraffe does one of her nervous-but-not-that-nervous headshakes and says, — A child protection plan might follow, to ensure Billy's well-being. His progress would be monitored, as would the family's.

Dad shifts beneath me. I squiggle sideways on his lap and see what I already knew: he's gone deadly pale. Stand back, stand back!

— What else? he asks. — What would this protection plan mean?

— There's no point in us second-guessing eventualities here and now, says Giraffe. — Let's take it one step at a time.

— But I want to hear you guess it. Go on. Do your *duty*.

— Please remember, we have Billy's best interests at heart, Mr. Wright. Giraffe spreads her long arms in a sweeping circle. — We really do.

— Enough platitudes. I want facts.

— Well, if the continuing risk is deemed serious, that is, if it is thought that Billy is likely to suffer significant harm, then of course we will have to take action to safeguard him, as I say.

Dad once hit his thumb with a hammer. We were in the garden because it was sunny and there was a stake for a new tree to knock into a hole. He used the big claw hammer and I kept out of the way because he told me to keep out of the way, and it was all all right. In went the pointy stick stake, bang, bang, bang. Then I helped put the root end of the tree in the hole next to the stake and we filled in around both with special mud called compost. It's nutritious. New tree slush. Watch out, worms. We stamped the mud down with our Wellington boots, only Dad didn't have any so he used his worst trainers. And that was fine, too. But then Dad had to knock a nail through a strap into the post so that we could tie the baby tree up straight like a prisoner about to be shot, Son. That was when it happened: the post didn't like being jabbed with a nail. It became a tricky customer, wobbly as hell. — Get in there you . . . said Dad, and sadly walloped his thumb incredibly hard with the big hammer by accident. I was right there. I saw his fist fold his thumb down and the redness spill out between his shut fingers, and I saw Dad's eyes go squinty as he bent over to hold himself superbly still, pressing it, a statue, pressing it, and pressing it harder, until he couldn't press it anymore and went — Fuck, fuck, cunting fuck! instead. Then he kicked the stake and tree so hard they both bent over and he hurled the hammer smack-straight through the wooden slut fence.

When Giraffe says the bit about *safeguarding*, Dad's eyes do the slitty hard-staring thing. He holds me. He holds me. Then very slowly he lifts me from his lap, using his good and bad arms, straight onto the kitchen table beside his chair and stands up.

— Which means . . . Dad growls louder.

— We're getting way ahead of ourselves, here, says Butterfly in a very cheerful twittery blackbird voice. She takes a step backward. — With Billy present, in particular, Mr. Wright, it's not appropriate to—

— To what? shouts Dad. — To what? To tell him the truth? That you're going to try to take him away from us? That's what this is about, isn't it? That's where it leads. I've read about you. You interfering fucking useless—

— JIM! yells Mum. — Shut up! Please, shut up!

— NO! This is my house. I'll say what I want. I have a *duty* to say it.

There are sharp red triangles in Mum's cheeks, and the corners of them have somehow jabbed tears into my eyes, and there's a gulp-sob fighting up in my chest. I try to wipe the tears away and push the sob back down but it's useless. Even if I could feel some force I couldn't use it: I'm too powerless to resist. And Mum has spotted what's coming, and she quicksteps around Dad who is swaying toward Giraffe, not as tall as her but two thicknesses wider and a hammer-split-thumb crosser, and everyone's talking high and loud and fast:

— Get out of here. Get out!

— This will only exacerbate—

— I don't fucking care—

Grandma Lynne: — Jim, please. He's unwell, stressed.

— I am not sick. I'm the only sane—

Mum, to me: — Come here, darling, shh.

And the sob comes, and Dad evolves on his heel and grabs hold of me, shouting at the women, — Look what you've done to him! Is this what you want? This is what you do!

— Leave him, Jim! pleads Mum, her fingers pecking at Dad's. I saw some ducks trying to jab through some ice once but they didn't manage it quickly enough and I had to go home before they did, if they did. — Just calm down. Let me take him upstairs. Calm down—

— He's not leaving! They're leaving! You two. Out! Get the fuck out!

Grandma Lynne: — He'll see reason. We'll do what's needed. I'll make sure that we —

— IT'S NOT UP TO YOU!

Butterfly's eyelashes are flapping above her "O" mouth as Giraffe grows taller all the time, advancing across the kitchen-tiled savannah toward us. Watch out for those hooves! Mum's peckety-peck fingers have less and less point because the sobs are still coming like bubbles swelling up through porridge, glup, glup, glup, and with each one Dad's grip tightens. It's like beer cans. Not the can bit itself but the plastic O, O, O thing that holds them all together before you throw it into the sea afterward so that it can strangle penguins or otters. There's something similar in *Watership Down*. Bigwig puts his head into it and they have to dig out the peg because the harder he struggles the tighter it gets.

I'm not struggling.

Dad stands up with me clutched to his chest. Mum stretches out her arms, very zombie, but Dad doesn't hand me over because Butterfly is saying something soothing about listening to Grandma and how this really isn't the way forward and Giraffe is all tilty-headed silent, looking down her nose at us out of one big brown unimpressed eye.

— Just get out, Dad says.

— No, no, don't, pleads Mum. — Stay!

Dad glares at her. — In which case, he says, and he barges us toward the open door, making Mum step back and Giraffe shy sideways and Butterfly flutter out of the way, too. Then we're through the gap in a very impressive instant and Dad even clips the door shut with his heel as he turns for the stairs. Up we go, three at a time. Explosive! Where now? His study-bedroom, of course, because we're Batmen, or a wounded animal, seeking the comfort of our lair!

Dad slumps down on the foot end of the bed, both of us breathing hard, then slower, lub-dub-lub-dub-lub-dub. Over his shoulder I can see his table with work papers all over the place. Very messy. And there's his computer screen glowing at me, too. The black and whites, eight by eight. He's been playing chess! I stare at the glowing squares and pieces trying to figure out who won and saying nothing.

★

I've already told you that I know exactly how to play chess and it's true, I do: I know how all of the pieces move, and I know about castling, and I even know the en passant pawn thing, which means I know all the rules, and that's an achievement in itself, Son; you should be proud. And I am! But sometimes the rules are annoying. Why can a pawn only do that and nobody but a knight jump and a queen do everything else? So from time to time I forget all about the rules and make up my own instead. Hey you, bishop! You can slide over there if you want. Go ahead, it's fine. Jump if you like! Why should knights have all the up-down fun? And you, pawn! Ever thought about going in a long curve instead of little plodding steps? No problem. Have a go at it. I've changed the rules!

Dad once saw me playing a game like that against myself.

— What are you up to? he asked.

— Playing chess against myself.

— But you know as well as I do. Pawns can't do that.

— They can in this game. I've made up new rules.

Dad's bottom lip pushed out a little to go with his nodding.

— New rules, he said. Then he scratched his head and the nodding turned to shaking. — But without the proper rules it's not chess.

— Yes it is.

— No it's not. It's just fiddling with the pieces. I mean, carry on, have fun with it, by all means, if that's what you want. But surely you see that without the rules you've got nothing. Just a pointless . . . can of worms!

— It's not pointless, I said.

He ruffled my head annoyingly so I went on:

— And neither are worms. Mr. Sparks put some into the school compost last week. He was wearing yellow rubber gloves because he didn't like the touch of them. But he said they were an important part of it because—

— Whoa, Billy. Back up a bit. School compost heap? What's that all about?

— It's where we put the scraps. From lunches without meat in them and from mowing the grassy bit. No biscuits or chocolate. One of us is allowed to do the putting-in every day.

— Then what? You stand around watching the worms and discussing the circle of life?

— No. Just the putting-in bit.

The nodding came back then and Dad's eyes went gentle black. — Fair enough, he said. — I expect it beats Latin.

We can hear them talking downstairs but because the door is shut it's impossible to tell exactly what they're saying. Gradually Dad's grip on me goes softer; if he was a python now would be the time to swallow me whole. He doesn't do that, though, no, of course not, because he has to answer his phone instead. It's in his pocket. He slides me off him and up toward the pillow end and fishes the phone out and smoothes down my hair with his bad hand, clunk, clunk, and answers it.

It's a work call.

I lie on my back and check the old ceiling crack. It's still there, streaky lightning, a bit longer than before perhaps. When I was a baby it was smaller because I was as well. Snakes have forked tongues. It makes them impossible to understand. I listen to Dad on the phone overcoming obstacles and finding new ways to push things forward but what he's saying doesn't really make sense either.

Yes, communication is extremely hard, and Dad does whole projects of it almost by himself, because it's his job, which is impressive. Quite often, though, I realize I don't really know what a communications project is, and that's fair enough because they're so difficult. But my brain is developing at a fantastic rate so every now and then I ask Dad to explain his job again just in case my powers have caught up. And when I ask, two things happen. First, whatever he says always makes sense. And second, it always sounds quite exciting. Actually, I was wrong about two things, because in fact there are three. The third is this: once Dad finishes explaining, the sensible bit stops making sense again very quickly, or rather, I realize it isn't actually true!

And to prove it, here are some of the answers Dad has given me when I've asked him — Hey, Dad, what are you actually doing? I've put the answers in groups because I've noticed that's where they belong; whatever communications projects involve it normally has to do with something else: either farming or building or sailing or cooking or sport or craft or party games or breaking laws or religion or fighting.

— I'm making hay while the sun shines, Son; I'm harvesting what I sowed; I'm counting my chickens before they've hatched; I'm trying to see the wood for the trees; I'm shutting the stable door after the horse has bolted; I'm casting pearls before swine . . .

— I'm building bridges; I'm reinventing wheels, Son; I'm mixing cement with a toothpick; I'm trying to build Rome in a day . . .

— I'm setting the sails; I'm keeping things shipshape; I'm sailing into a headwind; I'm trying to bail us out with a teaspoon . . .

— I'm cooking without gas, Son; I've got my head in the oven; I'm reheating the books . . .

— I'm keeping the ball rolling; I'm playing with ten men; I'm caught in the offside trap; I'm trying to keep my eye on the ball . . .

— I'm watching paint dry; I'm trying to make a silk purse out of a sow's ear . . .

— I'm pinning tails on moving donkeys; I'm playing musical chairs; I'm jumping through hoops, Son; I'm pushing a rope uphill; I'm running to stand still . . .

— I'm driving with the headlights off; I'm mugging old ladies; I'm doing thirty in the fast lane; I'm robbing Peter to pay Paul . . .

— I'm trying to walk on water; I'm dancing to the devil's tune; I'm feeding the five thousand without a fish; I'm going to hell in a handcart . . .

— I'm taking on allcomers; I'm fighting with one arm tied behind my back; I'm winning battles but losing the war; I could tell you but I'd have to kill you . . .

Dad has moved over to his desk while I've been remembering this list for you, talking on his phone the whole long time. And I've been watching him. His head is a silhouette because his computer screen is glowing round its cut-out edges. Once at school we made biscuits. Now Dad puts the phone down and his cookie-cutter head drops forward and his hands change the outline by making themselves into earmuffs. Who knows, maybe my brain has developed enough to understand what he means better now. There's only one way to find out.

— Dad?

— Yes, Son.

— What are you doing?

His shoulders shift and the earmuffs shrink to match his smaller voice: — I don't know, Billy. I really don't know.

We sit in the quiet after that, Dad at his table, me on the bed. Crocodiles do the same thing with their mouths open. It's fine, but slightly boring.

★

Eventually the voices are louder again in the hall. Good bye yes good bye, we'll be in touch. Then the front door raps shut. Dad pushes back from his desk. He squats down by the end of the bed and says, — Would you do me a drawing?

— Okay. What of?

— You decide. Something with teeth, perhaps. Just put lots of detail in it.

— Can I use a piece of paper from your dream?

— Ream, Son; it comes in reams. Of course. And you can work at my table. There you go: desk lamp on. Here's a pencil. Use as many sheets of this as you want. I'll be back up for an inspection a little later. Stay put until I do. Okay?

— Okay.

And off he goes, underwater slowly. It's a long way to the bottom of the ocean, Dad! Look out for the anglerfish; they'll help you see what's what.

Anglerfish have lots of teeth and a lightbulb on a stick sticking out of their nose. It acts as a lure. Come here, smaller fish, I'm luring you, luring you, luring . . . you don't know what's going on here, do you? Whap! I start drawing one. But I get it wrong, because halfway through drawing the mouth I remember that anglerfish have bigger teeth on the bottom than the top. Or at least their bottom teeth stick out farthest. It's called an under-bite and Raphael at school has one but you shouldn't point it out because Miss Hart will tell you not to. He wants to be a human, you see, not a deep-sea fish.

I do something very clever next: instead of allowing my crossness at the mistake to send prickles across my head, making me go downstairs to say I've done it wrong and need to start again, I use my memory and take another piece of paper because he said I could.

Ream, not dream.

The second drawing goes better. In fact, it is excellent. I do a fantastic underbite and incredibly sharp backward-pointing teeth, totally barbed, and I get the light-lure in the right place and even do some cross-patching on the belly where it joins the fins to make him look like he has three dimensions. It's an allusion and you don't even need cinema glasses to see it. But sadly, when I realize this I think about the film and see that my anglerfish isn't quite as excellently dimensional as the blue and red dragons, and before I can stop myself I go downstairs to show it to Dad because he'll probably make me feel slightly better by saying my anglerfish is actually better because there's a crack in everything.

It's nearly a disaster of tremendous portions!

I make it halfway down the stairs before realizing that I'm not supposed to be going down the stairs at all. The anglerfish has lured me into dangerous waters. I freeze. They're talking.

— I don't care what you think, says Dad. — They can stick their conference up . . .

— Just slow down for a second, Mum pleads. — Think of the consequences.

— I have nothing to hide. We've done nothing wrong.

— You have to help us prove that, Jim, says Grandma Lynne.

— No, they need the evidence, and there is none.

— These sorts of cases are different. They're—

— I'm still innocent until proven guilty.

— You're being naive. If they think a child is at risk they—

— Nobody's at risk! They can confer all they like.

Mum, very tired: — It's not as simple as that.

— You go, then. If that's what you think. *I'm having no part of it.*

Something bangs down hard on something else then, and there's mumbling and — oh no — footsteps. Before they make it to the door I run back up the stairs. Mink sometimes do the same thing when they hear hounds, and foxes have been known to flee up trees as well, because although they're mostly dog not many people know that they can in fact be the opposite of cheetahs, using their claws which are . . . retractable!

He comes thumping up the stairs. I've made it to the study-bedroom doorway. Before he can say anything I show him my drawing. He looks at it for a long time.

— Brilliant. Toothy.

He gives it back and leans two-fisted on his table staring at everything on it in turn, very disappointed. There's a gorilla at the Zoo that looks exactly the same quite often before it eats whole cabbages leaf by leaf. They should give it something more interesting to eat. Eventually Dad pushes himself upright, puffs out his gorilla cheeks, and claps his hands softly.

— Sod this lot for now.

— Can I help sod it? I ask.

He smiles. — It's half-term, isn't it?

— Yes.

— Fetch your trunks, then. I'll take you for a swim.

— Yes, yes, yes!

I sprint into my bedroom and grab my one-directional shark trunks and my green goggles which live in the same drawer under my pants and sprint back to Dad who is holding his bag open like a grouper's mouth. He stuffs a couple of towels in on top. Try saying something now, grouper-bag! It can't. Dad zips it up and off we go downstairs into the hall for shoes and coats. It's normal. But then, as I'm putting mine on, something funny happens. Mum hears us, leans out of the kitchen door, and catches sight of the bag in Dad's hand. That's not particularly funny I know. But her face is: it looks like somebody has taken a photo of her when she wasn't expecting it, only faces like that normally disappear immediately in real life, and hers doesn't: it stays fixed like it would in a photo, very fright-surprised, as if the bag probably contains an incredibly venomous funnel-web spider.

— Jim? Where are you going?

Dad doesn't answer. He looks at her and shakes his head and sort of laughs and says, — Unbelievable.

— Swimming, I say. — We're going swimming.

Mum's face blinks itself normal but only just. She puts a hand on my shoulder and says, — Lovely. When shall I make lunch?

Dad puts a hand on my other arm and speaks to Mum like he did to the man who came to mend the dishwasher. He was from Pole land. North Pole land, I expect, since nobody lives in Antarctica except emperor penguins, leopard seals, and, occasionally, David Attenborough, wearing a huge fur-hooded coat, because it's so in hospital there.

— I'm not sure, he says. We may have something while we're out. But don't you worry, we'll be back in time for tea.

We go swimming. Like normal it's great, only it's even better this time because Dad's red arm goes in a special plastic elastic sleeve thing. I'm not allowed to tug it. Have you ever played paper rock scissors? It's quite a good game to play on land if you're bored, and better still to play in the pool even if you're having a good time. We play underwater because you only need one hand. First Dad and I take deep breaths in our goggles and then Dad says, — Right: one, two, three, and on three we do submerging. Down we go, right down, until we're sitting on the black line, with Dad pressing one of his legs onto one of mine so I don't float off. Then we clench one fist each and knock them together: one, two, three; paper, rock, scissors; which is it going to be? Dad's scissors cut my paper in the first game but I'm not disappointed. We go up to the surface and he says it before me:

— Best of three.

Down we go again and I win this time because on three my rock blunts his scissors totally.

Up for a breath, and down again. Look at his hair waving about like Blue Planet seaweed. One, two, three. No, no, no. My rock is folded up by his huge paper hand and I feel desperate. We go up to the surface and as soon as I've breathed I ask if we can make it best of more than three but he laughs and swims off on his back, so I attack him viciously because I'm cunning, and ever since the lifeguard with the soggy trainers told us off I know Dad is in fact powerless to retaliate. Eventually he decides to listen to me.

— One more chance, please!

— But I've won.

— Another best of three.

Dad can make water squirt out of his hand when he wants to, and he wants to now because he squirts some at me. It goes in my eye. Luckily I'm not Casper in Mrs. Preddy's class because when you do that to him he screams.

— I wasn't playing my hardest, I say.

— Tough.

— And anyway I've got a better game. Paper, rock, scissors . . . Death Star. I put both of my hands together to show him what one looks like.

— What can a Death Star beat?

— Everything.

He laughs at me and shakes his head. — No. Escalation like that would upset the delicate balance of power.

— The what?

— The game wouldn't work.

— Yes it would.

— We'd destroy each other.

I can see what he means, nearly, so I concentrate on the bit I can't see; I did something similar when Tom at school explained about Father Christmas, and it worked, because he still came. And then I remember the bit at the end with the X wings and Red Five standing by and it makes everything more complicated.

— Actually there's Luke, too, I explain. — So you're even more wrong, because the Death Star *can* be destroyed.

But Dad's not concentrating. He's standing up pinching the water out of his eyes, muttering something else about escalators. And anyway I've got two hands of my own so I decide to have a go at the new version of the game by myself. Deep breaths. Down I go. Without his help I have to fight to keep the silvery wobbling water-lid high above my head. One, two, three: hand versus hand, victory. The sign for Luke is a finger pointing out like a light saver.

Later, in the showers, Dad thumb-pumps some green from the dip sensor thing into his hand and rubs it on my head, very like washing-up liquid; bubbles slipper off everywhere and down the drain, popping eventually. You have to keep pressing the water knob because otherwise idiots wouldn't know how to turn off the taps and everything would get wasted. It's tiring. I watch bubble scum drizzling in the drain gully, then look at Dad who has fur on his chest. Have you ever blown up a balloon? I have, nearly, and when I let it go the stretchiness breathed out, very hilarious and finally floppy. Dad's willy is pink and looks quite similar, unlike his arms and legs which have excellent knotted-towel muscles. Natural athlete, Son: don't worry, you're cut from the same cloth. If God existed, he would have an excellent pair of scissors. Thoughts are odd, like daffodils: the bulbs are inside you somewhere getting ready to pop up in your lawn brain from nowhere, and often they're shaped like questions, which jump out of your mouth in exactly the same way.

— At the end of wars do the losers congratulate the winners?

— What's that? says Dad. — Soap in my ears.

I repeat the question.

Dad half laughs. — Unfortunately not.

— But why? It's bad sport.

— Sportsmanship. Yes. But war isn't a game.

— There are winners and losers, though. So it's similar.

— Some winners, more losers. But no real rules. And yet . . . no. War isn't a sport, Billy. It's hell.

— But hell doesn't exist.

— Okay, it's the worst thing people can do to each other. It's people being horrific to other people on purpose. It's something we should avoid at all costs . . .

He trails off and I look at him out of my eye without water in it, and see him staring sadly at his red plastic-bag arm through the shower rain, shaking his head. With a bit more light we could have a rainbow in here.

— You know all that, he continues.

— Yes, I say. — And paper rock scissors Death Star isn't a real sport, either.

★

Instead of going home we walk to Cicely and Lizzie's house with a bag of food from the special small expensive shop, which I am allowed to carry. It's fine, not that heavy. Delicate essence. — Keep up now, says Dad, and I do, but every now and then I have to stop to check what Dad bought and by the time we get there I know: a pot of dirty green olives with little orange flickers in them; yes, they look like dragons' eyeballs. Some flappy bits of ham not even in a proper plastic box but paper instead, very folding. That big round crunchy crust loaf of bread without slices. And in this pot there's some humorous, which Dad doesn't normally like and I think is only medium so why did he buy it? But yes yes yes, there they are, there: two gingerbread men, I can see by their outline. Excellent!

Dad smoothes down his hair on the step. When Cicely opens the door he does a funny little bow which is quite embarrassing and says, — Sorry not to call.

Cicely touches her throat. — It's fine. Come on in.

— We've brought lunch, says Dad, pointing stupidly at the bag.

I explain exactly what's in it. You already know because I told you, so I'm not going to tell you again: use your memory.

— Where's Lizzie? I ask. Normally she's exactly behind Cicely's legs when the door opens, but not today, today she has evaporated.

— In her bedroom.

— Can I take it to her if we don't make crumbs?

— What's that?

Keep up at the back there, Cicely, lope! — Gingerbread man, I say slowly.

But Cicely is concentrating on Dad who is scraping his hand through his corn hair like perhaps he has nits. — I just needed to talk to you, he says. I should have rung ahead. But . . .

— Of course, Cicely says. — I'll put some coffee on.

And to me she quickly says, — She's doing a tea party for her animals. Crumb-free gingerbread men are definitely invited.

I jump the right-shaped package out of the bag and drop the rest on the floor and run off without coming back even when Dad says — Hey! because I can tell he doesn't really mean it, and anyway I have to go past the fish in their topical tank first to say, — Hello goldfish, remember me? But of course they don't because goldfish are not elephants and anyway Cicely was wrong: when I make it inside Lizzie's room I actually see that she is lying down on her back under a blanket in the middle of the floor with her eyes shut and a line of her animals spread out on either side of her as if she is the fuse large of an airplane and they are her wings.

— What are you doing? I ask.

She blinks at me.

Small children are interesting: it's not that possible to tell exactly what is going on inside their heads, and with Lizzie it is even harder because she still doesn't use words. Adults are also tricky to understand, but for the opposite reasons.

— Would you like a gingerbread man?

She knows what I'm talking about now. Good-bye wings and up she gets. I give the slightly-less-good-because-one-of-its-buttons-has-fallen-off-in-the-bag gingerbread man to her and hold mine up and take a bite which she unsurprisingly copies. But what's this? She's holding her headless man out to look at and here we go again: crumply mouth, melted plastic. I push the door shut with my foot because grown-ups will only make this situation worse and luckily I only bit the arm off mine.

— Here, I say, and I snap the head off my gingerbread man

and put it down on the floor next to her feet. — You can have my head if you want. Lay your body next to it and he'll be whole again, almost.

Lizzie wipes biscuit muck on her dress sleeve and stops crying and does as I say.

— But really the point is to eat all of him. I snap the legs off mine one by one and do impressive eating and it works: eventually Lizzie breaks a foot off her man and then I take back my head and we sit in the middle of her quite strange line of animal toys eating the last bits up pretty happily.

After that I do some explaining about things to her, because if you talk honestly to a person, Son, they'll soon start talking honestly to you, or so the theory goes, and my mission is to be the first to hear Lizzie talk. I am mostly honest about animals because I know many interesting facts about them, including cetaceans, which include massively developed dolphins. Did you know that their sonar communications are so-phisticated that they make mankind's look like toys in a shop? Lizzie starts playing with her slightly babyish blocks of big Legos when I tell her this. Mine at home is technical because my fingers are nimbler. I help her anyway: we build a square thing with a hole in it for her bean cat to sit in, plus turrets. Then I tell her about silverback gorillas who also have posable thumbs and weigh up to four hundred pounds and are therefore earth's greatest prime-apes.

— Did you know that they avoid fighting each other by doing imposing poses instead? I ask, even though I know she won't answer, because it is called a one-way conversation.

— And my dad downstairs does the same thing, a bit. You don't have a dad here, but if you did he might avoid fighting with your mum by not making eye contact and being imposing nearby instead before walking off.

Lizzie breaks up some of my turrets and swaps them with ones of her own which do look better, in fact, because they are in a repeating-color pattern of red then white then green. I tell her about how countries have colored flags. White is a very boring color and means stop, I surrender. Lizzie tries to make a bridge thing on the front of the round thing and can't and starts to cry instead. I don't help her with it either because what she wants to make is actually impossible. It's gravity's fault, and other laws of nature, like the one about four-dot Lego bricks not fitting into three-dot spaces. I think about surrendering but go to the kitchen for reinforcements instead.

Have you ever built a hide? I don't mean the skin you slice off a dead animal, but a hide you can hide in? I built one with Dad once, using a lawn-mower box. It was as tall as me: huge! And when Dad took the lawn mower out of it there was nothing left inside so it was empty. Waste not want not, Son: what shall we make out of this? Easy: David Attenborough's hide! First Dad cut a letter-box slit in it with Stanley's knife, and then we stuck the box behind the big bush next to the compost heap. After that, I spent the whole afternoon camouflaging it with branches and leaves and twigs and mud and colored chalk and glitter and sellotape. Then I hid in it. I looked out at the garden for a long time, whispering what I was seeing to myself, just like David Attenborough.

— There he is: our cat Richard, appearing from over the wall! And yes, just to the side of him, some bees are buzzing around by that lavender plant. Is Richard going to try to catch one? No. He's walked off.

I knew I'd probably have seen those things anyway, but I tried not to be disappointed. Catching a glimpse of something rarer — a buzzard with strips of flesh for its young, perhaps, or some fox cubs digging a hole — would simply require better technology. David Attenborough often uses a mote control camera when he wants to film a rattlesnake striking a mouse in the middle of the night, so I asked Dad if we had a mote control camera I could use. But he just laughed and said, — No, which made me shiver angrily, nearly cry, and go back into the hide.

Half an hour later Dad's face appeared in the letter-box window slit. — The closest we have is your old baby monitor, Son. I've charged it up. Stick the microphone here in the garden and take the receiver up to your bedroom. You can spend the evening listening to the grass grow . . .

Dad and Cicely are sitting with their knees close together across the corner of the wobbly table. His head is in his hands and she is stroking his arm with her thumb. It's posable.

— You poor thing, Cicely says. — You have to let me speak to her.

It looks like Dad's hands are shaking his head. — No, no, no.

— Or at least tell Mum to butt out.

— You mustn't get involved. Dad looks up at her. — Can't you see?

— Of course, but . . . you can't do nothing.

I fizz forward then, saying, — I can't do anything about Lizzie's Lego tower thing either and she's crying about it quite hard.

Dad rocks back sharply in his chair and takes a big breath through his nose; Cicely gives his arm one last pat and pushes herself up from the table, which squeaks.

— I have been telling her about dolphin sonar, I say.

— Lovely. Cicely smiles and pats me on the head on her way past, then pauses to look back at Dad. — See, communication, Jim. That's what it's all about.

*

Have you ever tried not to laugh? I have, and it's incredibly hard not to laugh if you're having to try not to, but if you're not thinking about it it's easy because you probably don't laugh most of the time anyway.

It's quite like catching a ball.

Dad is fantastic at catching balls but sadly I am not, and when he last tried to teach me I noticed that the muscles in his jaw kept crumpling up. Crocodiles have the strongest bite in the animal kingdom, which you might guess, but I bet you don't know what comes next? Snapping turtles! Yes, a turtle. Its jaw pressure is bigger than a Great White's, and a lion's, and even a hyena's.

— Relax, Son, just keep your eye on the ball. Stop thinking. Let yourself catch it.

It's impossible to stop thinking, too, when somebody says stop thinking, so I don't even try; I do try to watch the ball, though, and there it is, looping up and dropping down with the bright yellow hedge and crooked fence behind it. Ready, hands, ready! But as the ball dips right down close, getting faster, my knee sort of jumps up a bit and my shoulder goes with it and my face decides to twist itself away slightly in case the ball hits it. Go, hands, go! Too late. The ball hits my cheek and the eye that's looking sees it hop-run off right under the thickest bit of hedge. Tennis balls are bright yellow as well and Dad's jaw muscles start showing off again.

— It will be a tricky customer to find, I say.

— Yes. Never mind. We'll get it later.

— Sorry.

— Forget about it. You're okay?

— I'm fine.

*

Sometimes Dad turns the trying-not-to-laugh thing into a special game.

— Look at me and try not to laugh, he says. — You'll fail. I'll have you laughing in under a minute. Not with tickling or pulling funny faces. Just by sitting here looking straight at you. Don't believe me? Give it a try.

I normally get ready by shaking myself and moving my lips all around and crossing my eyes and blinking hundreds of times before finally looking straight at him. But even if I hold my breath and squint until I nearly can't see him, just his outline sitting there not moving but staring straight back at me without even blinking, I can only last for ten or twelve seconds. I don't know why. It's like popcorn in a hot pan: normal, normal, normal, normal, pop: totally funny.

And sometimes when I go pop and laugh I feel angry and growl as I'm laughing and kick him in the shin relatively hard, but he just sits there and says, — Come on then, tough guy. If you're that cross surely you won't laugh next time. Get yourself ready: let's go again!

Mating is crucial. Without it David Attenborough would have much less to do on the African plain. Every animal mates there and quite often David Attenborough watches through his camera so we can, too, and that is necessary for the survival of the fittest, otherwise everything would die out, including us. We don't live in Africa but in fact that doesn't matter because mating happens on every continent and even in the sea, where dolphins seem to enjoy it.

— Anthropomorphization, Dad said, when I told him that, which made no sense at all. — Who can tell anyway with those fixed grins?

Not everybody at school understands about mating.

Mum said I should wait until one of the teachers brought it up before explaining.

But Red Steve in my class does know a bit about mating in humans because he's seen it happen. Red Steve is called Red Steve because the other Steve has normal hair and Red Steve's is red like his brother Joseph's hair in Year Six. That's how Red Steve knows a bit about mating: he's watched it with his brother Joseph on their computer.

David Attenborough has never shown me humans mating. Mum said it wouldn't be right, seriously, and Dad stopped smiling to agree. But still I think Red Steve either wasn't concentrating or remembered it wrong, because his explanation didn't sound correct. He was right about the first part: it makes sense that mating happens when the man aims his willy up the woman's bottom, because vertically all mammals do that, but he got the rest wrong: it doesn't make sense to put your willy in a woman's mouth for the last bit when the sperms come out because the eggs are in the ovaries not the stomach; the pipes don't join up, so the sperms would be swimming in a pointless direction. Red Steve got that part wrong and that is why he only knows a bit about mating.

If you do mating wrong nothing terrible happens; it's just the end: dead sperm, dead eggs, no new young. The ingredients have gone stale. When one person's pieces can't move anymore in chess the same thing happens: stalemating.

Nobody in our house moves normally over the weekend apart from Grandma Lynne who goes away, which is normal, but then she comes back again.

And after that it's not half-term anymore but time for more school, and the strange thing about that is that although I don't want to go back to school at all, and nearly cry when

Mum first tells me it's time, a part of me knows that school will probably be more normal than home, and this is in fact quite luring. We have hot chocolate the night before as well.

But sadly I was wrong! School is not normal at all. Normally we have planning time after assembly but on the first day back they swap it round and then at lunch the packed lunch tables are up the other end of the hall. It feels wrong. Even the little scissors-in-the-tree thing has moved from the create corner to Miss Hart's desk, so that instead of just taking a pair to cut out with and putting them back when I've finished I have to go up to Miss Hart and ask to use them specially.

And Miss Hart is not quite normal either.

First, when I ask her about the scissors, she leans a bit close to me and blinks kindly before saying, — Of course, Billy, be my guest. And the way she says *Billy* is just odd; it's either as if she's not heard my name before or thinks I may have forgotten it, or for some other reason wants to make it sound special.

Then, after I've cut the teeth out for a model of a shark I'm making with Fraser, and I've left Fraser red-felt-tipping the crumpled bit of paper we're using as a seal carcass so that I can take the scissors back, Miss Hart says my name again, — Billy.

— Yes.

— How are you today?

— Fine.

— That's good. What are you up to?

Over her shoulder I can see Fraser finishing the coloring bit.

— Making.

— Making! That's great. And what are you making?

— A thing with Fraser.

He's crumpled up the seal paper now and . . . no, no, no: I

told him not to stick it into the shark's mouth until I came back. Paper teeth are delicate and anyway we agreed: it was my idea so it's my job!

— Great! What sort of thing?

— Can I go now, please, it's just—

— Of course, in a second. You can show it to me after school, perhaps. I wanted to have a chat with you then anyway. Okay? Nothing to worry about. Just five minutes after the day ends.

— Okay okay, okay, I say, and I immediately run-walk round her desk back to Fraser who is cramming the last bit of the whole dead crumpled red-seal paper through the shark into its cardboard tube stomach. And I can see that the teeth are all twisted and bent and . . .

— No! I told you not to! I try to grab it off him before he makes it worse but he just holds it annoyingly behind his back so I have to grip his arm. He yanks me toward him trying to pull away, and before I know what I've done, oh no, I've done judo, and Fraser is on his back crying incredibly hard. He is nice but weak.

Miss Hart arrives immediately, picking Fraser up and pulling us apart and telling everyone else to carry on carrying on because it's none of their business. She takes us to the corner by the chipped sink next to the stork cupboard and it's amazing how quickly Fraser stops crying: doing judo on him is like letting go of a balloon. Easy throw, scream, cry, stop: totally un-flated.

And shall I tell you why what happens next is not normal either? Okay, it's this. Even though it really was me who threw Fraser over and made him cry, and even though I admit it, because she probably saw it anyway, Miss Hart still listens carefully when I tell her my excuse about the bent shark's teeth and torn red-paper seal carcass model which Fraser broke, and when I've finished all she does is stare at me for a long time blinking, before telling Fraser he really should keep his word and asking us both to — Carry on nicely.

That's it! Just that!

No trip to Mrs. McCabe's office. No golden-time deduction. Not even a sad-face mark. Miss Hart is a brilliant teacher. Just *carry on nicely*!

But later, during cross-legged mat time for the story before the end of the day, my stomach feels like a pinecone: light and prickly. To start with I don't know why, until I stop listening to the story about the boring dragon that doesn't kill anybody or even get killed himself, and remember instead that she wants to see me after school. The pinecone pops. She probably knew I was about to be naughty before it happened, and that's why she told me I would have to stay behind later. Have you ever made a smoothie? I have, with Mum. Imagine if we'd put a dry old pinecone into the mixer thing. As the chunk of pages left to go in the dull dragon story grows thinner and thinner, my stomach mixer speeds up so much it makes me need the toilet, and by the time there are only one or two pages to go I am desperate.

— Miss.

— One moment, Billy.

— But Miss . . .

— The story is nearly over. Just sit tight and listen.

— But Miss I need—

— Shh, Billy. We'll talk later.

But I already know we are going to talk later. That's the whole problem. So when she tells me we are going to talk later again it just makes the pinecone blender whiz down faster from my stomach to my bladder balloon chipping sparks and did you know that pinecones are very flammable and no, no, no . . .

A flame of wee spurts out.

It just does!

Hot and wet and darkening the gray of my trousers in front and between and behind.

And now my eyes start itchy-hot sparking, too.

No, no, no!

When wombats sense a bush fire they dig down deep to hide away while the fire passes overhead, and when kestrels and other small birds of prey have made a kill they shield it with their wings so other bigger predators don't see it and attack.

Quick as I can, I yank my sweatshirt over the top of my head and press it down, little school crest thing first, into my terrible lap. Then I hunch my shoulders forward and stare down Superman-hard at my knuckles which go little and white with gaps in like Lizzie's baby teeth.

Somehow I stop crying before I've really started.

The wee-fire puffs out.

And everyone else is still listening to the story, so I sit there looking down while it ends and they all jump up to get their book bags and stand in line — quietly please children — for the lobby.

Miss Hart helps with the coats and sees them all out. While her back is turned I wriggle my sweatshirt around my waist and tie the arms tight and think my hardest what to say about judo-throwing Fraser and the dark patch on my trousers which she might still see. What would Dad say? There's not enough time! Here she comes back with her big friendly smile, ready to use her not-normal voice again.

— So, *Billy*.

— It wasn't my fault.

— What wasn't?

— Fraser crying. He was putting it on because he only fell over when I pushed him and it can't have hurt very much and even if it did my dad says a little bit of pain never hurt anyone because that's what happens in life you should expect it especially if you make people angry and if you do you have to deal with the sequences because pain will make you tougher in the end and anyway there's a crack in everything and—

— Whoa! Miss Hart holds up her hand. — Slow down. What are you saying, Billy?

— Nothing!

— Calm down. It's all right. Come here.

— Please no.

— No? There's no need to look so worried — it's just a chat. Come and sit at the table with me.

— I don't want to. It's not my fault. I had to go and you wouldn't let me so it just happened.

— What's happened? Come on. Sit down next to me here and explain.

I desperately don't want to do what she says but it's impossible not to, so I clutch the sweatshirt wings forward to guard myself from her predator stare and shuffle over hoping she won't notice. And it works. At least, she doesn't look like she's seen; she's too busy shuffling papers and pretending to clear up the desk when really it's obvious that she is in fact just trying to think what to say next to make me feel extremely bad about Fraser, and yes, I was right, because what she eventually says is this.

— Why do you say that a little bit of pain never hurt, Billy?

One wing of my sweatshirt flops sideways then. I have to

grab it quickly. The pinecone is on fire again burning through me, right up to my cheeks.

— Who told you that? she asks.

— It wasn't on purpose. He was spoiling my thing. I didn't mean to hurt him.

— I know that. The . . . accident with Fraser isn't why I wanted to see you.

— It isn't?

— No.

Suddenly I realize Miss Hart must have known I was going to have a different kind of accident altogether and when I understand that, it's like her predator talons are gripping into my arm wings, very mean.

— I wanted to ask you how things are at home.

Not just mean: nosy, too.

— Fine.

She does a little nodding smile and glances at our life-cycle-of-tadpoles display, which gives me time to sort out my wings again, but no, no, no . . . the patch has definitely spread. I shuffle forward onto the seat edge so I can tuck it over and keep the dark bit out of sight but then two things happen. First, I spot Dad peeping in through the door glass, and second, the smell of it swims up warm and yellow-nasty.

— Well that's good. And . . . she trails off for a bit, but then does a weird little I-can't-resist-that-last-slice-of-cake grin and blurts out — and everything is all right with Mummy and Daddy as well?

— Yes.

— Good. She does another long pause. — But if you ever feel you need to talk to somebody . . . about anything, then remember that's what I'm here for.

She cocks her head to one side next like Alan's spaniel; dogs have good noses so she must be about to notice.

— And of course there's the worry box, she says eventually, nodding at the wrapping-papered shoe box on her desk. — If ever you have a worry you don't want to talk about you can always put a note in the worry box.

— But what about spelling?

— Spelling doesn't matter in the worry box! She laughs. — It's just a place to put things you don't want to talk about. To get them off your chest!

— I don't have anything in my chest.

— Well that's good. Very good. She pauses again. — Nobody wants you to have worries. And, if you don't, then there's certainly no need to make them up! But you're sure you're okay, Billy? You do look a little . . . worried. Is everything really okay . . . at home?

I nod hard, hoping it will end, but she's still just sitting there waiting, and the Dad shape moves across the door window, and she's going to spot what I've done unless I say something to get away quickly, so I start talking fast. — Yes Mum and Dad are fine nearly but Grandma Lynne is helping with that because actually Mum and Dad won't move or speak normally anymore. They are stalemating. So Dad sleeps downstairs and does imposing poses the other way without eye contact when they're together to avoid violent behavior like prime-apes do.

Miss Hart's head tilts the other way hard now, blinking, totally spaniel-inquisitive-sad: she doesn't understand at all and her nose is twitching.

— It's like silverbacks, I explain. — They only do hurting when they have to, otherwise it would damage their genes. Please can I go now, please? Plea—

I slip off the front of my chair and my sweatshirt wings

come apart and she notices. She sort of pulls back a tiny bit and grabs her chin with her hand and says, — Gosh, Billy!

I want to say sorry, sorry, sorry, I didn't mean to and you wouldn't let me go so it's your fault really not mine and I'm incredibly sorry so please don't be cross I won't ever do it again it was an accident I'm wet, I'm wet, I'm wet . . . but Dad's face swims up to the door glass now, looking in, and suddenly I desperately don't want him to know about it too so I just say, — Please don't tell my dad, very quickly before the sob comes. Sobbing is quite interesting because it jumps your shoulders up and down as if you're a puppet on jerky strings.

— Oh, Billy. You poor thing.

— Don't tell anyone!

— But why didn't you let me know if you needed—

— Once it happened in the car . . . after I'd been pretending it might happen . . . and we stopped . . . and I didn't need to go really then . . . so the next time Dad wouldn't stop . . . and it happened . . . and we had to wash the car-seat cover thing . . . and he wasn't happy . . . so please . . . don't say anything.

— Breathe gently: it's all right. Accidents happen; he'll understand.

She nods after she says this but strangely the nod works backward, making what she's said seem even less likely to be true than it did before.

— Let me find you some PE kit, she says.

She retreats to the pegs to look for my dolphin bag with the stiff zipper, but I can't stop the puppet strings yanking on my shoulders even though I'm trying to do the gentle breathing like she said, and the next thing that happens is a knock on the door followed by Dad's head leaning in.

— Everything all right, Miss Hart? Billy? What's going on?

Miss Hart spins on her squeaky heel with her eyes wide and her mouth all round and I pull at my sweatshirt which I've somehow got tangled round my left leg. Miss Hart sorts herself out quickest; the "O" mouth disappears into her assembly face, very sit-still-no-wriggling-or-else.

— We're fine. One moment. I'll bring Billy through.

— Billy? says Dad.

— Please, Mr. Wright. Just give us a moment. I'll explain.

And I immediately horribly understand what's going on here: Miss Hart is pretending. She is finding my PE-bag shorts and saying it's all going to be okay but she isn't really meaning to keep it a secret at all.

She's admitted it! She's going to *explain*.

And what was I thinking anyway, idiot?

If I take off my wet trousers and put my PE shorts on instead, Dad will see I'm wearing PE shorts and holding wet trousers and say Hey, why are you holding those wet trousers and what are you wearing your PE shorts for? And even if I don't change out of my wet trousers into my PE shorts I'll still be wearing wet trousers and he'll just ask about those instead.

So do you know what? No, but I do! I decide I'm not going to answer any questions. None. She can do the answers anyway. I yank my sweatshirt wings off my lap and bury my head in them on the table to do my puppet jerky sobbing under cover instead.

— Son?

— Please, says Miss Hart. — Just give us a moment.

But Dad is already beside me bending down, big hand on the back of my neck. I wriggle a bit but he keeps it there.

— What's happened to you, Billy? I'm here. It's okay.

I say nothing.

— Come on, sit up. Let me have a look at you.

I hunker down harder.

— What on earth is it? Come here.

— No! I say. No isn't an answer because Come here isn't a question, and anyway I was right because Miss Hart is already doing it.

— Billy had a little accident, she explains. — He's upset.

— Accident, says Dad, worried. — What sort of accident? Is he hurt?

— No, no. He was just late getting to the toilet.

— I see, he says. — I see.

But the way he says this, all jelly-mold unserious, is wrong and angering! And anyway, Miss Hart is lying! I wasn't late getting to the toilet. She wouldn't let me go! Dad is rubbing the hair on the back of my head the way he tells me not to stroke our cat Richard, who doesn't like being stroked backward, and neither do I!

— That's not like him at all, says Dad. — Is it, Son? But never mind . . . next time you'll—

— Miss Hart made me do it! I shout into my arms. — She did! She's not telling the—

— Billy! Dad says sharply.

— But it's true!

I lift up my head and see something surprising. Both Dad and Miss Hart are looking at one another with similar shut faces. Miss Hart's eyes are narrowed and her lips are I'm-going-to-have-to-give-you-a-red-mark thin: Dad looks like he's biting the inside of his mouth to stop himself saying something mean. He takes my PE-kit bag from Miss Hart's outstretched hand and gives it to me. — Go and put your shorts on, he says softly.

I trudge over to the chipped sink area again and start

changing. It's not as easy to swap trousers you've wet for dry shorts as you might think: first of all, you definitely have to take your shoes off, and then you have to decide whether you're supposed to wear nothing under the shorts or wet pants which nobody will see instead.

— What happened?

— He had an accident, like I say.

I decide that it's probably best to take the pants off as well as my trousers because I don't wear pants under my swimming trunks. Why would you? They'd get all wet.

— But why? He doesn't have accidents.

— I'm afraid I don't know, Mr. Wright. He's clearly upset about something.

— Wouldn't you be? If he asked, why wasn't he allowed to go?

— He didn't ask—

— Yes I did.

— Or, if he did, I'm afraid I didn't hear him until it was too late. Obviously I'm sorry if that's the case.

— Didn't *hear* him?

— No.

— Did this happen in front of the class? Was it . . . noticed?

— No, no, no. But it wouldn't be the first time a pupil—

— Maybe not, but not Billy: he doesn't have accidents.

— Really? says Miss Hart, using her try-again-that's-not-quite-the-answer-I-was-looking-for voice. — Most little ones do from time to time. It's to be expected. In the car, for instance . . . Here she leaves a pause just like the ones she leaves in class which somebody — anybody — might like to fill with the actual true answer, before she eventually continues: — But as I say, he's clearly distressed . . .

— About what?

— I don't know. He had an argument with Fraser about a project they were working on together, but to me that seemed more of a symptom than the cause of the problem.

— What else has happened?

— That's what I was hoping you might be able to help with.

But hold on, I don't wear pants under my trunks because I don't want them to get wet, and these ones are already wet, so perhaps I should put them back on?

— Me? Dad's voice has knives in it. — Ah, I see.

Miss Hart, very assembly: — Has anything happened at home that we should be aware of?

Dad doesn't answer and I decide not to put the pants back on. After swimming we wrap all the wet things into a towel sausage. There's no towel here but I carefully roll the pants up inside the wet trousers. Then I unroll them because I did it from the wrong end. By starting with the wet patch the dry legs come last. It takes a few goes but I do some person veering and succeed by the time Dad comes to fetch me. The sausage bundle looks much smaller under his arm.

— Okay? he says very quietly, taking my hand.

— Fine.

Miss Hart: — Do feel free to come in and see me if you want to talk about how Billy's getting on, both in school . . . and more generally. No need for an appointment, just drop by at the end of the day.

Dad says, — Thank you, as he walks us past her desk again, but I can tell he means something else, very camouflaged knife tips, and at the door he stops. — Home's not the problem, he says. — We've had no accidents there.

It's not just accidents that have left home; when we get back Grandma Lynne and Mum are out, too. Dad looks at his watch and goes up to his bedroom-study to check his computer, and I put on some normal trousers to do drawing in. I feel better like that, and somebody has sharpened all the pencils which is excellent. I draw incredibly pointy claws first and then attach a giant man with two heads. One of the faces does a hilarious smile while the other opens its fearsome jaws wide to eat a stick person who has a speech bubble coming out of her mouth. *I am Miss Hart* is what the speech bubble says to start with, but after I've written it I read it and feel bad so I try to rub it out, but sadly I discover that I've written it in the wrong sort of pencil, black instead of gray. Black is part of the colored-pencil set and if you try to rub out colored pencils all you do is make a smeary mess. I don't know why: that's just the way life goes, Son. Luckily I am not downhearted but inventive instead: I color the whole speech bubble in very black indeed. It's strange. Even though I use bright turquoise and yellow and red for the rest of the picture the black speech bubble makes the stick person incredibly desperate. It looks like they have a storm coming out of their mouth. I draw Mum a seagull with a daffodil in its beak next because the clownfish the daffodil was supposed to be goes all wrong.

Dad comes downstairs eventually and yes, yes, yes, he decides I can watch some children's television if I want to, which I do. But sadly when he turns the television on it's the news which shouldn't be on at this time of day but is, and quite unfairly Dad sits down on the edge of the coffee table to watch it instead. There's an emergency debate going on to do with broken resolutions and the new clear threat. I'm confused: a resolution is a promise you make after Christmas which isn't for ages. Dad's head dips forward to listen carefully. Without conclusive evidence the Government will be acting illegally, says a woman with puffy white hair, and Dad nods in agreement. But then somebody more important-looking wearing an excellent yellow-spotted tie starts saying something I can't understand about sanctions not having worked and the rapidly approaching point of no return and Dad growls the sort of sad growl a leopard might growl if it had to abandon its kill to a pride of advancing lions. — They're going to get their own way eventually no matter what, he says, walking right up to the television. It looks like he might kick it. But in the end he just yanks the plug out of the wall.

— Dinner, he says. — What would you like?

— Fish and chips.

— Out of the question. How does chili con carne sound instead?

— Fine.

Dad likes cooking but he does it differently from Mum. When Mum finishes there's a lovely meal you recognize on a plate and nothing else to see; when Dad does it there are packets and spoons and knives and cuttings and pans and jars everywhere — because it's a kitchen, Son, not a bloody operating theater — and the thing you get on the plate is often surprising.

— Right, you can help, he says, giving me a bundle of carrots. — Peel these.

I love peeling. Here's a dirty old carrot. Here's a peeler. Here are the peelings. And here is a brand-new carrot. It's brilliant and it works with potatoes, too. Best of all, with Dad you can leave the peelings on the side. They are fiddly buggers to pick up.

While I peel, Dad chops onions and starts to cry.

Then we fetch out the biggest pan and heat up some oil and do really spitting frying. Onions, mince, carrots: they all go in. But then Dad decides carrots were a mistake so he fishes them out and puts them in another pan full of boiling water instead. Next, spices. There they are in their little pots, lined up like soldiers on parade. Let's have a tap of each one, shall we, and a good old shake of the chili. Back they go, retreat, retreat, retreat; not in a line anymore but safe again. Cans of beans and chopped tomatoes go on top when the frying is done, and the spots that spit out of the pan onto the cooker and tiles now are more gluey-red, like nosebleed snot. Magic ingredients next: a tin of tomato soup plus a mega-squirt of ketchup. And look at this — there's even a real chili in the back of the fridge. Chilies are peppers' hottest cousins, Son: they're related. Dad chops this one up very small and we both try a piece and my tongue is fine to start with until it's not, and then there's nothing to be done about it: even the glass of water Dad gives me tastes like malting larvae. He lets me stir the pot to take my mind off it, so long as I'm careful not to pull the whole boiling lot on top of my head and end up scalded and scarred for life, and while I'm stirring he puts the rice on and has a second bite of chili and starts crying again.

Simmering is quite boring.

But I'm allowed to grate the cheese so long as I do it without shredding my fingertips because nobody wants to eat pink cheese, Son, and before long there isn't any space in the sink which means we're nearly ready.

Dad frowns at his phone again. — We might as well make a start, he says.

We do, and it's fine: I can't even really taste the black twisty bits of onion. And since I know it makes him happy I manage to eat every last spoonful, which works, because yes, yes, yes: ice cream! With extras! This time it's peanut butter and chopped-up bits of something he fetches from his coat pocket: a Mars bar!

— Hell, we've earned it, Son.

I'm halfway through my bowl when Mum comes in. Dad turns and says, — Hello, but stops short of what he was going to say next when he sees Grandma Lynne walk through the door behind her. Both Mum and Grandma Lynne have a little look around the kitchen before anyone speaks next. It's Dad, pretend-happy: — I know, I know. We've been reenacting the Somme. Don't worry, I'll sort it out afterward.

Mum plants a kiss on the top of my head and all of a sudden I wish I'd finished my pudding before they'd arrived because what's left in the bowl makes me feel guilty.

— That looks . . . nice, she says.

I nod.

— Special-treat pudding again. On a Monday.

— Tessa, says Dad.

— Well, they do say the way to a man's heart is through his stomach.

— For God's sake.

— Shall I make a start on the washing-up? asks Grandma Lynne.

— No need, Lynne. It's our mess.

— But you're still eating. It's really no bother.

— I'll sort it out in a moment.

— Let me help. At least I can make a start.

Grandma Lynne puts her bag down on the side and squints at the buttons on her frilly cuff. She undoes them eventually, and rolls up that sleeve, and squints at the other, and Mum must be watching all this, too, because the hand that she's smoothing my head with suddenly grips my shoulder instead.

— For God's sake don't, Mum. It's just washing-up. Relax. Read the paper . . . watch TV. I'll bring you through a cup of tea in a moment.

Grandma Lynne spends as much time turning her sleeves back down again as she did rolling them up. My ice cream is melting. I have another spoonful when she finally goes: it wouldn't have felt right beforehand. But eating still doesn't feel normal because Mum and Dad are standing either side of me and I feel like something fascinating David Attenborough is showing to the camera.

— That does look delicious, Mum says gently. — Can I have a spoonful?

— Finish mine if you like, says Dad, edging his bowl toward her. Mum takes it and cuts out a half-moon spoonful of ice cream and mine immediately looks more normal and even tastes better because Mum says, — Mmm, delicious, so everything is nearly normal all right.

But then she says, —Good day at school, Billy? and the cold mouthful I'm swallowing turns pinecone prickly in my throat. Sometimes Richard has fur balls to cough up: they are nothing compared to this! I cough the ice cream back up into my mouth but spitting out is ugly so I swish it around until it goes back down again.

— Fine, I say at last, blinking at Dad.

He checks that Mum is still looking at me, then gives me an incredibly fast wink. — They've got tadpoles in the classroom, he explains to Mum. — What more could a man want?

— Great!

I nod hard enough to turn the tadpoles into dolphins, pliosaurs, even.

— And it must have been nice to see your friends — and Miss Hart — again?

I carry on nodding, focusing falcon-hard on the bottom of my bowl.

— Give me that, Mum says at last. — You'll scrape a hole in it!

I do as she asks but now that I've said fine and done nodding it's not nice sitting next to Mum with my wet trousers on the floor of my bedroom upstairs. I decide they would be better off buried quite far down in the washing basket.

— Can I go and play now?

— Of course.

I slide off the side of my chair and sprint out through the hall past the open front-room door, catching a glimpse of Grandma Lynne reading as I go. She's pretending to concentrate so hard on her paper that she doesn't even flinch, which means move an inch fast, but even though I only see her for a second I can tell that she desperately wants to look up, because her concentrating face is sadly unrealistic. Leaping stairs two at a time is easy when you're pretending to be an impala, and it's no problem pressing damp trousers down underneath Dad's dirty shirts when your hands have turned into a badger's paws. Once that's done I feel better enough to make a small stealth bomber out of technical Legos: I've made more or less the same thing hundreds of times before, but this one has a particularly impressive tail fin so I decide to fly it downstairs under the radar to show Mum and Dad.

But I only make it as far as the hall because Grandma Lynne stops pretending to concentrate on the news as I tiptoe past and says — Pssst, Billy, to me instead. — Leave them for a moment, she tells me. — They need some time to catch up with each other.

This makes no sense because they're right there together, not racing, but Grandma Lynne is quite old so probably hasn't done racing for a long time and therefore doesn't understand. She doesn't appreciate my stealth bomber either. I show her the loading-bay hinge and tell her how it can hold a new clear bomb with awesome powers of distraction, but she doesn't even look at it properly; she just keeps glancing across the hall at the half-open kitchen door. — Lovely, she says, flapping a new page of paper open on her lap. — Why don't you have a little play with it on the sofa while I read this; there's a good boy.

Grandma Lynne is nice but her questions aren't always real. There's no way of saying, — Because I don't want to now, even though that's what I want to say. Instead I sit on the couch next to her and both of us do pretending: she tries to look like she's reading again, and I fiddle my stealth bomber around in my hands as if it's incredibly fascinating when actually what I'm thinking is that it really does remind me of all the similar ones I've made before.

In fact what we're both doing is listening to Mum and Dad making up across the hall.

— Oh Jim, says Mum. — Of course I did.

— Why didn't you say so then?

— I didn't think I had to.

— Really?

— *Of course.*

I have no idea what they're talking about but that's not the point: the point is that they're using normal un-prickly voices again. Did you know that whales can communicate across whole oceans without any words? Our cat Richard can even do it silently, by rubbing his scent glands on the kitchen-table legs. Mum and Dad carry on for a while and I stop listening to their exact words: whatever they're saying it doesn't have to do with my wet trousers, so that's okay, until . . . it's not, because the sound of their conversation suddenly darkles.

— But you just agreed!

— I know, and I meant it: I believe you, says Mum. — We have to present a united front.

— Yes, by standing by me. You said you'd stand by me.

— I want to.

— There's a but, though. I know it. There always is.

— Don't start with that again.

— With what?

— You always say that.

— Because it's always true! Every concession you make comes with a caveat that effectively undoes it.

— It's not a caveat. I'm just being realistic. It's what we have to do to back one another up. If we don't go we will only make matters worse.

— In your opinion.

— And Mum's.

— Christ. Hers and yours, maybe, but not *mine.*

Grandma swishes her newspaper to a new page at this point, very rustling, but it doesn't do any good: when the voices come back they're almost speech-bubble black.

— I've told you: I'm not going. Full stop.

— But . . . how do you think that will help? It's just stubbornness. Insane, pigheaded—

— Here we go.

— But it is: can't you see? What you *don't* say will carry weight. Because it does! At best you're running away, at worst it's a tacit admission. It makes you look guilty!

— But I'm not.

— I know.

— And is that not enough for you?

— No, no, no! Because—

— Because what?

— Because it's not me that counts.

— But it is, isn't it?

— What's that supposed to mean?

— You don't actually believe me, do you?

— I haven't said that.

— Yes, but what you haven't said counts, too. You just said—

— Don't twist—

— We're back where we fucking well started!

At this point Grandma Lynne flaps the newspaper so hard it lifts her from her seat to shut the front-room door with a bang. The face she turns round with is very bright: it reminds me of the man who does the art show on television. He's okay but desperate.

— Can we watch some television? I ask.

— Good idea, says Grandma Lynne, scrabbling for the remote. — How do we turn it on?

I show her and it's brilliant because even though the quite desperate but okay bright-faced art man isn't doing any projects just then, Grandma Lynne says I can watch something else which has a cartoon fish in it which blows raspberries and says *what you lookin' at* the whole time instead. It's loud.

Fucking is quite loud, too. Dad explained it once: — Most words are quiet, Son, even if you shout them, but some are explosively noisy no matter how softly you whisper their name.

This made no sense at first; even Dad looked into his beer bottle to find a better way of explaining it.

— Some words are too loud for most places. For example . . . He looked around the kitchen. — For example, you wouldn't beat a big bass drum in the downstairs loo, would you?

I didn't know what he meant by that, either, but he did start to make sense about the operating theater and the instruments, because as well as being noisy and quiet, like instruments, words are in fact either useful or pointless as well, depending on where you use them, like tools.

— What I'm getting at is this, Son. You only want to use the right tool for the job. Tweezers are for pulling out splinters and sledgehammers are for knocking down walls. See what I mean?

— What's a sled hammer?

— Sledge. A big heavy one. You wouldn't use a big heavy hammer to cut your hair with, would you? No. And it's the same with words. He took a sip of his beer and put it back down very carefully onto the wet ring he'd made when he spilled it before. — What I want you to realize is that words aren't offensive in themselves. They're just offensive when you use them in . . . the wrong places. Like school. Never say the "F" word at school. It would be like using a pneumatic drill in the dentist's. Totally . . . wrong. In fact, come to think of it, children should never use pneumatic drills. Not without supervision, anyway. But that doesn't make pneumatic drills evil, does it?

— What's a new mat tick drill?

— You know, those horrible noisy things workmen use for digging up roads. You see my point?

— What about if a dentist was digging up a road?

— Precisely! Dad peeled the label off his bottle. — Clever boy. Now. You're supervised here, by me, so we'll do a demonstration. What word must you never say?

— The "F" word.

— Right. It's not a tool for children, or dentists. But when can you say it?

A trick question! But I am too quick for him, too clever!
— Never, I said. It rhymes.

— No. Normally you'd be right, but not here. The right answer begins with super and ends with vision.

— Supervision.

— Yes. Some tools children can only use under supervision.

— Like when Superman burns things with his eyes?

— Eh? Not quite. Like now, though. Now you're under supervision, so now you can say the "F" word. Say it.

— The "F" word.

— No. Actually say fucking.

— Fucking.

— Fuckity fuckity fuck fuck fucking.

— Fuckity fuckity fuck fuck fucking.

— Brilliant! And we're still here, aren't we? We haven't melted or gone pop.

— Fuck. Fuck. Fuck.

— That's enough. But essentially . . . yes. And there are more. Loads more. For example: Shit. Bugger. Wanker. Cunt. Nigger. Say them.

— Shitter bugger wanker cunter nigger.

— More or less. All of those are strong words, some viciously so, and you must never, ever say them in the wrong place; in fact just about everywhere is the wrong place for all of them when you're you. But they're only words at the end of the day, loud words, some louder than others, and here's the point . . . He jumped up and went to the fridge for another bottle of beer, then, which was great because I got the froth. — The point is this, Billy . . . he said when he'd taken the bottle back from me. — The point is that . . . what was the point again? Oh yes. It's this . . . The point is that all those bad words have a place and a purpose, and it's your job to figure out what that place and purpose is . . . and never, ever, use one when you're not sure . . . because if you get it wrong, if somebody finds you offensive, you'll wind up in trouble, serious trouble . . . but always remember . . . remember . . . yes, that every word has its right place and purpose . . . because they wouldn't be words unless they had one . . . they simply wouldn't exist.

— What's a fence sieve?

He rubbed the top of my head and dug a thumb and forefinger into his eyes when I asked that, and said — Priceless and laughed quite annoyingly loud for a reasonably long time.

Halfway through the strange cartoon with the raspberry fish I hear the front door slam and Dad's head bobs past the window.

And he's not back for stories at bedtime, or even my that's-it-the-end-of-another-great-day-lights-out-kiss later on, and that night I don't just have one dream, I have a whole load of little spiky ones followed by a big loud sad one. Like trailers leading up to the main film. I'm still not going to tell you what the dreams were about though, don't worry. I haven't forgotten what Dad said: hearing other people's dreams is boring.

Have you ever killed one of your pets? I have. Not our cat, Richard, which is lucky, because Richard is older than me and when he dies it will be sad. I'm talking about the goldfish Dad brought home in a plastic bag ages ago, when I was vertically four or maybe even three. He won it on a stag night. — No, Son; it's a night for staggering about on; there aren't any no eyed deer.

I was quite pleased with the goldfish, but couldn't understand why he was called a goldfish when he wasn't gold or even silver, and that's how we came up with his name: Orangey.

The problem was that we needed a proper tank like Lizzie has now, with filtered bubbles in it, not just the little round glass bowl Dad bought secondhand. I heard Mum telling Dad so. But he didn't agree.

He said, — Let's not add financial insult to injury, eh. If it's good enough for Tom and Jerry it's good enough for me.

— It's not you I'm worried about, it's Billy.

I didn't understand that — I wasn't going to swim in the bowl. I wouldn't have fitted in and anyway I couldn't swim yet because when you're three you aren't developed enough to swim properly or even move your body carefully, never mind think sensible thoughts, and that's why I thought it would be a good idea to take Orangey out of his bowl with no filtered bubbles in it: he probably needed some air. I know now of course that fish use their gills to eat oxygen from water, because I've seen *The Blue Planet*, but I hadn't seen that then. I didn't even know that wet fish are slippery customers. That's why I let Orangey flip between my fingers onto the floor and, when I tried to pick him up, I accidentally knelt on him.

Normally I go to school for the whole week but guess what? One morning before we've even arrived at the weekend Mum puts out ordinary clothes for me to wear instead of my uniform. I check my book bag: sometimes there's a piece of paper in it saying something like *No school uniform tomorrow, just pay a pound to keep earthquakes in Africa*, but not today, which is so great it makes me practice my sea-eagle swoops on the stairs. First I run up to the top on a thermal, then I glide back down to the fourth or fifth step from the bottom very stealthy, using my softest feet, then I leap-dive down incredibly banging loud on my imaginary un-expecting prey.

I manage three swoop-dives like this before Mum appears saying, — Stop it, stop it, stop it: for God's sake stop it!

— But I don't have to go to school. It's a day off.

— Not really, Billy. Come here.

I do as I'm told and sit down next to Mum on the top stair. She is holding her dressing gown tight into her throat and has red eyes. Jenna in my class can make her whole face go pink if she wants. Don't strangle yourself, Mum!

— Today is a serious day, she says in a very serious voice. — We have to go to an important meeting. You, me, and Grandma Lynne. The ladies from the Council will be there, and the doctor you went to see the other day, and there'll be more people, too. They're going to want to talk to me and they may well also want to speak to you.

I do some serious nodding back. — What about?

She twists the dressing-gown collar tighter, bites her lips, and looks away for a long time. It's quite boring waiting, so I ask what's for breakfast, which makes her say, — Just tell the truth about . . . how much . . . you love your dad . . . and how much . . . he . . . But she doesn't finish this quite easy-to-end sentence-question because she needs the toilet very intensively instead, which isn't really a problem, because Grandma Lynne is already downstairs and she lets me have Saturdays-only chocolate spread on toast.

Have you ever been to a pantomime? I went once, and my trip to the meeting with Grandma Lynne and Mum is reasonably similar in two ways. First, because Grandma Lynne and Mum took me to the pantomime on a bus without Dad as well (— Slapstick isn't really my thing, Son, you'll have a much better time without me) and second, because they both wore stuff on their lips for that trip, too. Apart from those similarities it's different. Less happens; this meeting is quite a lot more boring.

When I knelt on Orangey I was sad. He stopped wriggling and became much less fiddly to pick up and I knew what had happened: he was dead because I had killed him. I still hoped Dad might be able to mend him because I was only three or four and an idiot at the time, so I took Orangey up to the bedroom-study and asked Dad to help me make him better. When he said he couldn't I got quite angrily upset and he had to calm me down by putting Orangey on his mouse mat and bear-hugging me. In a bear hug you can't kick or struggle because everything is wrapped up tightly. I know it's unrealistic: bears don't really kill prey that way: they scoop Alaskan salmon out of rivers in slow motion with incredibly nimble claws.

— But why can't you make him alive again? I asked when the bear hug stopped.

— Because it's impossible, nobody can. That's what dead means. Gone for good.

— Gone where?

— Nowhere.

— But if I don't go anywhere I'm still here. He's still here. Look. He's on your mouse mat.

— That's just his body. The Orangey part of Orangey has gone.

— But where?

— I . . . He trailed off. I did not know it then but now I've been to school I think he was thinking about Jesus and God, because they own the heaven where Christians think people go after life has ended if they've either been totally good, or bad-and-said-sorry. But sadly we are not Christians or even members of other less good religions. All of them have something like heaven, too, but we don't, so when our pets die that's it, they're gone, and we don't know where. End of story. Put the book back on the shelf and lock the library door, Son.

— I wish I could tell you, Billy, is what Dad said about dead Orangey eventually. — I wish I believed something nice that I could tell you to make it easier. But the honest truth is this: I don't. Orangey is gone forever.

After that we put Orangey's body in one of Dad's work envelopes. It had a little plastic window. If he'd been alive he could have looked out, and even though he wasn't and couldn't we could still see his body by looking in, right up until we buried the envelope not deeply enough in the garden and somebody, probably our cat Richard, dug it up and ate it. I didn't mind. He was dead anyway.

Here's what happens at the important pantomime meeting.

First of all, we take the bus and arrive at the big building early so we go for a walk to a shop instead. Inside the shop there is a rack of chocolate bars which I don't ask about and yes, yes, yes, Mum buys us all Kit Kats anyway. That's right: a whole one each, no split-it-three-ways sharing! Better still, she then spots some sticker activity books on a shelf, and there's even one on the animals of the Arctic, and when I don't ask for that either she buys it plus a brand-new pack of colored pencils because, she says, they may well come in handy, too.

And then we arrive at the meeting in a room with a lovely carpet which you can see the joins in because it's not one big piece but a whole chessboard of little squares, gray and brown, like in the hospital, only there it wasn't carpet, excellent. I decide to move like a knight and I manage one dogleg forward and another sideways before Mum says, — No, please come here, Billy, in a mouse-hole voice.

Here's a timid mouse peeping out.

Zip, back it goes in again.

I do as I'm told, very reassuring.

There are some other people in the room and Mum wants me to say hello to them. I recognize Butterfly and her cow sill friend, Giraffe.

— Hello, I say to them, because I am polite.

Giraffe does her long-head-sideways-blinking thing with her Hello back, and yes, yes, yes, Butterfly actually has her butterfly roach thing on again today, perched on her chest. It still looks too woolly-heavy to fly, but I'm pleased to see it all the same, and she's pleased to see me as well because she says, — Well hello, Billy! How are you today?

— I'm fine.

— That's a good boy.

I *am* a good boy, it's true: I've eaten a whole Kit Kat on my own to prove it, and I've been polite, but I'd be an even better boy if I could do a long bishop diagonal move from that corner of the room beside the letter-box bin thing right through the gaps between the tables with plastic bottles of water lined up like soldiers on them, over to that droopy plant in a pot with pebbles around its roots on the far side of the board.

It's good to give your bishops an angle of attack early on, Son, because they're commanding.

But I can't, because somebody else is in the way now: the doctor! He is wearing a very white shirt with the sleeves rolled up showing his excellent black arms and the supershiny big wristwatch. When he smiles at me his teeth glisten like his watch, and he also has some silver pen-clip things in his top pocket. Black and white and shiny: a magpie. They are intelligent, which makes sense, because to be a doctor you have to know exactly where the bones are in everybody's body. And he unfolds a serious-big-newspaper as he sits down to prove it!

And it's very funny thinking of magpies and chess because over in that corner sitting down there's a policewoman in a black-and-white uniform, holding a hat on the table in front of her. It's a chess hat! Look, proper black and white squares, even better than the gray-brown carpet tiles!

What we should really be doing here is setting up a pawn pyramid of defense, but we can't, because somebody is arriving late. The doors are like the ones we have in school: they have big pushy metal rod things on the top to shut them with a squeak after you've come in or gone out, which therefore must be nice for Miss Hart because it will remind her of her own habitat.

Miss Hart?

Oh no, no, no!

She's here! And she's seen me! Which means she definitely knows I'm not at school or ill! My ears are hot because I feel very intensively guilty and embarrassed.

Miss Hart looks straight at me as she walks over and does that thing she sometimes does if somebody is upset in class or doesn't understand the thing on the board: she goes down on one knee and looks at me super gently and says what she has to say in a lovely quiet voice.

— Don't you worry, Billy. Everybody's here to make things better.

— It wasn't my idea, Miss Hart, I'm sorry.

— Idea about what?

— Coming! And it was my turn to count the tadpoles! I really don't want to miss . . .

Miss Hart does a smile-glance at Mum then gives my hand a pat.

— Don't you worry. The tadpoles can wait.

But she's wrong! They can't wait. They will develop whether they like it or not because of metamorphosis which isn't evolution. But I don't have a chance to tell Miss Hart these things because she's already standing up to say something else to Mum instead.

And now Grandma Lynne is chatting to a small woman who looks like a starling because she has speckles on her face and flecks in her jacket and she even pecks her nose forward a bit when she speaks. She must be Grandma Lynne's friend, who is going to help Grandma Lynne with something, because Grandma Lynne beckons me over and says, — Remember I told you about Jean, my friend, who is going to help.

— Yes.

— Well this is Jean. She's going to help.

I still don't really know what that means but it's obvious from the way Grandma Lynne is speaking what I'm supposed to say so I say it anyway.

— Thank you very much.

The lady, Jean, pecks her nose at me and says, — You're most welcome. But no, there are no clues about what I'm welcome to do: she just pecks back at Grandma Lynne and says, — No Jim then?

— Perhaps it's for the best.

Starling Jean shrugs her wing shoulders and starts unpacking her briefcase. It's large. Extremely! I spot Butterfly watching from across the tabletops. She must be quite upset: her own briefcase is miniature compared with that! Still, she digs some papers out of it for Giraffe, who thanks her sideways as usual.

But there's something more interesting going on behind Giraffe's long head: a big yellow crane arm is moving in an arc above the half-built next-door building top. It's taller than a real giraffe even, way taller! And there's a chain hanging down, very black and tight, so something is probably on the hooky end, but although I stand on tiptoes I can't see what it is, so I do a few almost invisibly small steps forward to see if I can see it then, but Mum still notices, because very quietly she says, — Billy!

I have to stop. It's frustrating! I really want to know what's on the end!

And it's strange because normally I'd just ask Mum if I could go and have a look out of the window, and Mum is not Dad so she's much more likely to say yes if you must even if she would really prefer me not to, but today it feels as if asking to look out of the window would be like asking to open Christmas presents early, which means even Mum is bound to say No way, don't even think about it, so there's no point in asking, so I don't.

The crane cranks round a little nearer anyway. And everybody in the room is pretending they're busy with something because they don't really want to talk to each other until the thing they're all waiting for happens, so nobody talks until the silence feels like the deep end of the swimming pool. Magpie doctor jumps in first. He shows his paper to Giraffe and says something about pointless posturing and the new clear capabilities. She can't believe the Government will use force without conclusive evidence either, and Butterfly leans in to have a look at the pictures. I decide to keep an eye on the crane because it's less boring than everything else and the thing on the end may come up on its own anyway.

Then everyone jumps up for an orangutan!

Not a real one of course. The orangutan is actually a man who comes through the door bum-first because he's holding a massive coffee cup in one hand and a folder of papers under the other arm. Squeak goes the hinge. He has a circle of messy orange hair round the back of his head with only a few wisps on top, and when he turns round I see that the circle joins up with an orange beard, almost exactly like King Louis's from *The Jungle Book*. I want to be a man, man cub, and walk right into town. Well done, you've succeeded!

The orangutan apologizes for being late, but he doesn't sound sorry; he sounds cheerful instead. He plonks his papers down and takes a big slurp of coffee and a deep what-have-we-here breath, then tells us all he's called Bill Pearson twice, and works his way around the room saying hello to everyone with lots of nodding and smiling, calling people by their name at least twice, too.

— And this must be Billy! he says, when he arrives at Mum and me. — Now I'm sure Mum has told you, Billy, what today is all about. Everyone here wants what's best for you. That's what we're going to try and work out. It's a *What's Best for Billy Meeting*, do you understand?

I nod. He seems very nicely in charge, this man, with excellent orange wire hairs poking out of his ears, too.

— Good! he says. — Now. I'm sure you also understand that some of the time grown-ups have to talk to other grown-ups about grown-up things, yes?

I nod again. The crane swings back across the window gap.

— And it's not always possible for children to be part of those grown-up chats, is it?

Another nod. Sadly the hooky end is still out of sight: boring!

— Well, today will be a bit like that. I know you've already spoken with most of the people here — Dr. Adebayo, Mrs. Hudson, and your teacher, because I've read about what you said to them in the notes. That's why I'm a little late, in fact:

because there was such a lot in that folder to read! And I want to thank you for answering their questions so sensibly. You've been very helpful.

Orange hairs. Yellow crane. Nod, nod, boring nod.

— So . . . he turns to Mum . . . — so I hope that Mum has brought somebody with her to look after Billy while we have our grown-up chat? As we discussed.

Grandma Lynne and Mum turn to each other for a moment: it's obvious that Grandma Lynne would prefer to stay in the grown-up room but in the end she picks up the arctic sticker book and waves it cheerfully instead.

— Great. Thank you. There's a chance we may need to ask Billy a question or two later, but I hope it won't be necessary. You saw the lobby area down the hall? Well, if the two of you could wait there for now, that would be just great.

Orangutan rubs his hands together: there are orange hairs on his knuckles as well. And Grandma Lynne is nodding her head off beside me, hoping to win the best nodding prize perhaps, which is sad, because I've already won it, and the crane is cranking whatever-it-is back across the window again anyway. Imagine if it swung right into the room and lifted one of us up. Me! Yes, I could be a chess piece and the crane arm might swing onto my square. Up I'd swoop. It's for the best. The crane has taken me! With what, though? I feel suddenly sad that I won't ever find out which piece is really on the hook.

— Okay then. No need to look so worried, Billy. You understand what's happening, yes?

Nod, nod, nod. What long arms. Did you know that an orangutan is four times as strong as a man? That's why they don't need cranes, probably: they can reach and lift massive chess pieces on their own.

Mum bends down next to me, very sparkly-eyed. — Billy? Say thank you to Mr. Pearson.

— Thank you, Mr. Pearson, I say.

And that's all that happens in the meeting, or at least that's all that happens in the meeting when I'm there. Much more must happen when I'm not because it takes ages! I do every single arctic sticker and complete the word search and drink so many tiny plastic glasses of cold water from a machine with a big glugging jar-bottle thing on top that I have to go to the toilet down the corridor a few times.

The third time makes Grandma Lynne nearly cross. — If you must go yet again, Billy, you know where the toilet is now, so you can go on your own!

She's right. I do know where it is. And I am able to go on my own. But sadly everything is different backward. After I've finished I take a wrong turn and get lost. It's not my fault! The corridors are long and they all look the same because of their chessboard carpet tiles and blue plastic-padded chairs and little low tables with seashell fans of leaflets on them.

Have you ever been lost? Of course, because everyone has, and that includes me. The thing is not to panic, Son. Just retrace your steps if you can, or stay put if you can't. I'll always find you. Always.

I do some tracing but it's no good so I do it faster to cover more ground but sadly all that happens is I end up back by the toilets again with a fluttery feeling in my chest. A man comes out as I'm standing there trying to breathe slowly. He has crispy light brown trousers with oh no a small patch of wet just there, and he's still doing up his belt, and no, no, no, he asks me if I'm all right or need help. No and yes! But I can't say that because you should never go with strangers, particularly when you're lost, because that's when you're at your most venerable. So I turn round and do a sprint of tracing back the way I've come again past the big notice board with the smiling-wheelchair-people pictures and words in capital letters.

The fluttering is a crashing feeling now. It makes my head swivel like a meerkat's. And there's the fat-water-bottle glugging machine, but no, no, no: it's not the right one because it doesn't have a torn label! Somebody else is walking round the corner up ahead with a Tesco bag, so I run past with my head turned the other way and start to cry. What if everyone goes home without me? They wouldn't do that but then again that could be what they think is best for me. What's best for Billy? Billy who? He's not here anymore because he ran away. It's probably for the best. Let's all go home. My legs are itchy and they use horrible soap on the walls or carpets or door windows here: the whole place smells like a cross between the lavender plant in our garden and petrol from when Dad overfilled the tank. Just calm down, Son. Where's Mum? Door window. Door win . . . yes, yes, yes. Just like at school, you can see through the door windows here, so I have a peep straight back into this one and the next and round the corner there's another and . . .

Yes, yes, yes.

Big room. Mum. With her back to me: pale neck. Mum, Mum, Mum.

Starling Jean is speaking, flapping her wings at Giraffe, who shakes her long head and looks sideways at Butterfly, which makes Butterfly do a sadly-I-agree nod. Orangutan spreads his long arms hold-on-now wide, but his hands turn palm upward, very what-can-we-do? The woman with the chessboard hat is reading something boring and the magpie doctor is looking out of the window, at something shiny, probably. I can't tell you much about Mum because as I've said she's sitting with her back to the door and anyway her head is dipped forward in her hands, very weary: even prairie dogs tire out eventually.

There's a skittery noise in the corridor then, and Grandma Lynne is suddenly right next to me with puffing cheeks. — Oh thank goodness, she says.

I look down at my shoes. My feet are in them. They do a little jump.

Grandma Lynne says, — But where have you been?

— I don't know.

— You don't know? I've been running around like a . . . She shakes her head. — Not to worry. It's okay. Just . . . don't go off on your own again, promise. She takes my hand. Under her breath she continues, — Particularly not today, of all days.

— But you told me to go on my own.

Grandma Lynne doesn't reply to that because she's looking over my head through the door window. I turn to have another look, too. Mum's head is bent farther forward and her shoulders are quivering, but it's okay because Starling Jean has a wing around her.

— Come on, Grandma Lynne murmurs. — Let's go and wait where we were told to wait.

Mum and Grandma Lynne don't talk much on the journey back home. Mum is so incredibly tired her eyes have gone night-shifting puffy: to begin with she has to blink a lot and take deep breaths to make the car go. But Grandma Lynne's hands won't sit still in her lap. They're itchy. They make her lean across the front seat before Mum has gone over the humps where the road goes narrow and loud-whisper, — Well?

— Not now, Mum.

And do you know what? I can tell, when Mum says *not now*, that it's all an act. Keeping quiet for the journey has nothing to do with being tired. It's to do with keeping something quiet from me! The meeting was all about what was best for me, after all: they must have come up with something so important Mum has decided to keep it a secret, for now.

I decide not to pester. It doesn't work anyway, Son, ever. Instead I form a plan. As soon as we're inside I go up to my bedroom and put the microphone bit of the old baby monitor inside my school book bag. Idiot! I take it out again and switch it onto green lights and put it back in again. Very stealthy, I carry the bag into the kitchen and hook it on the back of the spare chair; it often hangs there: nice camouflage! Not long afterward Mum says — Why not go up to play in your room until tea, and I knew she would, and when it happens I just smile and quite loudly ask Grandma Lynne for my excellent new pencils and arctic activity book and say what a good idea, I'm off upstairs to color in the picture of the northern lights. I'm in genius.

I don't actually color in the picture to begin with.

Instead I take the other part of the baby monitor and plug it into the socket behind the end of my bed. It's quite tricky to stretch under there. You should never hold the metal bits of a plug: if you do you'll be electrified. Don't worry, though, you can touch a Scalextric track if you want, but not at my house because I don't have one, and anyway, remember never to stick a fork in your toaster. The lights on the monitor thing flash green like a dragon's eyes. They can see all the way downstairs! And David Attenborough would be proud of me because here's some evidence: straightaway Mum and Grandma Lynne are talking under my bed. I lie down next to the monitor and listen carefully for the secret of what's best for me, but sadly all they're talking about is something else quite a lot more boring instead.

— He'll never agree to it.

— He'll have to, Tessa. He has no choice.

— I know what he'll say, though. And you know what, he's right. It's absurd.

— But it's not forever.

— Doesn't matter. A day is too long. It just won't work.

— You've agreed now, though.

— Only because the alternative was worse. If it hadn't been for Jean they'd have gone for a court order.

— And they haven't done that. He'll realize he's had a narrow escape.

— Come on, Mum. You know he won't. And anyway, even if he agrees, how on earth are we supposed to make it happen? He has Billy more than half the time. He takes him to school, collects him . . . My shifts . . .

— This is temporary, though.

— Yes, but so what?

— They'll soon see there's no need . . . on their . . . visits. You've only got to spend ten minutes with Billy and Jim to understand. It's just supervised contact . . .

— Yes, but under a child protection plan.

— Like Jean said, they could have applied for an exclusion order. Everything will be back to normal before you know it.

— They're monitoring us, Mum. My son.

— And they'll stop monitoring you — us — again soon.

— They think Jim hit him with a brick, or dragged him over a wall.

— Well . . . but . . .

— What am I going to tell him?

— He should have been there himself. It's his fault, not yours.

— How has this happened?

— Look. Tessa.

— How? *My son.*

— Darling.

The monitor goes quiet then so I open up the activity book and even though coloring-in is really quite boring unless you're coloring things you've drawn yourself, I find my new pencils and make a start on the northern lights page. You never know, Mum or Grandma Lynne might ask to see the results. If I haven't done what I said I'll look like an idiot, or worse still a liar. At least the colored pencils are sharp. The ones at school are mostly blunt and often don't have lead poking out at all. I decide to overlap the colors in the segments to create interesting effects, because life doesn't come in neat squares, Son. Sooner or later Mum and Grandma Lynne are bound to start talking again and when they do they'll get to the point and give away the secret surprise instead of talking nonsense about super vision.

— What am I going to tell work? Mum asks eventually. —How am I going to get the time off?

— They'll have to give it to you.

— But I'll need to explain. I can't. I just . . . can't.

— I'll help.

— Oh, Mum.

— We'll get through this. I'll take him. Or I'll be here . . . whenever is necessary. I can do that. I want to help.

— No, but, Jim . . .

— If he can think of a better solution, let him. The time off isn't an issue for me: I can work around it. You'll have to take your holiday. For as long as I'm needed, I'll be here. Between us, we'll manage.

After that there's some clattering. When you lie on your stomach for a long time on the floor it's quite funny because it actually feels like there's something heavy on your back, not your front. Eliza in our class can do a cartwheel but I am better than her at forward rolls. The secret is to keep yourself rolled up into a defensive hedgehog ball for ages: don't go straight until everything has stopped. My back feels heavy so I wriggle out from under the end of the bed and do a few practice forward rolls, which turns out to be really stupid of me because after about seven I open my eyes and see Mum in my doorway.

— What's all the banging about?

I try not to glance desperately at the monitor under the bed

— PE. Sorry.

— Ah.

But I can't help looking at the bed-end! Luckily, when I do, I see my northern lights picture just there, so I cunningly pretend I was looking at that by diving on it quickly. I pick it up and start telling Mum all about the cross-patched shading quite loudly. — Let's take it down to show Grandma Lynne, shall we? I say.

Mum's eyes still look puffy tired, but she's definitely narrowing them at me. — Is everything all right, Billy?

— Yes fine brilliant let's go sorry.

— What are you apologizing for?

— I don't know. I'm not.

She puts her hand round my shoulder and strokes my cheek as we walk downstairs. — You've done nothing wrong.

— That's what Dad keeps saying.

— And you know what he means?

— Yes.

— Promise?

— Yes. What's for tea?

Luckily Mum seems keen to move on to the tea stage very cheerfully. She nearly nods her head off, and down we go, and

I'm allowed to choose exactly what I like. Excellent! Sausages of course and smashed potatoes, and just to test whether she actually means it I ask for some peanut butter instead of gravy. Mum and Grandma Lynne have a who-can-grin-the-hardest competition when I say that, and Mum fetches the jar so quickly I nearly see whether they'll give me chocolate sprinkles on top of my carrots as well, but just as I'm about to ask, I don't, because chocolate-sprinkled carrots would actually be disgusting.

Did you know that there are rules about eating?

Well there are. Lots. And here are some examples. You have to eat with your bum on a chair pushed up to the table, saying please before things you want and thank you after them, doing your best all the time not to spill things all over your uniform because washing it costs money. If you don't like something you have to try it anyway without making a huge fuss. Spicy food sorts out the men from the boys, Son: I like it and so will you if you try hard enough. Whatever you do, when your mouth gets pins and needles have a sip of water instead of spitting everything out like a baby. There are no alternatives in this house: if you don't like what's on your plate it's tough because there are hungry children in Africa so you mustn't put your elbows on the table, but do ask for help if you're having trouble cutting up your food. Fingers on the buttons. We're not pirates. Yes, peas are tricky customers, but you'll manage if you scoop them up carefully. If you have to, use some smashed potato cement to keep them from jumping all over the place. Spinach makes you strong and carrots give you curly hair and chocolate makes you fat and too much ketchup rots your teeth but everything is okay if you eat it in modern nation.

Normally the rules are like toasters: I don't actually want to stick my fork in them anyway; but something funny about Mum makes it hard not to prod about a bit today. It's as if her wide smile is saying Go on, try stretching me, I won't snap! My legs slip-slide off the chair and I hold my knife like a stabbing dagger and say, — I don't want these carrots today after all; what's for pudding?

Mum pushes her thumb and finger into her eyes, but asks, — What would you like?

— Ice cream with . . . something in it.

— What sort of something?

— I don't know. Chocolates sliced up. And jam. Mum's smile flickers so I quickly explain, — You asked so I said. It's not fair! But I don't think I needed to say that anyway because she's already shaking her head and fetching the ingredients.

The funny feeling carries on: Mum gives me my pudding and it *is* ice cream with a some jam and a chocolate square, very tiny, on top, and I say, — It's not big enough, while eating it up quite fast without bothering to lean forward over the bowl, and nobody says anything at all about the small mess I make; Mum and Grandma Lynne just sit either side of me watching like I'm a really lovely experiment until the door goes click and there's Dad behind us rumpling his cornstalk hair, staring down.

— That looks nice, he says, a little too loudly.

— It is.

— Good! Great!

— Jim. I'll make you some coffee.

— Coffee. Dad drags the spare chair out from under the table as if it has done something wrong, and sits down on it heavily. — That'd be lovely. Make us all a cup. Lynne would like one, too, I'm sure, seeing as she's here. Of course she would. Lovely.

We sit quite quietly for a moment while Mum fiddles with the coffee thing which always needs emptying before you fill it. Hurry up, Mum! My pudding is less good now, but I finish it, leaning right over to catch any spills which I don't make anyway. When I look up Mum has her head cranked over her shoulder, face headlamp bright, ready to say, — Good boy, Billy! Now, upstairs and get yourself ready for the bath.

— But Mum . . .

The headlamp blinks shut when I say that and the funny feeling shrinks away immediately. No buts. Dad grabs me as I slip down from the table, gives me a rough but lovely three-beer-cuddle, then says, — Scoot.

— I'm scooting.

— I'll be up in a bit. We have things to discuss. Okay?

— Fine.

Undressing is easier than getting dressed but watch out for done-up buttons: they make it vertically impossible to take off your shirt by pulling it over your head. I tug quite hard but the neck just bites my face even when I turn my head upside down. Some dogs wear funnels that look quite similar. When I was small I thought the funnels were to help the dogs catch balls but they're not. They're to stop dogs biting themselves. Dogs are less well developed than me: I wouldn't bite myself. But actually, I am wrong, because here I am using my done-up shirt button to bite myself! As soon as I realize this I pull my shirt back down and undo the button using my opposable thumbs. Ha! Take that, dogs.

And since I am doing nicely without asking for help I decide to do another grown-up thing as well: run the bath. If you're an idiot you forget to put the plug in. I'm not and I don't. The little grille thing is quite like a Lancaster bomber's turret, until you cover it with the plug, which reminds me of a miniature dustbin lid instead. Done. I slosh some bubble bath down the bath's white side and turn on the tap full steam ahead! Scooping up my clothes I run out on to the landing to put them in the washing basket. Ali Baba lives in it with forty sleeves. I'm pushing some of the arms and legs back under the lid when I hear a strange clattering noise in my bedroom. What could it be? Suddenly, I remember: the baby monitor! The voices downstairs make no sense but they're louder when I'm through my bedroom door, with Mum saying, — Please! and more washing-up crockery noises and a long spell of hissy-water silence leading to nothing.

Then Dad starts laughing.

It's a long low rumbling nothing-funny-here four-beer laugh: ha bloody ha bloody ha bloody ha! And it grows louder. Once a nasty man in a hat — because he's a jumped-up little bastard, Son — gave Dad a parking ticket when we were just on our way back from the doctor's: the laugh he did when he tore the ticket off the window and got it stuck to his fingers as he tried to throw it at the man's shiny shoes was quite similar but less bad.

Ha bloody ha bloody ha bloody ha!

I dive at the bed legs, pull the monitor plug out of the wall, and push the whole thing with its dead dragon eyes out of sight.

But as soon as I'm back up on my knees I hear a door bang open and footsteps on the stairs. Quick! If you were a red squirrel and you'd just buried a walnut you wouldn't sit there staring at the place where you'd just buried it while a more dominant gray squirrel stood over you telling you that you were supposed to be in the bath, would you? No and neither would I, so with explosive acceleration I leap up from the foothills and sprint across the landing and bang through the steam-pouring door and do a two-footed jump-slide straight splash into the bath.

It's hot.

Hot.

It's hotter than hot: it's almost immediately incredibly burning: so shockingly malting-larvae hot that I jump-slide straight up the bath side again, screaming. But sadly baths are wet and so am I and everything has gone viciously slippery. I crash back into the water on the side of my leg, the steaming-hot water everywhere, screaming.

Dad's there.

He's above me yelling, — Christ! and yanking me by the leg and arm clear of the fire water.

I'm screaming.

He rips the shower from the wall and turns it full-cold straight at me there on the carpet where I'm rolling to get away from myself.

Screaming.

And Mum's here, too, yelling, — What?

The cold shower water is full of needles. They jab me. My red legs. Red side. Red hand, like Dad's. And Dad is covered in water as well because he's holding me. It's up the wall and squelching beneath me in the gaps between screaming.

— Empty the bath! shouts Dad. My face is pressed into his soaked shirt shoulder. He has the shower head held high above us. Mum yanks out the bath plug. I shut my eyes and see fiery bullets called tracers streaming from Lancaster bomber turrets. There's a picture in a book. The bullets are tearing holes in my skin. Somehow or other somebody yanked the shower curtain down: the see-through starfish covering it are rumpled over Dad's legs. He lies with me on the plastic sheet aiming the water across us both, going, — Shhhh! while the bath drains out and fills up again.

I stop screaming and sob instead.

And then he's lifting me back into the bath, but the cold water makes my hot bits sting so I scream again. Dad looks like he's trying to twist his hairs out of his head when that happens, so I try to stop, and manage to go back to just sobbing again.

The bath looks funny with no shower curtain above it. Up by the tap there's a plastic submarine. It used to be clockwork but something went rusty inside it and now the winder is stuck.

And Dad is still holding my shoulders, half leaning into the bath with Mum above him, and Grandma Lynne bobs in and out of the doorway so fast her helmet hair shakes. I shut my eyes. It sounds odd when you cry through chattering teeth. I bite the inside of my mouth until I can't feel the twisty flame bits of my leg. I open my eyes again. The submarine is made of two plastic halves. The crack between them has gone black: I hadn't noticed that before.

Dad's face is still just above mine, very worrying: he looks like he's lost something brilliant down a drain, and he's shivering, too, saying, — What do we do? What do we do?

— What we're doing, says Mum. — We cool him down. Which bits hurt, Billy?

The moaning noise rattles out of me again. I don't actually know the answer anyway because my body has gone blurry. The black crack along the submarine looks like a smile. It's no use: I can't smile back at it.

— We need to get him to hospital, says Dad.

— Wait.

— Get us some dry clothes. What should we put him in?

— Just wait.

— He can't lie in a cold bath indefinitely. He needs looking at.

— Is the hurt going away, Billy?

I say, — A bit, yes, but roll toward her as I say it, and when I move my leg the twisty flame gets me again, so I yelp, — No! as well.

— Clothes. Car keys, says Dad.

— Please, Jim. Give it a few moments. We have to be sure!

— I am sure. It was bloody hot water.

— Yes, but—

— He doesn't cry like that unless he's hurt.

— I know.

— Should I wrap him in that, then?

— I don't know . . . look. He's probably shocked. We cool him down. We all calm down. And then, then we decide what to do. If we take him to A&E . . . we can't just take him in . . . not today . . . Christ, they'll . . .

— *They?*

— You know what I mean.

— You're worried about how this *looks*?

— Think about it.

— I'm not thinking about anybody other than him!

— Neither am I! I'm just looking beyond—

— I'm sorry, I say.

— Oh, Billy.

— Will I die?

— No, no, no, whispers Dad. — Don't be daft.

— Will my leg skin fall off like a snake's?

— No.

— It hurts.

— I know, Son. I know. Tessa, fetch me some clothes.

— You can't drive. You've been drinking.

— You drive then, for fuck's sake!

Once, I picked the submarine up and black water dribbled out of it, which was interesting; at school I had a nosebleed, too: drip, drip, drip. Miss Hart gave me a new worksheet. Dad is still rocking me a little bit, saying, — Shh, even though I'm not saying anything myself. Have you ever been for a walk in windy cold rain? Did your chin go tingly-numb? That's what everything is like. I try to sit up and Dad says, — Shhh! to me again, and — Don't just stand there, to Mum.

Mum's eyes are full of light. She brushes some of it away with her thumb heels. But as she turns to go she's stopped by Grandma Lynne, who says, very quietly, — I've called an ambulance.

Mum takes a deep breath and sinks back against the wall.

Dad stares over at Grandma Lynne. Slowly, he nods. — Thank you, Lynne. Thank you.

You can't see the flashing lights when you're inside the ambulance, or hear the siren even, particularly when they don't turn it on. I'm disappointed. Still, the lady with the green coat is friendly, but her teeth overlap strangely. Dad sits with me stroking my head. A lot: careful you don't stroke a hole in it, Dad! In ambulances they have lots of things clipped to other things. Sometimes there are straps. One of the strapped things is a mask for your face attached to a fire extinguisher with laughing medicine in it.

— Are we both allowed some? Dad asks the lady.

— For a fee, she says.

It tastes funny but feels funnier, like the moment just after the tickling stops, combined with when you realize everything's actually a dream.

— What's that you've got there? the woman asks.

I hold my dolphin up for her to see but the words that come out don't make sense. — My smiling nosebleed.

The doctor in the hospital asks about it, too, when he's tapping his syringe, which he tells me to look away from, so I immediately can't, but at least I tell him the truth.

— It's my submarine.

— Marvelous, he says, pricking the needle in.

My arm hurts so I say, — My arm hurts.

— Brave boy.

— I'm durable.

— What's that?

— Tough.

— You are. He looks at Mum as he goes on. — Must have been a hot bath.

— Accident, says Dad.

The doctor nods and takes off his glasses. There are excellent red grooves above his ears. Some people keep pencils there. Jesus was a carpenter's son. He did miracles including curing the sick by helping them pick up their beds, but sadly it was probably a trick. The bed I'm sitting on has wheels and brilliant suspension, like Mr. Sparks's bicycle. The doctor looks very young because his skin, apart from the red grooves, is lovely and pink.

— Accidents do happen, he says. — He's lucky you pulled him out so quickly. The upper leg, this small area here, may blister, but it's a little early to say. Mostly he's got away with it. The erythema — redness — should calm down pretty quickly. He's a lucky unlucky boy, so to speak. We'll keep him in overnight, see how he does, top him up with pain relief as necessary. His leg may need dressing: the nurses will show you how. You're a tough a little chap, though, Billy, yes? No more diving off the hot tap. I'm sure you'll be fine.

— Great. Thank you, Doctor, says Dad in a job-done-let's-move-on voice.

Mum pinches the ridge of her nose.

— Not at all, the doctor replies. Now, I just need to sort out the paperwork. He takes a clipboard from the foothills of the bed — Butterfly would be proud — and continues, — What's Billy's full name?

Mum says it slowly.

— And his date of birth?

She gets that right, too.

— Home address?

Correct. Well done, Mum.

— GP's name?

She answers. He nods, scribbles.

— And where does he go to school?

This doctor has very impressive fast writing: he puts his head on one side to admire what his pen is up to, only pausing when Mum replies to his *and finally* question, — Does the family have a health visitor or social worker?

— Yes, Mum says. — We do.

— I see. Okay.

Dad, under his breath: — Jesus Christ.

— You're in good hands, then. The doctor smiles, flipping up pages in his pad. — I'll be back in a moment. There's a green form I need to fill out, too.

I'm allowed to spend the night sleeping in my bed with suspension in the hospital, but sadly Mum and Dad have to do it sitting up on chairs with wooden arms. Chairs are interesting. They have backs and legs and arms and feet and bottoms, too, but no heads or hands. You wouldn't believe the dreams I have about chairs during my night in the hospital! Incredible dreams: just incredible! Don't worry, I'm still not going to describe them. Just because something is incredible for me in a dream doesn't mean that it won't be totally boring for you.

Have you ever fallen over playing tag in the playground wearing shorts and a T-shirt? I have, quite often, and the worst thing that happens is when the skin grates off my knees or elbows, with bits of grit left in. But even if I cunningly avoid that by breaking my fall with my hands it normally means my hands smack down on the tarmacs very hard and sting horribly for a reasonably long time until they stop stinging and start throbbing instead. Well that's exactly what happens to my boiling-leg-splashes when I wake up very early in the hospital after my dreams, only in reverse: gentle throb, throb, loud throb, almost sting, stinging, very stingy . . . actually hurt. I nearly cry so Mum fetches the nurse who gives me some more medication which is just a special way of saying medicine: normal pink stuff from a bottle you have in a white plastic spoon. It tastes nearly as nice as Calpol. I lie with Mum's and Dad's hands taking turns in my hair as the hurt gradually turns stingy and then to quiet throb again.

You can eat food in hospital without getting out of bed. They have a tray thing on wheels which rolls over the top of your legs at exactly the right height. Excellent! The vegetables have water under them but there's custard.

Sadly you're not allowed to lie there eating the food definitely. They send you away from hospital as soon as they can so that somebody else can have a go in the bed. The doctor looks at my side and legs again after breakfast in the morning. It's Cheerios: excellent. The doctor is also pleased; I know because he says, — That's good, I'm pleased. Everybody's very pleased in fact. Well done, Billy's body; still a bit blotchy, and that is a small blister on the side of the upper leg, but it's not as bad as expected. Overall: impressive powers of healing. Luke Skywalker has a brilliant fake hand but when the farmers shoot off Fantastic Mr. Fox's tail that's it, it's gone for good. Unfortunately, as soon as we've all smiled at each other the doctor takes Mum and Dad out through the curtain flap and explains something disappointing to them about a follow-up visit from so shall services. So shall we? Why not. Curtain flaps are much less muffling than walls. When they come back through the slit they prefer not to look at one another again, and sadly that's it, we've got to go home how. Cheerio. Don't come back unless you forget to check the temperature of the boiling bath before leaping into it like an idiot again. No need to worry: I won't.

We drive home without talking. The radio fills up the car with noise for us anyway. There's a song about tying something to a tree with yellow ribbon. Rope would be stronger. Then there's one about angels which don't really exist. Afterward, a lady gets excited about the traffic jams. All normal. I'm sitting on the backseat behind Dad so I can't see his face, but using observations I can tell he's concentrating very hard on the road: he doesn't turn his head at all. Sadly that means he doesn't see when Mum shudders a bit and smears a line of tears into her cheek. I lean forward to pat her arm but I can't quite reach because my leg hurts when I stretch out that way, so I have to sit back normally again.

*

Excellent! Grandma Lynne's car is still parked in our street! I see it first and tell everybody but grown-ups are unpredictable creatures, like orcas, egg-shaped rugby balls, and the weather in Wales on holiday. Orca is just the right way of saying killer whale: one moment they're fine but watch out because, whap, the next they're likely to eat their trainer. Dad's good hand thumps the steering wheel and he stops the car with a jerk; Mum looks out of her window at the scaggy bush as if its leaves are made of something unusual, like green icing, perhaps, or shavings of plasticine.

One of the best things about scalding your legs in the bath is that you don't have to go straight back to school. Instead, you're allowed to do vertically what you want at home, which is actually more difficult than it seems. Choice, Son; it's not all it's cracked up to be. Does the same thing ever happen to you? What do I fancy doing? you ask. Well, what are the choices? Anything at all. That's fantastic! But hold on; it's so good it's actually bad because . . . I can't decide.

It definitely happens to rabbits crossing roads in the dark, and when it does it's often fatal.

I start by reading a chapter of a book about an eagle, up to the bit where the eagle's family arrive for a visit in the snow quite boringly, which makes me build most of another Lego stealth bomber with a loading bay, until I realize it's just the same as the last one I made, so I watch half of David Attenborough's *Life in the Freezer* instead. It makes me want to look at my arctic activity book, which I do, but I've only been looking at it for a few moments when I realize that I'd actually prefer to be doing another drawing of my own instead.

I go to fetch some more sheets from Dad's dream of paper.

He's in his study-bedroom staring at some tiny writing on

his computer screen, so I take the Sellotape dispenser across into my room as well and stick some sheets of paper together to make a giant canvas. Sellotape can be a tricky customer, especially if two bits of the sticky side stick to each other; when that happens you're buggered, Son, just start with another piece.

I do.

It's okay, but by the time I've made the canvas I've forgotten what I wanted to draw on it. That is called having no inspiration, and the best tactic for dealing with it is to look at great things you've done before, which makes you remember you did them and think hey, I did that, so I can definitely do something else as good again!

I dig out my most recent pictures, including the one with the black cloud scribble coming out of Stick Woman's mouth. The black cloud looks something like an explosion. Kakaboom. Since my piece of paper is massively Sellotaped together I decide to do a whole battlefield of war on it, with hundreds of similar explosions, plus fire dragons, a red river, and a flock of tiny blue birds. Chuffinches. There are twenty-six until some explosions go off in the middle of the flock. Kakaboom, kakaboom, kakaboom.

Feathers everywhere!

Our cat Richard catches birds sometimes. There are more feathers on a sparrow than you think. Once Richard caught a sparrow and only nearly killed it before Mum chased him off. We walked up slowly but the bird didn't fly away; it flippered sideways into a bush instead. We pulled the leaves back to have a look and it was interesting to see a sparrow so closely at first, then sad, then confusing, because Mum didn't know what to do. Its beak kept opening and shutting. Calpol is very effective medication, but sparrows don't eat from spoons. When Dad came I suggested we could use a box full of holes instead of a cage, because all you need is a sharp pencil, but sadly he told Mum to take me inside so I didn't see what happened in the end.

Curiosity is a wonderful thing, Son, but sometimes ignorance is bliss.

I have a wooden box with things in it.

Valuable things.

For example, there are four bottle tops I found with Ben's dad's metal defector when we went on a picnic with them. You have to sweep the silvery round bit very low to the ground. Slower than that. *Very* slow. It's quite boring. But if you're lucky the round bit sees some metal and goes beep. Ben's dad knows a man so lucky he found a Roman thing in a ditch once. They put it into the museum and let him go on the news to tell everyone. It was brilliant. I wanted to find an arrowhead or another sharp thing, but the bottle tops were excellent anyway because they came from Spain, near Rome, with Spanish writing written on them. It hadn't even faded much. Modern shops still sell San Miguel beer and I've seen empty bottles of it in the recycling.

Another valuable thing I have is an ammonite. Do you know what one is? Miss Hart didn't, and neither did anyone else in my class, so I was allowed to bring it in for show-and-tell. I stood at the front. Everybody else looked at me and I looked at them. All their hairs were golden and wiry because of the sunny window behind: it's how you get real halos. I decided to sit down again because I didn't want to say anything anymore, but Miss Hart did encouragements on me, so I started by explaining that ammonites are extinct. Samira said they couldn't be, because I had one just there in my hand, but

I told her that I didn't, and Jacob said that meant I was lying, so I told him it was only a fossil. He asked why I hadn't said it was a fossil instead, then, so I told him what a fossil was and that I was showing him a fossil-eyed ammonite. After that some people stopped looking at me and talking was easier. You can't please all of the people all of the time, Son. I explained that ammonites have a spiral shape and that in the olden days people thought they must be the fossil-eyed bodies of curled-up snakes. Luckily those people were wrong, or else there would have been no ammonites. Normally they lie for millions of years between layers of rock for archaeologists to discover, but I got mine at the beach in an ice-cream shop.

I have a snow leopard called Philip in my valuables box as well. He's full of squashy beans, but unlike the beanbag downstairs he doesn't have a zip, or even a hole for the bits to come out of. I've had him since we were both brand-new, which means he's six, too. He looks older. His white spots turned gray a long time ago because I used to carry him around everywhere, dropping him out of my buggy like an idiot. Once Dad had to drive all the way back to Tesco. Nowadays I keep Philip in my valuables box because Samuel came round and saw him on my pillow. Have you ever watched *Doctor Who*? I did once, just before bed. There were whispering vampires with curved fangs and pale faces, so I got Philip out of the box again, just for one night. He still smells excellent.

When I didn't see how Dad was helping the injured sparrow I knew I didn't know everything that was going on and felt annoyed and reassuring at the same time. For a few days after the hospital it feels the same at home. Blissful has nothing to do with blisters. Grandma Lynne stays living in the spare room when Mum has to set off for her night-shifting, but sadly she doesn't come out of her room as much as normal, and when she does, if Dad's there, they do strange headlamp smiles at each other. See, I'm smiling: can you see? Dad mostly does his work on the computer in his bedroom-study with the door slightly open. It's an invitation. If you're quiet as a mouse you're allowed in, so in I creep to do things on the floor, for example a drawing of a praying mantis. Mice are actually quite noisy, like colored pencils. Scratch, scratch, squeak, squeak. Owls are much stealthier. Unlike other birds, their feathers have no oil coating, and that's what makes them vertically silent. I am not an owl. Out you go now, Son: I have an important call to make.

Have you ever run out of milk? Sadly that's what happens next to us. Actually it's not really that sad for me because I've already had some hot chocolate earlier in the morning. You never get two cups. But Dad is allowed as many mugs of coffee as he wants and Grandma Lynne is normally very thirsty about tea. I'm sitting under the kitchen table adding some more wildebeests to the migrating Serengeti picture I'm secretly drawing on the table's underneath — it's a lovely big flat surface, and the right color, too — when Dad walks in and starts doing coffee things. You always have to wash the pot out first. It's quite clattery. But once the black graduals are in and the pot is on the cooker there's nothing to hear except the tickling flames. I sit very still. Drawing on the furniture is illegal, even the underneath bits, probably. When you have to sit very still everything goes electric almost immediately. Luckily, just when I can feel that the fizzing is going to make me make a noise, Grandma Lynne also decides to be thirsty. She arrives in the kitchen reading some papers from her work. You're not allowed to draw on the backs of them either, until she says so, or make airplanes. She isn't expecting Dad to be here now: when she looks up from reading, it takes her just a little bit too long to light up her headlamp smile.

— Oh hi! she says.

I wriggle some electricity out of my left arm. This one. Dad's face is already set to bright.

— Hi, he says. — I'm doing some coffee.

— Actually . . . Grandma Lynne points at the kettle . . . — I've come down to make some tea.

— Of course.

I judder out some more sparks in the noisy bit where Dad watches Grandma Lynne fill the kettle quite loudly. She clicks it down on the black circle thing as if it's a new one, very special, and they both stand there watching the coffeepot and kettle take ages boiling, until Dad realizes there's something else he could be doing in the fridge. He rummages around in it for a while helpfully noisily, then thumps the door shut with a look on his face that says, fridge, you disappoint me. I have seen that look myself because I am not the best at catching.

— No milk.

Grandma Lynne looks nearly cheerful about this sad situation. — No bother, she says. — I'll nip to the shop.

— Would you? says Dad, smiling more normally. — I'm expecting a call.

— Leave it to me.

Grandma Lynne disappears into the hall. Dad slumps back against the cupboards. They're also called units. We count in them at school, which makes sense, because the bit above them is called a counter. Steam starts fluffing out of the kettle. But instead of the front-door sound Grandma Lynne comes back into the kitchen and puts her handbag down on the side.

— Jim, she says.

Dad knows what she's going to say already. I can tell. He's gripping his forehead as if he's trying not to let the next words in.

— I'd forgotten, says Grandma Lynne.

He knows what, but still asks: — Forgotten what?

— The supervision—

— Jesus, Lynne. You're popping down the shops.

— Yes but—

— It's ridiculous, anyway. No offense, but I've never been more likely to commit an act of violence than I am with you here now, constantly breathing down my neck. Do they really think putting a family under this kind of pressure could possibly help?

— It must do. In some circumstances. Otherwise they wouldn't—

— Yes but not in these circumstances. Not here.

— No.

— Then please. We need some milk.

Grandma Lynne grips both flopped handles of her bag and lifts it up an inch. But she puts it down again. The coffeepot is rattling on the cooker and my sore leg is starting to throb. If he doesn't turn the knob down soon the spitting will start. I've seen it happen: the blue flame squirts orange.

— You're right, Jim. But why take the risk?

— It's not a risk. It's a point of principle.

Grandma Lynne puffs air through her lips and shakes her head. It's a mistake. When wolves are doing dominating they use tiny body-language signals. Leopards do the same thing probably. By puffing out air through her lips Grandma Lynne is really saying, — You, Jim, are quite an idiot. In response

Dad's good fist knots up behind him on the counter. Very slowly, he leans over to turn off the cooker.

— You've done a lot to help over the past weeks, he says.

Grandma Lynne says it's no bother by shrugging her shoulders.

— But I really think we've imposed for long enough.

— Don't be—

— Your work . . . Dad nods at Grandma Lynne's papers . . . — must be suffering. I know mine is.

— Tessa asked—

— And we're all grateful. Really, we are. I won't forget what you've done, particularly when Billy had his accident. But I can't accept anymore . . . help. I just can't do this anymore. It's tantamount to an admission of guilt. I've done nothing wrong. You know that. Sooner or later they'll understand, too. In the meantime, I need some space. I just . . . do.

— I can't leave.

— Please don't make me ask you to.

— I promised Tessa.

— I'll explain to her.

— That's not the point.

Dad straightens up and takes a small step nearer Grandma Lynne. He slaps his red cast into his open good hand. His eyes are screwed into slits and there are two lines either side of his mouth. Grandma Lynne leans back without letting go of her bag handles, but trying not to pick the bag up. Plants grow toward the light no matter where you put their roots. We did sunflowers in Reception. The electricity is still buzzing but the sore bit of my leg is sort of drowning everything out and anyway I'm not about to move.

Dad, very quietly: — It's my decision, Lynne.

— Let me call Tessa. I can wait for her to get back.

— No.

— Look, I'll fetch the milk. You're right. Ten minutes won't hurt. I'll come back. Let me come back.

He takes another small step toward her; the bag comes off the surface but she stays where she is, saying, — Please.

Can't she hear? Can't she see? I want to scuttle out from under the Serengeti and explain: when Dad's voice goes all sandpapery like this you just have to do what he says. Immediately. If you don't . . . Have you ever seen those twisty things they use to hold bags shut? My insides feel very wound up tight like that. Dad moves forward again. The mouth part of me wants me to say something but I manage to keep it shut, and luckily Dad swerves around Grandma Lynne into the hall. He's moving funny. Jerk jerk. I suddenly recognize something: the electricity is in him, too; it's not quite the same sort but it's definitely related.

I know you, Son: I can see your soul.

Dad makes it to the front door. I lean across to watch him step back from it, the door swinging in slowly. It's as if he's opening it for a magnificent queen. He's looking very hard at his socks. Don't worry, Dad, they're even.

Grandma Lynne says, — Just some milk then. Her voice is un-Grandma-Lynne-ish, like she's not a quite old grown-up with carefully cut black wing hair, but someone small forced to answer a Miss Hart question she thinks she's probably got wrong instead.

Dad doesn't reply.

Grandma Lynne takes her coat from the pegs, puts it on slowly, and slides her bag handles up her arm. She opens her mouth but closes it without speaking. Down the front step she goes. Dad sock-watches a moment longer. Then his face lifts slowly to the ceiling and he flicks the door with the fingers of his good hand. The door swings shut with a clunk. He folds his arms and leans back against the hall wall. Maybe it's the gray light coming in through the window over the door: his face is the color of the smashed potatoes they give us at school. He shuts his eyes. You can't sleep there, Dad: it won't be comfortable. He opens them again, looks the door up and down slowly, as if it's wearing an excellent superhero outfit, including mask plus boots, then gently slides the metal thing at the top of the door across.

It's not the lightning kind, but still it's called a bolt.

He leans his forehead against the door.

Then he says, — It's all right, Billy. You can come out.

— I'm not—

— Come on. Out from under the table.

— But I'm sorry. I'm sorry, I'm—

— It's all right, Son. Come here.

I stand up a little too soon as I'm coming out and scrape the back of my head on the table lip. He swings round quickly.

— I'm fine.

— Good. He rubs my head. — Upstairs then, to the study. Let's play chess.

I nearly win.

But not because I play well: more because Dad isn't concentrating. He spends less time looking at the board than at me. It wasn't just the hall light, either: even up here where there's a yellow bulb in the lamp he still looks white. His fingers shake when he moves his pieces. Mostly he puts them right in the way of mine so that even an idiot would know how to take them, and when I do an experiment and leave my knight right in front of his queen he just ignores it.

He ignores the doorbell as well.

And his phone.

He looks at the face of it, mutters, — Christ, and switches it off.

I don't like that: it's not normal.

So when the doorbell rings again I say, — That's the doorbell. I can answer it if you like.

— Stay where you are, Son.

— But it's the doorbell.

— I know.

— So we have to answer it.

— No we don't. Now come on, it's your move.

— But—

— NO BUTS, he roars. Then he immediately steps round the board and grabs me to his chest and says, — Sorry, sorry, sorry. I didn't mean it. You're okay. You're okay. Are you okay?

— I'm fine.

We sit there for quite a few moments more. The doorbell gradually gives up ringing. There's a dog down our road that sometimes barks at night until it stops. Our cat Richard never says anything: he doesn't even meow. I know who is ringing the doorbell and Dad knows who is ringing the doorbell but neither of us say who is ringing the doorbell. It makes me sad. And angry. I look at the pieces on the chessboard, including my excellent pawn wedge of defense, and suddenly they all seem so incredibly stupid that I want to knock the board over. But I don't, because I did once and it only made things worse, and anyway, even as I'm thinking about it, the doorbell starts ringing again.

— Ho-hum, says Dad, but it's not a real ho-hum because a real one means never mind and I can tell that Dad actually minds very much indeed. He shakes his head. He goes over to his computer. Then he flicks a switch on the stereo. Lights glitter on the black box and the speakers on the bookshelves do crackly hissing. Here comes the music, the crackles say, get ready, it's going to be impressive! And they're right, because that's what comes next: swelly loud music. It's like the sea, with us under the surface, and all the roaring and crashing going on overhead. Dad wasn't concentrating beforehand and neither can I, now, so we're even, which makes it all the more spectacular that after another twenty-thousand-league journey under the sea I *nearly* win.

I don't, though.

Just when I've almost got him with my queen and castle he suddenly stops fiddling with his fingers, looks at the board for a moment, says, — No you don't, and does something sneaky with that pawn there. A move later he turns it into another horrible queen. The same thing happens to Doctor Who's enemies occasionally. The Doctor never fails, though; he's a Time Lord so he can always sort things out. I can't. Next move, I'm dead.

— Close, but no cigar! Dad says over the music.

I've lost, so I'm cross, but I know I'm not supposed to be cross that I've lost, or at least I know I'm not supposed to let anybody know I'm cross I lost, but I can't help feeling cross I lost, so I shout, — The doorbell is ringing again! It is. I can tell.

He twists the music softer and stands there with his hands on his hips.

— That was a good game, Billy, he says. You did well. I'll never throw a game, though, and you'll thank me for that eventually. It's only a matter of time. When you win, you really will win.

There it is again: brrrringggg.

His eyebrows pinch down. — You're right, he says.

— It could be Mum, I say. — You did up the bolt thing.

He checks his watch, squints back at me, drags the fingers of his bad hand through his hair. There are gray marks just inside the cast's rim. I'm not sure whether you get soot inside volcanoes.

— If it is her she's back early.

He goes to the window and looks out. I do, too.

— I'm right, I say. — That's Mum's car.

— Where?

— Parked next to the skip.

We both bound down the stairs to let her in. And as I'm bounding I don't even care about my sore leg because everything is great. When prairie dogs reunite they lick each other's faces. All pack animals do it, I think, except the ones killed on the hunt. Skips have nothing to do with skipping. I somehow squiggle past Dad so that he has to lean forward above me to undo the lightning bolt, and by the time he's done that I've already turned the latch-lock thing, so it's really me who pulls the door open to let Mum in.

It's not just her on the step, though.

There's a little party looking in.

Mum's up front, holding hands with Grandma Lynne, and Butterfly and Giraffe are there, too, right behind them.

Dad's hand is still on the top of the door, which slides forward just far enough to make me think he's going to shut it again. But he doesn't. Instead he sort of uses the door to steady himself for a moment before he says, — Hello, very quietly, followed by, — Come in, come in.

Mum leads the way. Her mouth is a line which only crinkles when I grab-hug her round the bum and leg. By the time we've all made it into the kitchen, though, her face is fixed again. She stands very still, like the fridge she's wedged herself against. There are three ways a prairie dog can react when it's impossibly cornered. One, it freezes in a sub-missing pose; two, it flees away at top speed; three, it fights back like a Tasmanian devil. Which is it going to be, then? Giraffe and Butterfly are standing quietly either side of the kitchen table, looking at one another, being very polite about whose turn it is to speak first. Dad slumps down on his chair, head bent forward. And Grandma Lynne, coming in last, does something surprising: she goes round behind Dad, puts a hand on his shoulder, and murmurs, — It's okay. I'm sorry. Don't worry, Jim.

— Don't worry? snaps Mum. — *You're* sorry? He's had you sitting in your car for . . . and you're apologizing?

Dad shoots Mum a very worried look. Hold on, the look says, please don't let it be you who starts throwing spanners here.

And Grandma Lynne says, — Really, it was no bother. I was able to catch up on some reading. Right in front of the house. Just outside.

— Okay, says Giraffe, very I'm-in-charge-here. — I really do suggest — this time — that we find something nice for Billy to do while we're talking. She has a go at smiling while looking sideways from Dad to Mum to me, then her eyes drift up to look for some more acacia leaves.

Dad does some of-course nodding at Mum, and says, — Come with me, Son. Let's find something interesting to watch on TV. But although when he says that it's normally yes-yes-yes time, today the words make me feel like I've just landed slap in the hot bath again, all instantly no-no-no NO. My leg actually begins to throb. Has he forgotten what he said last time? These people are here because making me sad is what they do. It concerns me! I can't do anything about it, though, because there's a man on television who can bend spoons with his eyes, and it feels like every eye in the room is powerfully saying the same thing to me now: go and watch something that isn't as amazing as it sounds, like spoon-bending, on TV. It's just metal fatigue.

I don't even look at Dad as he switches the boxes on. Doesn't he realize I can do it myself?

— What do you want to watch?

— I don't care.

— Come on, Billy.

— Anything.

— Anything it is, he says, pushing buttons.

I nearly say, — Anything but that, when he finally chooses, but his fingers are all twitchy with the mote control so I don't.

He pulls the door to as he leaves, and I hear the kitchen door shut beyond it. Pulling the door to is a stupid saying. To where? To not quite shut. I stand up and open it again. The TV shows a stupid boy who is probably only five, with blue hair and a water pistol. I have a better water pistol than that. He can't even aim his straight. Last time Butterfly and Giraffe were here Dad said fucking because the situation must have called for it: he was incredibly cross with them. Why? Because they wanted to take me away. On cat-feet, very stealthy, I run upstairs to my bedroom to find my water pistol. It's not actually a water pistol at all: it's a pump-action water shotgun. In the olden days people were killed for things like setting off fireworks beneath the House of Parliament, and they went to prison for tiny things like borrowing bread without asking. Nowadays we actually give it to pigeons. Some of them roast in Big Ben.

I haven't stolen anybody's bread, but that's not the point. The point is that the people who can't cope with their children aren't allowed to keep them in case somebody gets hurt. And what have I done? I've run away across the playing pitches and hurt myself on a wall without railings and nearly had a fight with Fraser at school and weed in my trousers afterward. Then I didn't go to school even though I wasn't ill and Miss Hart saw. And after that I jumped into a stupid hot bath and stayed away from school again until I nearly got cross about losing at chess. I've already had one smack which made Butterfly cross. But it wasn't enough because since I had it I've done more bad things anyway. And now they think I can't cope, so Grandma Lynne had to stay outside in her car and Mum came home early and Butterfly and Giraffe are here to do what people like them always do, Son: take people away. I fill up my water shotgun in the bathroom and take it downstairs.

I know exactly how the TV mote control works. On and Off are the same button, but I'm not even going to press it. I'm going to press this one instead: Mute.

I creep up to the kitchen door and listen at the crack, very stealthy.

— But I was just outside, says Grandma Lynne again. — In the car, right in front of the house.

— That's not what the child protection plan says, though, is it? Supervised contact means supervised contact. Mr. Wright isn't supposed to be alone with Billy . . . for now.

My shotgun is dripping slightly. It's one of the rules: I'm not allowed to use it inside. I take my sock off the foot attached to my unburned leg and wrap it round the end of the barrel to catch the drips.

— And the very fact that Grandma was in the car at all is

evidence that the plan isn't working. Mrs. Wright hasn't been able, as she hoped, to persuade Mr. Wright to do as we agreed, have you?

Mum: — No.

— Listen. It's not her fault, says Dad. — It's mine, of course. I've been an idiot. I *am* an idiot. But I'm sorry. I'll . . . comply from now on. I promise. It's just been hard to take in. But I've got it, now. I'll do what it takes. I'm sorry, I'm . . .

Butterfly: — I understand.

There are lots of shotgun rules. Dad made them up quite quickly on the barbecue day when he bought it. I was looking at it in the huge supermarket we went to for charcoal and beer. There was a whole wall of water toys and Dad saw me looking at them and said, — Cheer up, it may never happen.

— What won't?

— I don't know. But in case it does, we should probably be armed.

— What's *armed*?

— Tooled up.

— What's—

— Never mind. Look . . . He leaned into the trolley, took out a box of beer, and put it on the floor. — Choose one, he said. — I've made room.

— That didn't make sense because there was enough room anyway, but I didn't argue. I chose the orange one nearest me very quickly instead.

Giraffe: — But the next step may well be out of our hands. We have a duty to report what's happened, just as we must let the team know about Billy's accident. These things are material.

— What does material mean? Dad asks quietly.

Mum, loud: — For Christ's sake, Jim. What do you think it means? I told you. Ignore the child protection plan and they'll get a court order to stop you seeing him entirely.

— That may not happen, says Butterfly swiftly.

Dad, almost too quietly to hear: — *May not?*

Dad put a hand on my shoulder when I chose the orange water pistol and said, — Are you sure?

— Yes.

— You'll be filling it up faster than you can shoot it, though.

— What?

— Look at this one.

— But it's . . . massive!

— So what? I've made room in the trolley.

We bought the big one. I was pleased and so was Dad, and Mum thought it was excessive, too.

— What Sheila is saying is technically correct, Giraffe begins, — but—

Mum: — But it *may not* matter. Christ, they spelled it out in the meeting. If you'd only deigned to come . . .

Dad: — I've done nothing wrong.

Mum: — Oh my God.

— Nothing, Dad repeats.

Mum: — The broken record again. It. Doesn't. Matter. What part of that don't you understand? Forget them banning you from seeing him; now you've fucked this up they're likely to take him away entirely. But that's probably what you wanted you selfish—

— Tessa! says Grandma Lynne.

Mum, still loud: — Well I just don't know anymore. It's probably true.

*

By the time the barbecue started, Dad was less massively happy about my shotgun. It fires a jet of water as thick as a reasonably fat carrot, and when it hits you it makes you immediately completely wet.

I hit Dad in the back when he was setting up the charcoal and he yelled, — Jesus! quite loudly which made Mum laugh.

By the time he'd changed his shirt he was smiling again, but he still said, — Okay. We need some rules for that thing.

— Come on now, says Grandma Lynne. — Tessa's exhausted. We're all very, very upset. Listen, Ms. Godwin — Rommi —what can we do to minimize the impact of this . . . unfortunate . . . setback?

— Well, I—

Dad: — I—

Have you ever tried to talk when you're just about to be sick? I did, once. I'd gone all gray and shivery and Mum kept saying What's the matter, and I didn't want to say anything at all but in the end she was sounding so worried that I forced myself to say I think I'm going to be sick and then Whoa! I *was* sick. Dad sounds similar now.

— *I'll go.*

Grandma Lynne: — Jim, be careful what you—

— No. I'll go. Tessa's right. It's . . . all I can do. I'll go, and I'll stay away until everyone's convinced I . . . until I can come back.

Grandma Lynne: — Don't offer what you're not willing to—

— I am willing. She says they might take him away. If it's the only way of stopping that, I'll go.

*

By the time the burgers were done I was not allowed to fire the shotgun indoors or at the windows or at cars or over the neighbors' walls or our cat Richard or at people wearing clothes or anyone who said stop or looked annoyed. Mum laughed at Dad when he made up that last rule and said, — Lighten up. What did you expect?

— Okay, okay. Why not shoot . . . insects . . . off the plants, Dad suggested.

I did. It was excellent, until I decided to have a go at a bee on the lavender even though I didn't really want to because I like them. I was so cross I'd squirted it I did it some more.

The bee drowned.

Butterfly: — Hold on, hold on. Nobody's asking anyone to make decisions here and now.

After a pause, Dad replies, — No, but what's the point of delaying the inevitable?

Butterfly: — Nothing is inevitable.

— Will they or will they not take Billy away from us?

— Nobody has said that's going to happen. What we want . . . what everybody concerned wants, is what's best for Billy. That is all we've said all along, and it hasn't changed.

— But it's a possibility, isn't it?

Mum, sobbing: — It was a possibility from the moment you belted him!

Pause.

— It's one of a number of possibilities, says Giraffe. — But it's by no means a foregone conclusion.

Butterfly: — By no means at all. There are many avenues open to us. And if you're willing to help with the process now, and we can demonstrate that, then despite this setback, the prognosis will be so much better.

★

After I drowned the bee I was angry so I walked up to Dad and blasted his back at point-plank range, soaking another shirt. This one was checkered, with rolled-up sleeves. He didn't say anything. He just spun around and ripped the gun from my hands quite harshly in front of everyone and threw it on top of the shed. Then he asked if anyone wanted another drink. I could have got it down if I wanted to, because of the branch on the tree at the back, but I didn't. I went inside instead.

At bedtime that night he brought the gun up to my room with a many-beer sad grin. — Look, I'm sorry. I was a prick.

— What's a—

— I wasn't nice. I was nice to buy the damned . . . blunderbuss, but I didn't think it through. Then I wasn't nice.

— It's a pump-action water shotgun. I like it.

— I know you do. And I like that you like . . . Anyway, what shall we do with it?

— Not fire it.

— Not for now, no. But tell you what. Next hot day we have, we'll have a proper shoot-out. I'll use the hose. Unlimited bullets.

— Can I keep it, then?

— Of course.

— Where?

He scratched his iron-filings chin. — There's only one place to keep a shotgun, he said.

There are scraping-chair noises from the kitchen. My scaldy leg aches and my sock is wet. The hand muffling it round the gun barrel has already started dripping. I need a wee. I need a wee and I know what they said in there. I know what *I'll go* means. I mustn't fire the water shotgun inside, but Son, rules are there to be broken. The difficult thing is knowing when and where to break them. You mustn't wee in the street, for example, but it's okay to wee if you're desperate . . . behind a car in the street. I grip the door handle. I could charge in and wet Giraffe and Butterfly. Drenching is the same as soaking. They would have to leave to fetch dry clothes, and then we could not let them back in again. It's a rubbish plan, I know, because I've only got water. If I had time I could empty out the water and wee into the shotgun instead, and then they really would have to leave because of germs. But I don't have time. Butterfly is going on about nobody jumping to conclusions or taking brash decisions, and saying how great it is that everybody will be keeping in touch, and there are more footsteps, and sooner or later somebody is going to open the door and find me there.

No they won't.

The boring thing about Enid Blyton is that everything in her stories turns out like you expect. Dad doesn't like reading them to me because of that. But confusingly if there's a shotgun up against the wall in act one, Son, it better go off by the end. Unless that's one of the rules it's okay to break.

The door handle quivers.

De-frying expectations, I run upstairs and slide the shotgun back under the bed.

And I lie on the bed well after the grown-ups have walked about downstairs opening and shutting doors and eventually saying good bye. It takes ages. I wait for somebody to come up and see me afterward, but nobody does, only our cat Richard, and even he hasn't brought anything interesting to show me. Nothing dead or wounded. Just his normal belly fur, which is at least quite warm if you stick your fingers into it when he's lying purring on his side. I stroke him quite carefully for a bit. Not backward.

Then I jump up, fetch my swimming bag from the hook on the bathroom door, empty it out in the corner, and pack it again. Not with the same stuff. More useful things. My ammonite, some pants, a jumper with a hood and a pocket your hands can feel each other in, four pieces of paper for drawing on, a sharp pencil, and my snow leopard, Philip. When it's full I hide the bag in my bed. It's quite bulgy, but when I runkle up the duvet the bed looks almost normal.

If he's going, I'm going with him. To help cope.

And he definitely is going. I know, because when I go downstairs he is making tea quite slowly and when he's made it he gives a cup to Mum and a cup to Grandma Lynne, saying, —Here you are, I've made us all a cup of tea. But we've all been watching, Dad! It's not news. And even though we all knew what he was doing because we saw it happen ever — so — slowly, Grandma Lynne still says, — Great. That hits the spot. A cup of tea!

It's so obvious, I nearly ask, — When are you off, then? But Mum is fetching the biscuit tin so I don't, in case it stops her offering me one.

I needn't have worried. The rest of today is not just normal, it's especially nicely normal, right from the have-another-biscuit snack through to no-need-for-a-bath-tonight bedtime. Mum reads me two extra chapters of my *Blade the Stallion* book before I go up. It isn't particularly realistic because the baddies could just have hobbled Blade when they caught him after the brushfire, and then he wouldn't have been able to escape by gnawing through the rope, but it's still a good enough story, especially when Mum reads the suspension bits in a hushing voice, very slow. I almost don't have to do any reading myself after that, but when Dad comes in to say good night he sits down on the edge of my bed and whaps my schoolbook on the duvet like usual.

— Where were we? he asks.

— Can't remember.

— Right then. The start it is.

It's an extremely boring book about twins who go to a fair. One gets frightened by the ghost train. The other one doesn't. The frightened one takes flight. Then the not-frightened one goes around again and this time he looks up high and has a fright, too. Finally the one who was frightened first comes back and stops them both being frightened by turning on a bright flashlight. After that they both sigh happily. There's no real reason for the story: it's just an excuse to write "igh" in a lot of words. But Dad listens very carefully as I'm reading, looking at me rather than the words. It's like I'm a chess puzzle on the computer. If Dad just stares hard enough at me, he's thinking, he'll work out the right move.

I shut the book and neither of us says anything for quite a long time.

Then he leans over — nearly putting his hand on my swimming bag, which I've sort of half got my leg on under the covers for lumpy camouflage — and kisses the top of my head. It's normal. But he's not fooling me, particularly when he forgets to say anything at all to me after he turns out the light, because that's not normal, not normal at all.

Have you ever counted sheep? It's supposed to put you to sleep. Even though horses are better at jumping fences, and dogs are, too, there's no point counting them because they don't rhyme. Sleep. Leap. Sheep. Actually, there's not much point counting sheep, either. Not for me at least. You're supposed to count one after another again and again until you get bored enough to make your brain think, Christ I've had enough of this I'm going to switch off for a bit, but my sheep aren't in fact properly boring, because I can't make them jump over the fence normally. Some of them will, but every now and then one does a backflip or trips up or says bugger off I'm not jumping that and sits down instead or explodes. It's not fascinating, but it's interesting enough to keep me wondering what's going to happen next, and if you're wondering that then you're not actually sleeping because you're staying awake to find out what's going to happen next instead . . . which I do.

A very long time is called a neon.

After Dad says good night I count sheep for at least a neon, probably two.

It helps me keep awake as I listen to the mumbly conversations downstairs, and the dishwasher chuntering away, and the feet back and forth across floorboards and that rug, the one with the pattern that looks like a dragon upside down grinning in the hall. Then there's the voice from the television, and hundreds of people laughing on and off in a biscuit tin, and louder advert music, all *buy some toilet ducks now* now!

Ducks for your toilet: very strange. We keep mine in the bath.

I lie on my good-leg side with an arm looped through the strap of my swimming bag, one eye shut for the sheep, the other open watching the landing slice through the gap in my door. And yes! I was right! Because there's Dad now, gathering up clothes from the airing cupboard. Why? To put in a bag of his own, of course. A couple of sheep trip up. He goes in and out of his bedroom with things in his hand, including a towel, and there's no way I'm going to sleep now. Backflip. I'm just not. Somersault. And I'm not jumping over that, either. Explosion. No way, no! Explosion. No way. Explosion. No.

I wriggle nearer the bed edge and stick a foot out, then pull it back, then grab the bag tighter, and watch, watch, watch, as nothing much new happens for a while, either out on the landing or in the sheep field. Gray carpet. Green grass. Dad. Naughty sheep. Everything in modern nations, Son, because even exciting things get boring after a while.

Explosion.

Ex pollution.

Expel lotion.

Ex pillow shin.

Ex plow shone.

Ex pull low shun.

Ex. Pull. Low. Shun.

Ex. Pull. Low.

Ex. Pull.

Ex.

Boom! I'm suddenly awake in the dark with something wet on my face. Sweat. No, tears. Tears because he said he'd go and I saw him packing an invisible suitcase before I fell asleep and now he must have gone. The landing light is off and so is the TV. My room is blackly dark, except for some streetlamp glow by the window, and it's totally quiet except for some tire hum over there. Which means it's middle-of-the-night normal. So he's left. I sit up in bed and take a deep breath. Human infants scream when they're terrifically upset, and timber wolves howl to bring back the moon. I take a huge breath.

But before the howl comes: whap!

There's a hand over my mouth and — Shhh! in my ears.

I freeze.

The — Shhh! goes soft to a whisper.

My duvet lifts itself off me, the hand comes away from my mouth, and two rustly arms bundle me up.

But something's dragging me back.

— Swimming bag, I say.

— What? Not now, Dad whispers, working to untangle the straps. One of my cheeks presses against his normal sharp chin, the other feels cool against his gore tricks coat. — An adventure, though, he goes on. — Just keep quiet until we're in the car. I'll explain.

— But I packed. It's all inside my bag.

— We're not going swimming, Son.

— But my bag.

— Christ! Okay. Just . . . shh!

The hand works its way up over my mouth again as Dad cat-foots to the head of the stairs. It means going quietly. A horse will never tread on you if it can help it and even elephants can walk softly when they want to. Down we go, with a question I manage not to ask out loud using incredible powers of concentration. It's there, though, bubbling up as he swings a rucksack onto his other shoulder in the hall, and it nearly asks itself while he checks his coat pockets, and slides back the lightning bolt, and hushes us through the door. The street-lamp has an excellent halo. *Ask*, it says. I'm about to, but the — Shhh! purrs softly in my ear again. Dad strides us down the pavement past the skip. Skips. I don't know why they call them that, but I do know that you can fill them fuller if you put big flat things up the sides and in the ends. Planks of wood or old doors. Don't try with plasterboard: it goes soggy in the rain. And anyway, here's the roof of the car full of wet reflections. Dad sits me on it all the same. Then I'm in my excellent padded seat with a damp pajama bum and his coat over my chest and our bags down there in the footwell. There's no bucket. Dad even clumps the doors shut gently, like he's closing egg-box lids. Hand-breaks are to stop you running into obstacles and breaking things, your hands included. That's ours, there: down it creaks when Dad does it and here comes the question as the engine flutters us off up the road.

— Where's Mum?

No answer.

— Where is she?

— Go back to sleep, Son.

— Isn't she coming, too?

— We'll chat about it in the morning.

— I want—

— Sleep, Billy.

— Mum.

— *Sleep*.

We drive for a long time and even though he's told me to go to sleep I don't. Not immediately, anyway. I watch instead. To begin with streetlamps do slow jellyfish pulsing in the car, all tangerine. Then their orange bits flicker faster across the back of Dad's headrest, like flames. Eventually they flutter out entirely. The car goes nice and black except for the dashboard lights which are excellent light-saver green. Feel the Force, Dad. It will guide you to a rebel spaceship where they may finally take off your plaster cast revealing a brand-new hand! That will be good because right now the cast is obviously annoying him: the fingers of his good hand keep digging into the stinky crevasses while the bad hand steers. Crevasse is another word for a crease so big you have to stick a V in it. Did you know that an itch is like a yawn? It's true: they're both catching. Dad scratches so hard my eyes need rubbing, too.

They're very heavy and puffy, like Lizzie's pull-ups first thing in the morning. I shut them. It's easiest. The road hums. I don't know where we're going, but wherever it is it's at the end of the longest-ever torn-off Cheerios-box lid.

When I wake up we've stopped. My body feels as if somebody has taken a rusty spanner and tightened up all my knee and elbow and hip and shoulder joints while I was asleep, and that feeling is normal if you've spent a long time asleep in a car seat which is nicely padded but still a chair. So I know we've come a long way. I also know that we're not *there* yet, wherever *there* is, because where we are is a massive car park like you have at the shops, and there's no way Dad would plan an adventure in a shopping center.

— Where are we? I ask.

Dad straightens up from leaning forward and stretches his good arm out, and I realize that he was probably asleep, too.

— Service station.

— Can we go in? I need the—

— Sure, mumbles Dad. — Of course.

Yes, yes, yes! Excellent! A service station! Fantastic! All my joint-nuts are suddenly incredibly well adjusted and oiled. I ping my seat belt — good-bye snail — and jump out of the car, then realize I'm wearing my pajamas and jump straight back in. But, amazingly, Dad doesn't mind about clothes today. He just rummages my coat and boots out of his bag and says, — Stick these on. Let's get something to eat.

— In the . . . service station.

— Yes.

— Do they have real hamburgers in this one?

— I imagine so.

— And can I, can I, can—

— Yes.

Just *yes*? Not even a *for breakfast*? Oh yes, yes, yes! Hamburgers in service stations are excellent. Not only because they are quite nicely flat and come in buns full of gunky ketchup, and not just because you normally get a massive milk shake and some excellently thin chips to go with them, but because they come with an actual toy as well. It's true. I know because I had one once. The toy was in a little plastic bag at the bottom of the big paper bag everything else was in. I didn't even ask for it: it was just there, a whole tiny red baddy plastic-figure thing, with a gun.

And that's not the only reason service stations are excellent. There are lots. Like the fact that they have huge cardboard cups of coffee. I don't drink the coffee, but Mum and Dad do, and when they do it makes them talkatively pleased and very likely to buy some sweets. In a service station! Which is excellent! Because the sweets there don't come in normal rolls; they come in massive plastic bags instead. You can eat them when you've dried your hands after going to the loo in one of the hundreds of loos they have. Not on a towel. In a brilliant wind-tunnel machine called an Airblade. It's made by the man who makes all the Hoovers, Son. Dyson. Clever bugger. You can actually feel the air drying your hands off! Then, when your hands are clean and dry, and you've had some sweets, you can mess about with the massive computer games they have in the dark bit. Not actually play them, no, because they're a rip-off, Son, but you can sit on that motorbike and push all the buttons you like and watch the racetrack picture come at you like an excellent endless snake.

But sadly today the service station isn't as good as normal.

We walk across the parking bit in the rain and go in, with Dad looking at his phone most of the way. He's still looking at it as we queue up to get a burger for breakfast, and he doesn't like it when I interrupt to tell him it's the wrong kind of burger place because it's not a McDonald's but Burger King.

— Same difference.

— But—

— Don't start, Son, or you'll be eating a muesli bar quicker than you can say Soft Mick.

I don't start. I say Soft Mick in my head a few times, though, hoping that it will help, but it doesn't: my burger comes on a tray and I can see just by looking at it that there's no free toy, or even a milk shake, because he's bought me orange juice instead: the sight of it makes my sore leg throb.

We sit down at a little table to eat, but Dad hasn't ordered himself any food, just black coffee in a small paper cup. He winces when he takes the first sip. My burger is actually quite nice, but still, I can tell there won't be any sweets.

Dad stops squinting at his phone to press it against his ear.

— Cicely, he says.

Then he lurches up and nods at me to stay put and walks over to the corner of the restaurant and stands with the phone in his red hand while the good one squeezes the ridge of his nose and runs down tight into his cheeks. Every now and then he shakes his head. I can't really hear what he's saying because his voice is leopard low and there is strange music everywhere. He only growls up loud once when he says, — That's why I'm asking you to tell her.

There's lots of mayonnaise up my pajama sleeve. I don't try to clean it off, though, because I'm keeping my eyes on Dad. When an animal is in a corner it might do anything. Dad finishes speaking to Cicely and stares at the phone for quite a long time, then walks over to the rubbish bin and . . . drops it in.

I open my mouth in the middle of a bite and a triangle of lettuce flaps out onto my napkin plate.

Then Dad's leaning over me saying, — Are you done?

— Not yet.

— Well get a bloody move on. We need to . . .

He trails off, looks round the restaurant like it's all very new, then suddenly slumps down in his seat to rub at his bristles and slowly shake his head.

— Sorry, Billy, he says eventually. — Take your time. Enjoy your . . . burger thing.

— It has pickles, I tell him.

— Good.

— Why are we here anyway? I ask.

— Why are we here?

— Yes. Why?

— Well.

— Yes?

— It's an . . . adventure.

— What sort?

Dad looks up at the menu-board thing above the people who find the food in its hutches. I don't think the adventure ingredients are written up there, Dad. He looks out of the window at the car park. No help there, either. It's up his sleeve instead, inside the scraggly rim of his plaster cast.

— A safari. We're having a safari adventure, he says.

— Great.

— Yes, it'll be fun.

— But where are the animals?

— They're hiding. We have to find them. It'll take skill.

— Why?

— Because they mustn't see us coming.

— Why?

— Because they're very shy. They're not just ordinary lions and zebras and whatnots, you see. They're shyer. If they see us coming they'll instantly disappear. Because they're . . . magical.

— Pretend, you mean.

Dad looks at me for a long time when I say this. The onion rings in my burger probably made the cook cry, but it's okay now, Dad, nobody is going to hit your thumb with a sled hammer. He wipes his face and shakes his head in a very tiny way, then bigger.

— No, Billy. Not pretend.

— But you said—

— *Magic.*

— But—

— No buts.

— Really?

— Yes.

Dad squeezes the rim of his little coffee cup. The shapes inside it bend. Our moon is actually an oval, too: it just looks round and full of craters. They're important: like the cracks everywhere else, they let the light in. How else would nocturnal animals see? I finish my burger. There was a crack in its bun, too, but all it let out was mayonnaise.

— Okay, I say.

— Good. Now, to catch sight of these magic animals we're going to have to be cunning, says Dad.

— Stealthy in our heads.

— Very.

— Okay.

— And we're going to have to be patient, too. We may only see their shadows. But trust me, they're out there. And if we keep quiet when I say, and hide ourselves away from time to time, in the right spots, of course, then we may well catch a glimpse of one or two.

— Are there any here?

— Possibly.

I look around very obviously, as if I'm searching for them, but in fact I'm white-lying: I don't really expect there to be any magical animals in the service station because I'm six, not an idiot. It's ever so slightly embarrassing pretending to look, but Dad's doing it, too, so I carry on for a bit until I really do have to stop.

— Dad, I say.

— Yes.

— Why did you throw your phone in the bin?

— What? Oh. Because . . . He squeezes his oval empty coffee cup until the rim pinches shut. — Because it gives off a signal, a radio signal, and the animals, these magic animals, well, they can detect radio signals from miles away. We won't stand a chance of seeing them if we're carrying a phone. Yes?

If only he'd talked about bats or dolphins I might have believed him. They use echo location. But magic animals? It's obvious he's really talking about Butterfly and Giraffe. We don't want them interrupting our adventure. But somehow I can't bring them up. It would be like saying are the flames very hot to a person you have put in some flames. Isn't it obvious?

Instead I do changing-the-subject by saying, — There's mayonnaise up my pajama sleeve.

— Right. Well, never mind. Come here.

Did you know that it's impossible to walk straight across a desert? If you try, your uneven legs will defeat you. Not because you jumped in a hot bath. No: one leg is always longer than the other. This means that without a proper landmark for navigation you'll go round in longer-leg circles and eventually you'll die without any water.

It's better to take a camel because they have four normal legs, a hump, and an excellent sensor direction.

Dad's phone had navigation on it, too, but he threw it away, and that may be why, after we leave the service station and drive for another neon along motorways that all look the same, we actually end up going around in a circle.

Dad doesn't spot this mistake, but I do, because of Legoland. They have a sign for it next to the motorway. I see the sign once. Then, a long time later, I see it again! I still don't ask if we can go. But after we've eaten some sandwiches in triangle packets which Dad buys from another service station at lunchtime, and the same brown Legoland sign pops up a third time, I think maybe I should suggest a visit. Dad likes Legos, after all, and he's obviously not enjoying this driving. I know because normally he puts some music on quite loudly and overtakes most things. Out of our way, we're coming through! Not today, though: today even the lorries go round us spraying up dirt.

— Shall we go to Legoland then? I ask.

His head jerks up. — What's that?

— Legoland. Jamie went at half-term. He said it was amazing.

— Really.

— We keep *nearly* going there today. Why don't we *actually* go instead?

— No. Not today, Billy.

— Why?

— We're . . . on safari, remember?

— Oh, yes.

I look out of the window. The white lines are dotting backward. That line of hedge there is the same color as the road. Yes, everything I can see is incredibly boring.

— But we haven't actually spotted any magical animals and . . .

— And what?

— And I think the car's wheels aren't all the same length because we seem to be going in very slow circles.

A coach blares round us: Dad has slowed down even more. He flicks the indicator and trickles us onto the cold shoulder. We stop and sit in roary silence. Every time a big thing tears past, the car rocks to the side interestingly. Dad leans his arm on the headrest and looks back at me with his dandelion-hole eyes. — You're right. We've been dawdling. It's time to get a move on.

He starts the car rolling while he's still looking at me, which feels wrong. Then his face snaps to the front again and we swerve out in between some crossly howling lorries. We don't stay with them, though. Dad soon has us ripping Cheerios out of the fast lane. He even pushes the CD into the letter-box slot. But it's some of Mum's flickety-pickety guitar music and when that starts up he turns on the radio instead. Here is the news. An emergency meeting has happened in a cabinet somewhere, to do with the new clear threat. A cabinet is a very small cupboard. The tiny people in it think, in the interests of national security, that there are no options left. I look at Dad and see that he is crying. It makes me stare immediately out of the window again at some crows flapping nowhere in the wind. What they're doing about the new clear threat is like onions to Dad. Whichever way you cut them it stings. More news: some soldiers have been killed fighting an earthquake in a financial system, but their team is through to the next round anyway. Sport is not the same thing as war, and sometimes it's best to bite your tongue, Son. I do, for a long, long time.

Poor Dad.

Give up, crows.

There's no point flying against the wind or arguing about things you can't change.

I can't change which way the car is going. Not back to Legoland, that's for sure: even though we've listened to the same sad news three or four times, that sign hasn't come back. Here's one about boats, instead. Big boats: it looks like they eat cars. Jonah was a man in a whale in the Bible, but that story wasn't very realistic: even though most whales don't eat meat a person wouldn't survive very long in a whale's stomach because of the acid. The sign people are serious about the car-eating boats, though: here's a picture of one again, and again, right over the top of us. Dad does his seat back up a notch as we come off the fast road. His good-hand fingers are white on the steering wheel. The cars in front of us have slowed down, and over the top of them through that gap there, yes, yes, yes, there's a slice of brownish . . . sea!

— I can see the sea! I say. It's what we always say when we see the sea, and normally when we say it Mum gives out mints.

There are no mints today. Dad just squints harder at the queue of traffic ahead and says, — Keep quiet, Billy. Please.

— Are we going to the beach?

— No.

— Why n—

— Billy, he growls. — Shhh.

The sea slice disappears as we rumble forward. Then all the car lights go red again. Dragons' eyes. There's a big barrier thing ahead, beneath a bridge you drive through past a glass box with a person in it. Even though we're quite a few cars back, I can see that the lady leaning out is wearing white gloves. Perhaps she's cold. The car in front opens up a wider gap and Dad's good hand fiddles something out of his shirt pocket: two small booklets. They're a darker red than his plaster cast, and each has a golden crown on the front. He turns to a page in one of them but I can't make out what's on it because he's holding it too far away. I can see that the car in front has gone farther off, though. Pay attention, Dad, don't dawdle, keep up with everyone else, lope! But he's still staring at the little book, and when he holds it like that the light bounces off a little picture . . . of me!

Not me now. Me when I was vertically four and reasonably useless. Back then we went to Spain which is across the sea near America and before we even got there Dad forgot my booklet and we had to drive back incredibly quickly for it with Dad chewing his lip and Mum half wincing and half smiling and eventually bursting out laughing, saying — Imagine the stick if it had been me!

I liked Spain. They had mosquitoes in the tents there, and I was allowed to peel some dead skin off Dad's shoulder while he drank beer and Mum put on a yellow dress. Dad said she was stunning. You stun fish to kill them and fishy rice is called paella.

But we're not going to Spain today. For a minute I think it's a possibility because of the little me-picture book which is making Dad bite his lip all over again, but the gap between our car and the one in front is just too large. It makes the big white van behind us beep. Dad flinches. Even though the radio is on I can hear him panting. Dogs do it to cool themselves down with their tongue but it's actually immediately quite cold in our car because Dad has undone his window and is waving the van past. Once it's gone Dad reverses, turns the car round out of the queue, and drives back along the road out under the big car-eating boat sign.

He doesn't go far, though, not back onto the motorway, just into town, very jerky. He seems to have un-learned how to drive the car properly, so he sensibly steers quite sharply into a multistory car park. We're not on bicycles, that's the problem, because once you've mastered riding a bike, Son, you never forget. Round and round the pillars we squeal, searching in vain for the storyteller. He's not here, but there are loads of spaces. Dad slams the car into one of them and tells me to jump out.

I'm still in my pajamas. Perhaps I'll be allowed to stay in them all day: it's nearly dark again, after all. Dad is scooping all our stuff into his rucksack, putting me in my coat, and slipping my wellies onto my feet gently, because of my leg, muttering all the time about being a pointless fucking idiot. Suddenly he lurches away to the front of the car, leans on the bonnet, and throws up. Sick spatters the wheel quite loudly and for a fairly long time. I don't know what to do at first, but then I remember Mum leaning over the yellow bucket with me, stroking the back of my neck the last time I threw up, so I go sideways like a crab to Dad and do the same to him. It's hard to reach. At least I'm wearing wellies. After a while the sick dribbles out of him in smaller doses. Finally he finishes, turns round, and grabs me to his chest. It smells nicely of normal him in bed, with only a bit of yellowness added.

— Sorry, Billy, he growls, shaking his head.

— You won't be allowed to go to school for two whole days now, I tell him. — It's the rule.

He grins at me unhappily. — No rules like that on safari. We'll just soldier on.

— You should tell Mum, I say. — Last time I was sick she brought me a glass of water to help take the taste away.

— Did she?

— Yes. But it didn't really work.

— Perhaps a different drink might have.

— Or toothpaste.

It's a very safe car park even without the storyteller. I know, because Dad slams the car door shut without doing the window up or taking the keys out of the hole. He just swings the rucksack up onto his shoulder, takes me by the hand, and leads me out of the car park to a lift. Interestingly it also smells of sick. Somebody with a rubbish pen once wrote something on the inside of the lift doors, but it's mostly rubbed off now. We're not allowed permanent markers in school . . . in case they leave marks that are permanent. Dad kneels down in front of me to do up my coat before we head off into the wind, but he leaves his own coat open. Perhaps it's because he knows we're not going far. Just round this corner and down this smaller street to a building with a high-up flapping sign.

It's a pub.

But not just any old pub, because when Dad finally gets to talk to the woman with no neck behind the counter he doesn't ask for a pint of this or that, but a room. That's right, a room which doesn't belong to Cicely or another friend or us, a room to stay in for a whole night! Excellent! Perhaps this will turn into a proper safari holiday after all. I once saw a fat yellow Labrador with a head which went straight into its body like this lady's. It was wearing a red harness thing because a normal collar would have slipped straight off, but this lady is a human who stands up straight and that's why she's still allowed to wear lots of gold chains. They would only fall off if she did a headstand. She repeats everything Dad says to double-check he means it, then asks, — In what name?

— Attenborough, says Dad, squeezing my hand. — First initial "D." Before I can ask him why he said that he carries on: — And this boy here would like a Coke. With ice. Am I right?

— Yes. Yes. Yes.

— Good. He turns back to No-neck. — I'll keep him company with a pint of Guinness.

— A Coke and a pint of Guinness?

It's not that hard, Labrador. Keep up! He might change his mind. But she's already started pouring, and Dad is steering me past the end of the bar to a table in the corner behind the fruit machines. I know that's what they're called, and I also know there's no real fruit in them, just money people have put in to make the lights light up.

I wait while Dad goes back to fetch the drinks. There are lots of little cardboard squares to stack up and spread out again on this table, but they don't slide well because the wooden surface is wetly smeary. Occasionally at home I try to put my pajamas on before I've properly dried the backs of my legs and that doesn't work either because of damp friction. If I lay the cards out like this they look like bricks. Friction. Legs. A wall. Bricks. A thought is nearly thinking itself, but it won't quite say itself in words: it feels similar to when I feel like I need the loo, and try for ages, and nothing happens. That is called con-stupid. Being unable to think is just stupid. I'm not going to have a problem pulling my pajamas on today, though, because they're already on, beneath my wellies and coat. In a pub. I feel suddenly strange and small, like an arctic fox cub might feel if it wandered onto the Serengeti. No use having two coats of dense fur here. But Dad is concentrating his way across the dark-planks floor now, and yes, yes, yes, he's not just bringing our two black glasses, because he's also carrying snacks. Lots of them. There are a couple of packets gripped to the glasses, one between his cast-elbow and side, and he even has a bag of something hanging from his shut teeth. He sets the drinks down and tumbles the snack packets down in front of me.

— Dinner, he says, ripping things open. — Dig in.

It's fantastic: there are two kinds of peanuts and a big bag of pork scratchings and a packet each of beef and mustard crisps. We crunch without talking for quite a long salty time, after which Dad goes back to the bar. My drink isn't finished yet but I don't say anything. It works. He comes back with more Coke and Guinness, and a whole separate extra drink for himself. It's trans-parrot, not water, but very thirst clinching anyway: he gulps it down fast and fetches another to go with the next Guinness.

After a while the packets are empty and the pub is full and Dad starts talking about when I was born. It's confusing. First he says it was the happiest day of his life, but then he says it was also the day he first knew real fear. I am a miracle, he says. His love for me was instantly bottomless, yet it deepens with each passing day. The fear, too. I don't know what he means but I make sure he is very reassuring by telling him it's okay, I didn't mean to do frightening. He wipes his eyes and drinks some more and says no, no, no: he's not frightened *of* me, he's frightened *for* me. I don't understand that either. He tries to explain something about destroying the thing you value the most, which makes me think of Orangey, the goldfish I knelt on, so I remind him about that, but apparently it's not quite the point.

What the point is, I never find out. He changes the subject

and starts telling me a story about never having actually seen some white cliffs, but I can't really concentrate because I suddenly desperately need a wee. When I say so his eyes take an unusually long time to understand. Eventually he says, — Oh yes, of course, help yourself, and nods in the direction of the back of the pub where there's a door. Not all women wear skirts, but if you're a woman and you happen to be wearing trousers I'm sorry, you're still not allowed in here. It's for men: look, urinals. I know: they should put a willy hanging down between the legs on the sign, then there'd be less room for confusion.

Have you ever noticed that when you desperately need a wee and stand near a toilet you need it even more desperately? It's true, and standing by a urinal is actually worse. Sadly I'm wearing my coat with the long zip which is a tricky customer. My fingers take ages dragging it down and off the end, and by the time I'm ready to go it's terrible because I've already started going. There's wet in the crutch of my pajama bottom: for some reason it makes my sore leg throb. And just then two more men bang through the door behind me laughing and I don't know what to do. My coat is on the floor. I can actually feel some warm wet in my welly boot.

One of the men says, — King hell. This isn't right.

The other says, — They'll be serving Oompa Lloompahs next.

I'm quite frightened. The urinal smells of flowers turned into permanent pens. If they had an Airblade I might be able to dry my pajama bottoms, but I look around quickly and they don't. The next-best thing is to hide what I did in my coat. I pull it on and start trying to do the zip up but my hands are relatively useless. Dung beetles are strong: they could do up zips bigger than a house. One of the men is making a very loud wee. The metal urinal sounds like the news music. Drumerty-drumerty-drumerty: there's been an earthquake. But the other man is still just standing there with his hands on his hips.

— Who are you with?

I nearly tell him, but even though not all strangers are bad, Son, right now seems like a good time not to speak.

— Well?

My fingers are scrabbling at the zip but it won't zag up. That's nearly part of the thought, too: a zip, a brick, a wall, a leg, friction. And stairs. They're useful, too. But this man here is cross. He's squatting down in front of me with his belly, trying to look cheerful, but his shaven head, which is belly-round, too, is shaking as if somebody has told him a horse normally has three legs.

— It's not right at all, he says again. Then, — How old are you?

It just comes out: — Six.

— King hell.

Now I've started it's hard to stop: — I'm in Miss Hart's class.

— Who's brought you here tonight?

— My dad.

— Right.

— We're on safari.

He looks up at his friend. — I've never heard it called that before.

— Is your dad in the bar? asks the first man, wiping his hands on his jeans without washing them first, and not waiting for me to answer before saying, — We should have a word.

I'm just about to tell the jeans man I'll take him to Dad,

because that seems sensible, when the door bangs open, and here he is lurching in anyway, saying, — Billy, Billy? even though I'm standing on the tiles right in front of him.

— Christ! he says. — Come here.

He quickly bundles me up, coat and dribbled pajama bottoms together, and looks hard from one man to the other, and interestingly even though they've just been saying they should have a word, now Dad's here Smeary Jeans suddenly decides to wash his hands after all, and the Belly tries to make the wall tiles explode with his laser stare while his thumbs work at the buttons of his fly.

Fly.

Flies.

— Is it fly or flies, and why is it called that anyway? I ask Dad as he spins us back out into the pub.

He doesn't answer. It's as if he hasn't heard, but something many-beer about the not hearing stops me from repeating the question. We're on the move, anyway, heading back to our table, though when we arrive we don't sit down. Dad just glugs back the last of the trans-parrot drink, then snatches at his rucksack strap. Sadly, he knocks the glasses off the table. One smashes. I nearly say, — At least it wasn't full, but don't. Everyone is looking at us. Sunflowers all face the same way in the day but what about at night? Dad doesn't pick up the pieces or ask for a dustpan and brush or say sorry, he just stares back at everybody for a moment, then drags me to the end of the bar where Labrador has her fat arms crossed. If you barbecue sausages without pricking them first they split.

— Room key, says Dad.

— I already gave it you.

He sways. — You gave it to me.

— Yes.

— Yes. What?

— I. Gave. It. To. You.

— You did? You did. So, where do we go?

— Up the stairs, second door on the left. Bathroom's opposite.

— Bathroom's opposite.

— Like I said.

— Like you said.

— Yes. *Sleep well.*

This woman is annoying me now: she started the repeating-everything game, and now Dad is joining in she's being so cat sick. It means saying hello, hello, how nice to see you, when what you really mean is no, no, not you, just go away.

We push through the people to the door. There's a hand hanging down with a word on its knuckles, a glass held so that the yellow liquid is about to slop out, a huge belt buckle, and a — Mind yourself! as we shove past. Out in the hall there are swirly carpet stairs. If you dropped a plate of spaghetti here it would be nicely camouflaged. For a second it seems Dad has forgotten the instructions again, but just as I'm about to remind him I see that in fact he's stopped to look at a phone tied to a big silver box on the wall. His good hand jabs in his front jeans pocket as the red one steers me to sit on the bottom step. He's about to put money in there instead of lighting up the fruit machines, which is a shame, and yet the hand with the coin pauses near the slot. Don't do it! But he does: he thumb-slides the coins into the machine in a rush, and punches the numbers, and suddenly I feel like my toothbrush: it's an electric astronaut one, but sadly its batteries ran down ages ago, so now when I put it in my mouth and turn it on the astronaut just judders the brush very weakly as if he's exhausted. I drop my head onto my arm and lean low to the spaghetti carpet which smells of Dhiren's wet dog up close, and Dad does some talking and listening and gets cross.

— Safe? What the hell is that supposed to mean?

Easy, Dad. It means not endangered. Like tigers. Or like a tiger in a strong box with a lock you can't crack. A safe. Actually, it's hard to crack metal. Much easier to wear it out by bending spoons. That's called fatigued, which means so tired you fall in half.

— Did you say *police*?

I didn't say anything. If you crack a safe, though, you'll be a thief, so yes, they'll call the police. Cops and robbers. Copper is a metal: it can also suffer from fatigue, particularly if your tiger escapes.

Slam goes the phone. I jerk up startled-meerkat fast.

— You're okay, Billy, he says quickly. His face folds itself back together, very concentrating all of a sudden, as he takes me by the hand and leads me upstairs, and even though it's incredibly late he runs me a shallow bath in the little bathroom with black stuff around the taps, and says nothing about my pajama bottoms, just gives me a clean pair of pants when he's finished carefully drying the backs of my legs, sore one especially gently, and up they go smoothly, no problem at all, and my teeth squeak with his excellently sharp grown-up minty toothpaste, and the fingers of his good hand even have a go at doing some combing through my damp hair.

He peels up the bedding.

He lies me between the sheets.

The bedsprings chirrup as he rolls in, too.

And he pulls my back into the warmth of his chest.

I'm so, so tired. My body feels like it's falling as soon as I shut my eyes. Sheep, sheep, exploding sheep . . . and I still can't sleep. His breathing makes me think of waves falling onto a pebbly beach, and the high-tide line is full of nutritious scraps for a whole ray of likely scavengers. Dad isn't asleep either, but he doesn't sound properly awake. He's muttering. Words fall from him like conkers off a tree.

— Tried.

— All.

— Cards.

— Hard.

— Stacked.

Then a little flock of them tumble down in a flurry: something to do with it being no use changing the rules of a game, and having to play with one hand tied behind anyway. Next:

— Give.

— Bent.

— His.

And then he talks for a bit about not being pushed around, and seeing them all coming because there's one on every bloody ridge.

— Up.

— Dead.

— Job.

— Joke.

— End.

— Hang.

— Left.

There's a pause, before he says, — Communications projects fucking farce, then something about a slow-motion train crash. His grip around me tightens and he says we're connected whatever they do. Conkers again:

— Blood.

— All.

— Out.

— Hands.
— Back.
— Think.

He repeats this word a few times with *can't*, *impossible,* and *pointless* thrown in. Then a snort of laughter brings some fresh conkers rattling down.

— Veins.
— Bitch.
— Plug.
— Know.
— Fall.
— Else.
— Pull.
— Matter.
— Fault.
— Point.
— Walk.
— Failed.
— Up.
— End.
— Give.

He goes on about the car window for a while next. I knew we should have wound it up, but he starts talking about the exhaust pipe, which reminds me that I'm exhausted. Ex horse dead. His grip on me slackens off again as the last three conkers thud into the pillow.

— White.
— Love.
— Cliffs.

Have you ever eaten a full English breakfast? Neither have I, not all of one. But after only eating snacks the night before,

I'm impressively hungry as soon as I wake up and roll over to see Dad already dressed and sitting there. He doesn't say anything, just looks at me funnily with the apple thing in his throat bobbling.

— I'm extremely hungry, I explain.

He rocks back in his chair an inch and says, — Of course. Let's have a proper breakfast.

He dresses me. It's lovely but odd: lovely because it's a friendly treat, and odd because even though I'm not good at clothes I'm supposed to do them so that I improve because I'm six. After I'm done, he folds up my pajamas and packs them into his rucksack, doing everything very calmly and gently, like a Slow Loris. Once the bag is zipped up he makes the bed and pulls back the curtain. There are some dark bricks and a slice of purplish sky. Still very early. He doesn't mention it, though, just waits patiently while I pull my boots onto the wrong feet, take them off again, and put them back on properly. We tiptoe down the stairs. We're still on safari, then, but never mind magic animals, there's nobody at all in the bar or hall. Dad has to undo the catch on the pub door before it will let us out. He pauses in the doorway to pull up my hood and take my hand. Then he leads me slowly down the street in the opposite direction from our car in its many-storied parking space.

We find a café. It's not like the one near our house with its gold chocolate coins and marvelous-smelling warm-air door thing. It's better. There's ketchup in tomato-shaped bottles on every table, and there's no lady to queue up for; you just sit down and a man comes to write what you want on a tiny piece of paper. What we want turns out to be excellent: tea, hot chocolate, two orange juices, and two full English breakfasts. One of the man's thornbush eyebrows spikes upward when Dad says this. — Really? he says, nodding at me. — They're big.

Dad doesn't look up, just repeats, — Two full English.

— It's your money. The man shrugs and walks away.

While we wait Dad looks at me so carefully I actually feel shy. He can tell, because he reaches out for my hands which I didn't realize were electrically fiddling with the little salt and pepper things and holds them loosely on the little tabletop. When Dhiren's dog had puppies I had to hold them softly, too.

— Shh, says Dad, even though I wasn't saying anything. —Everything is going to be all right. He nods to himself and pumps my hands three times. Everything *is* all right, so that doesn't make sense either, but I don't say anything. After a patch of silence Dad goes on.

— How about a story while we wait?

— Yes!

— Okay then. Who should be in it?

— A leopard.

The apple bobs in his neck again. — What does this leopard want?

— To escape.

— Who from? he asks. But before I can answer he goes on himself. — Hunters, I imagine. Yes. There was once a leopard who wanted to escape from a pack of hunters. And the thing was, this leopard wasn't alone. He had a cub with him. His only cub. In fact, it was the cub the hunters wanted. That's right, they wanted to take the cub out of the jungle and put it in a zoo. A nice zoo, where the cub would be well looked after, very safe, but a zoo all the same. Do you understand?

Of course I understand, so I nod quite hard and ask, — But what happened next?

— The leopard didn't want the hunters to capture his cub.

He decided he'd do anything to stop them. Anything at all.

— And?

— Well, the hunters wouldn't give up. They kept chasing. They chased the leopard out of the forest and right up a mountain. They cornered him and his cub there. And . . .

— And what?

— What do you think should happen?

— Maybe the leopard should fight the hunters.

— He can't. There are too many of them.

— Then he should run further away!

— Impossible. They've got the leopard and his cub surrounded. They're watching him, high up on the mountaintop. The hunters have nets. They want the leopard's cub. They advance up the mountain. The leopard climbs further, right to the edge of a precipice. They keep calling up to him, the hunters, saying he's endangering his cub, that they're going to take it away for its own sake, and telling him there's nothing he can do to stop them.

— But there must be! Otherwise . . .

— Otherwise what?

— Otherwise it's not a good story.

— You're right.

— So?

— Well . . . there is one thing the leopard could do.

— Great! What is it?

Dad's pupils are not lizard-straight but roundly black and as big as chocolate coins. He blinks, then his gaze jerks up as two plates swoop down over my shoulder onto the table.

— There you go, Rudyard. The man chuckles to himself. — Two full English. He pats me on the head and says, — Good luck.

I desperately want Dad to tell me the end of the story, but

my stomach is giddy all of a sudden. The plate of food in front of me is the biggest I've ever seen, a sea of baked beans with oily toast islands, two egg suns and three fat sausages and a mushroom hill here, some glistening potato slices there, and a bleeding tomato lake in the middle, all crisscrossed with wetly pink bacon strips and . . . I grab up my fork and start jabbering hot mouthfuls in.

It's tasty.

I eat faster.

Watchmakers have to be careful, otherwise they lose whole cogs of time off the ends of their tweezers. It's called being precise, and we saw a thing on TV at school where they did it magnified. When I next look up I notice that Dad is eating like he's making a watch. It's a sausage, Dad, just stab it up and bite the end off it! But no: he's slicing as if he thinks something might ping out the end if he does it wrong. I do some bean scoops and carve a bit out of the mushroom hill and I'm actually beating Dad here; I've eaten more than him.

Excellent!

I keep going.

The radio is playing a song about a man who doesn't know how many roads he has to walk down to get there. A grown-up version of "Are We Nearly There Yet"? I don't know, and even if I did I couldn't tell him because it's a radio, not a phone, like Dad's, which is in the bin. The man should sing in a service station or perhaps look up the answer himself in an atlas. It's called researching and you can do it on the computer or in a library. Come to think of it, there's another man who sometimes plays his guitar outside the library at home. It has a big yawning to combat rain. You're occasionally allowed to throw coins at the man's hat once he's taken it off, to stop him playing and make him go and buy something to eat instead. It's very unusual to have two drinks at one meal: I have to work hard to drink some orange juice after my hot chocolate.

I'm stuffed.

I tell Dad, using politeness: — Thank you but I'm finished.

He says nothing: he's still listening to the radio. It's the news, and the woman telling it is very importantly saying that the Prime Minister will shortly announce something. We have to stand up to the new clear threat now, says a man, before it's too late. Evidence is never conclusive. Resolution or not, we must act with our allies. Surgical strikes at this stage will avert a possible catastrophe down the line.

Dad's good fingers are jabbing into the rim of his cast. Anteaters can prize open termite mounds as hard as concrete with their claws if they feel like it, but termites aren't ants. He is staring at his plate, which looks like it has more on it now than when he started. Suddenly he shoves it to one side and says, — What's the point? embarrassingly loudly.

— It's breakfast.

— It's a total stitch-up, Son. March? You'd have thought we'd learned! Whatever we say or do, it makes no difference. They'll just . . .

The man who gave us breakfast is looking across his counter thing. — Dad, I say, but once he's gulped and wiped his face he goes on just as loudly.

— No need for evidence. 'Course not. If it suits them, they'll drop bombs. Never mind the consequences. *Surgical.* Jesus. You think they've got it in for *us*? There'll be whole families . . .

His face goes into his hands and he takes deeper and deeper breaths and I'm worried he's going to shout whatever he has to say next. But when his head comes back up he sees something through the window with the funny half-curtain and goes very still. It's . . . the back of two policemen's heads. They're coming nearer the door. Inching, it's called, but at school we use centimeters. A bell tinkles as the first policeman comes into the café, still talking to the other one about something being impossible without a change of heart.

— Manager, you mean.

— He inherited the problem. He didn't create it.

— Morning, the first policeman says to the man with bristly eyebrows, who smiles over the big teapot he's already aiming at two clinkety mugs. The policemen sit down. They have excellently black jackets with amazing belt stuff, plus clips. You could speak to the Are-We-Nearly-There man on that walkie-talkie, I bet. George and James at school have a pair with a three-mile range, easily bigger than the Infants' playground, though they were only allowed to demonstrate in the classroom during show-and-tell, which was stupid, because we could all hear what they were saying anyway, and so could they.

I look back at Dad. Even the bobbling apple in his throat is stuck still. Through the food steam I catch the itched-out smell of his plaster cast.

Without looking at me he whispers, — We must go, Billy. Finish up.

— I am finished. I already told you.

— Good boy.

He slips some notes from his wallet under the rim of his mug, the slowest magician ever, totally obvious! Then he takes hold of my hand. Together we leave, me trying not to spark electricity, him walking like a deep-sea diver with incredibly heavy air in his tanks.

⋆

Why is it called on foot when you're walking: surely it should be on feet? You use both of them, after all. Still, I could probably hop faster than we walk through town this morning. We're like a real safari team stalking through the jungle, creep, stalk, creep, except there isn't much foil age to hide behind, just a bus shelter here and this shopping arcade and that row of recycling banks. If I shut one eye I can make those things into a rock face and a cave tunnel and some boulders. Round the next corner there are two workmen admiring a lamppost in wet cement and again if I think about it another way they look like they're pleased to see it's sprouted. Dad nearly walks into the orangey barrier thing but he is holding my hand so I'm holding his, and for a change I do the steering, pulling him sideways at the last minute.

What he's being is called unnerving.

So I say, — Come on, Dad, can you finish telling me that story?

And he blinks at me and says, — What story?

— The leopard one.

He shakes his head.

But the question works, sort of, because we start walking more quickly with Dad leading the way like on a normal hike, the sort where there are warmish drinks in little bottles and the occasional treat to keep us going, Son, because an army marches on its stomach. I don't ask for any treats today. I just concentrate on keeping up as we cross some bigger roads full of growling top predators and go out to where the town is windier with the buildings farther apart.

We climb a gray hill.

We cross a wooden style.

We follow a grassy path.

It starts to spit, which is rude, but footballers do it and so does nature. Dad doesn't pull my hood up. I can manage anyway. There's a raggedy hedge next to this path, tassels of dirty green grass, with the sky like a brownish lid above. Then, through a gap, I see the sea. Right there! Right *down* there, chewing on the far-below stones. I only glimpse it, but I'm right, because we cut through a gate and zag across a fieldy bit and there it is again, with extra wind and rain, a strip of whitey gray hushing at the shore.

Shhhh.

Shhhh.

Shhhh.

I can't help saying it: — I can see the sea.

— Yes.

— Are there any mints?

— No.

I don't ask again. There's a huge boat over there, and another one off to its side, both leaving slow silvery trails behind them, like snails. And we're going to have a closer look, because we're leaving the path, which is really just a narrow bit of more nibbled grass, and heading nearer to the edge.

Quite a lot nearer.

This is two things. First, it's excellent, because I'm never normally allowed near steep edges, including the far end of the garden wall. But second, it's actually worrying, because this cliff is higher than the highest wall, and we're only a few steps away from its edge.

Dad's silence suddenly turns worrying, too. I look up at him. The worried feeling worms over on itself horribly in my stomach.

He is crying again.

Not proper crying with sounds, but tears all the same, wet tracks down gray cheeks, and red eyes.

I can't feel where his hand ends and mine begins.

I know you, Son, I can see your soul.

But he doesn't know what I'm thinking and I don't know what he's thinking either because mind reading is impossible. I'm suddenly annoyed by his statue tears. I pull my fingers out of his.

And I wish I had a hammer, because if I did I could hit his thumb with it, and he could say fucking, and that would make sense because of the blood which you would see coming out the split nail. Everybody liked seeing the wall cut inside my leg, too: the doctor, Butterfly, everyone, because it also had dried-up blood. It was a sure sign. Just crying about nothing isn't helpful because it makes everyone cross with you without giving them a real reason to be angry. Like running across a road. Or standing too close to the . . .

I take some large steps forward, right up to the very edge. Do you know what serrated is? Like a holly leaf or bat's wing. Well, the very edge of this cliff is a bit serrated. Over there I can see a dagger of white dropping down into the beach. And the sprouts of grass beneath my feet spike out over the lip, with the last needles jabbering at the waves way below. Sometimes in the kitchen I rock back on my chair. It's a stupid thing to do because when you go beyond the counterbalance of a cheetah's tail the chair tips up entirely, whap, and if I take another step here that's it, good-bye, I'm gone. The wind is streaking up at me. It smells of Tesco: the bit where you buy the fish. And that big boat's horn comes with its own echo. I went to Wookey Hole once. The spears of cliff dropping down either side of me look a little like stalactites. But before you dive into the pool you have to put your toes over the edge. I put one foot half over the lip and turn sideways and see that Dad's face is now white-gray plus a line of snot. His mouth is working but there's nothing coming out. It's called speechless. Good. He's got something proper to say nothing about now.

— We're not really on safari, are we, Dad?

He shakes his head.

— We're the prey instead.

A bigger wave hits the pebbly beach below us, and the sound of it, *whump*, drifts up.

— We're the prey, and Butterfly and Giraffe, the orang-utan, all of the cow sill people, they're the hunters, aren't they?

He drops to one knee and reaches out toward me. I won't let him have my hand yet, though, because I won't.

— Why are they hunting us?

— Billy, he says, and shakes his head. — Just come—

— Why?

Maybe it's the wind, but his voice sounds small and scratchy, like a mouse in an egg box. — Please. Come here. They think I hurt you, Son. That's what this is about.

— Why?

— They want to keep me away from you, to prevent it happening again.

He's on his hands and knees now, reaching out, his hand an inch from my arm. That's about two centimeters. My bad leg throbs. He won't grab for me, though. Because if I jerk back . . .

— Pretend what's happening?

— Not pretend. Prevent. Stop. They want to stop me hurting you.

— You're not hurting me.

— No, and I'm not going to. I promise . . . I wasn't about . . . I won't. But they think I did. They think I hit you with something. They think I—

I drift my arm into his grip, which shuts ever so gently. Puppies again. It's fine. He's talking. It worked.

— I just can't bear it, Son.

— But you did hit me.

— No I didn't.

— Yes you did.

— I smacked you.

— It's the same.

— No. It's not. At least . . . not like they think. Christ, they think I hurt you with something.

— You did.

— What?

— With a brick. A wall brick. You were chasing me so I jumped over a wall to get away and the brick bit me. It was your fault. And mine, too, slightly. Then there was a road and you smacked me incredibly hard for that as well.

— Is that what you said to them?

— I was cross that you told on me. You said it was behind us, but you lied. So I said it all to them.

— That I hurt you with a brick?

— Hurt. Bit. Maybe. I can't remember. But anyway. What did *you* tell them?

Dad's face is the same flat gray as the sky, which has no edges. It's just one big lump of cloud rushing along behind him, or maybe we're moving and the cloud is staying still. The world is like a basketball on God's finger, Son, if only he existed.

— Nothing, Dad says.

— What?

— I told them . . . nothing.

— Why?

— Because . . . it's not their business, Son.

— I don't understand.

He gentles me closer to him. It's called drawing but not the kind that has to do with sketches, more like a string in the neck of a bag. One arm-loop tightens round me, pulls me down onto the grass tufts, the wetness of his face pressing into my forehead. Normally my snot tears do it to him, in reverse.

— We are nothing to do with them, he says.

— But you told me something different. You said *just tell the truth*.

— I know.

— So why don't *you* just tell the truth, too?

— I—

— Tell them the truth.

— I—

— Tell them the truth. All of it. Explain about the crack and the light and everything being all right because it has some wrong. When they know it they'll say thank you. They'll go away and leave us alone. It's incredibly obvious. Just do what you told me to do! *Tell them the truth.*

— It's not always so simple. The truth doesn't always work.

I pull away from him. Not far, not back toward the edge drop, just so that I can see his face. — Not always doesn't mean never.

This is the last bit and shall I tell you why? Because it comes at the end. But don't worry, it's not like most last bits. In most last bits everything finishes, and normally it finishes happily, and if it's a book for children it normally finishes with everybody going to bed. Stock trick, Son. End of story, lights-out, bed.

But I'm not finished.

Neither are the fish in Lizzie's topical tank. They're still swimming round and round and round and round. Well done, fish. They must have been at it ever since I was last here, but does a tree fall over in the forest if you're not there to see it crash down? Yes, of course, obviously! Look, there it is, on its barky side, all smashed up. That fish just did two back-and-forths in different directions, which equals a figure of eight.

Through the tank a bendy version of Lizzie is lying on her belly making a garage for her cars out of wooden bricks. It's never going to work because the bottom bit is wobbly and it's not just the glassy water's fault. I decide to help her. Together we put some bigger bricks down first which is called laying foundations. We build a pretty good wall, but small children are incredibly clumsy. It doesn't matter: I explain how all houses have roots in the ground except for the ones which fall over because of hurricanes in Africa. Hurricanes have names. Watch out, here comes Lizzie. End of garage. She stares at the ruins.

— Not to worry, I tell her. — We can build a new one.

Sometimes, Son, there's nothing for it but to start again.

The adults are talking in the kitchen. Cicely is there, and that's normal: it's her house. Mum, too: not so normal; even though they're sisters I hardly ever used to come here with just Mum. And there's also the new horse man. He's a new man because he's new, so he's not yet normal, not at all. He is definitely a horse, though, very long-faced with a stringy mane and polished wet eyes. Even his talking is horselike: he sort of whinnies in between whatever Cicely or Mum says.

Everything changes, Son, apart from that fact.

And to prove it's true I'll give you an example: my shoes, the ones which flash, don't fit me anymore. My feet grew because everything changes. The little heel lights still go wink, wink, wink when I whack the shoes on the bottom step, though, and my feet are still here, so it's more complicated than that, Dad: everything changes, yes, but nothing goes totally away.

It's obvious Cicely likes the new horse man. She kept patting his arm when she introduced him to Mum and me in the kitchen, and do you know what her other hand was doing? I'll tell you: its long fingers were winding themselves round the necklace which came in that blue-velvety box. The one Lizzie unwrapped. Well done, horse man, good gift! Cicely likes it nearly as much as Lizzie enjoyed tearing off the paper. Time for another whinny!

And Lizzie likes the horse man, too. Some birds perch on water buffaloes, and there's even a type called a plover which pulls strips of rotting meat out of the gaps between crocodile teeth. I've never heard of an owl sitting on a horse before, though. But while we had our healthy boring snack Lizzie sat on his lap, very contented, using her slow owl blinks. Like Dad,

I'm not a huge fan of humorous, particularly not with strange knobbly crackers. But I ate the snack up so that Lizzie and I could go and play because everything changes and I wanted to see whether my experiment might finally have worked.

And it had!

I said to Lizzie: — Isn't it strange. Normally when I'm here I have a dad with a lap to sit on, not you.

And she looked at me and slow-blinked and said: — Yes.

Yes! She spoke!

She didn't stop there. She asked: — Where's yours gone?

And even though I think I may have heard her saying something behind the front door before Cicely let us in, it still feels like Lizzie's started speaking because of me, which means all the running comment trees I did for her helped. So I do some more.

I explain that Dad isn't here today because he's copulating. He's been doing it for a while now, ever since we came back from the white cliffs.

— It's called jumping before you're pushed, Son. They can't order me out of my own house if I've already upped and gone.

Everyone was very pleased with him for taking this wise precaution. Even Giraffe. She told Mum, — Despite the recent setback, so clear a signal of Jim's new constructive attitude toward the process can only be favorably interpreted, which sounded nice, whatever it meant.

Either she or Butterfly comes round for a chat quite often. Last time it was Butterfly and we watched *Life in Cold Blood —The Dragons of the Dry* episode — together. I drew a picture of two skinks fighting. She liked it a lot: in fact she said it was really very helpful, so I gave it to her. I didn't mind: the legs were wrong anyway.

This second block garage is much better than the first one. While Lizzie keeps on adding new bricks willy-nilly I'm doing very careful adjustments here and there to keep the balance without her noticing. It's called using subtlety, and while I'm using it I carry on telling her everything, not just about how it might be better to use what we're making as a zoo for plastic animals rather than a boring car park, but also explaining about Grandma Lynne, who left our house when Dad did, but only so she could make up her own spare-room bed for him to sleep in until he found his feet. He's still there. They're on the ends of your legs, Dad! It's all right, though: I can go round to see him more often there because Grandma Lynne is allowed to use her super vision on us both, just until we're able to put this whole sorry episode behind us, Son, okay?

I stop.

Lizzie's heels squash out pinkly as she sits back on them. She smiles because she's pleased with what we've built. It's okay. We do nothing for a moment. There are normal car Cheerio noises outside and the smell of coffee from across in the kitchen pushes a feeling of Dad into me. The doctors took off his plaster cast the other day, so neither of his arms is warning-red anymore. His bad hand is still oddly thin. I try to pass Lizzie one last brick. She lets it skiddle between her knees and sits there blinking from me to the garage-zoo with her marmalade eyes. Bicycles also have spokes. Mine sparkle in the sun when I'm riding magnificently along the pavement behind Dad without even nearly falling off.

I'm Billy Wright.

I'm six, not finished.

Here is the real ending.